IORICH

STEVEN BRUST

IORICH

TOR®

A TOM DOHERTY ASSOCIATES BOOK

NEW YORK

IORICH

Edited by Teresa Nielsen Hayden

A Tor Book
Published by Tom Doherty Associates, LLC
175 Fifth Avenue
New York, NY 10010

www.tor-forge.com

Tor® is a registered trademark of Tom Doherty Associates, LLC.

Library of Congress Cataloging-in-Publication Data

Brust, Steven, 1955–
  Iorich / Steven Brust. — 1st ed.
      p.   cm.
  "A Tom Doherty Associates book."
  ISBN 978-0-7653-1208-2
  1. Taltos, Vlad (Fictitious character)—Fiction.   I. Title.
PS3552.R84I57 2010
813'.54—dc22

2009040414

First Edition: January 2010

Printed in the United States of America

0 9 8 7 6 5 4 3 2 1

For Meridel Bianca

ACKNOWLEDGMENTS

Thanks to Reesa Brown for potato pastries and other things too numerous to mention, and to Kit O'Connell for computer and research help. Anne K. G. Murphy provided some emacs help for which I remain grateful. Thanks to Brad Roberts and Thomas Bull for significant help in surviving until this was done. Finally, my thanks to Alexx Kay for continuity checking.

THE CYCLE

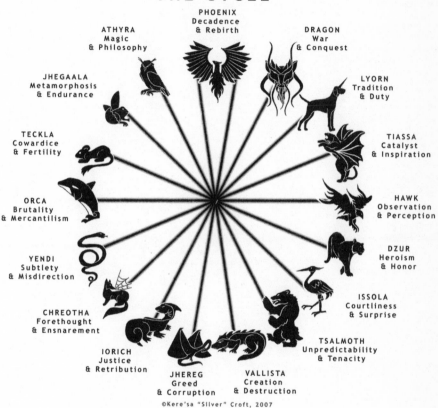

PHOENIX
Decadence
& Rebirth

ATHYRA
Magic
& Philosophy

DRAGON
War
& Conquest

JHEGAALA
Metamorphosis
& Endurance

LYORN
Tradition
& Duty

TECKLA
Cowardice
& Fertility

TIASSA
Catalyst
& Inspiration

ORCA
Brutality
& Mercantilism

HAWK
Observation
& Perception

YENDI
Subtlety
& Misdirection

DZUR
Heroism
& Honor

CHREOTHA
Forethought
& Ensnarement

ISSOLA
Courtliness
& Surprise

IORICH
Justice
& Retribution

TSALMOTH
Unpredictability
& Tenacity

JHEREG
Greed
& Corruption

VALLISTA
Creation
& Destruction

©Kere'sa "Silver" Croft, 2007

IORICH

PROLOGUE

Even if things don't work the way you'd planned, it's good when you can take something useful away from the experience.

They jumped me just as I was entering a little village called Whitemill at the southern edge of the Pushta. They had concealed themselves behind the long, broken hedge that bordered the Whitemill Pike before it turned into the single road of the hamlet. It was a good place for an attack. The nearest dwelling was perhaps a quarter of a mile away, and night was just falling.

There were three of them: Dragaerans, two men and a woman, wearing the colors of no special House. They all carried swords and knives. And they knew their business: the key to convincing someone to give up his cash is to be fast and very, very aggressive; you do not stand there and explain to your client why he should do what you want, you try to get him into a position where, before he has time to think, much less respond, he is at your mercy and hoping that somehow he can get out of this alive. When he hands over his purse, he should be feeling grateful.

Rocza took the man on the right, Loiosh flew into the face of the woman. I drew and disarmed the one in front of me with a stop-cut to the wrist, then took one step in and hit him in the nose with the pommel of my rapier. I took another step in and kicked the side of his knee.

He went down and I put the point at his throat. I said, "Intent to rob, intent to assault, assault, and failing to be selective in your choice of victim. Bad day for you."

He looked at me, wide-eyed.

I gave him a friendly suggestion: "Drop your purse."

The other man had run off, Rocza flying after him; the woman was doing what I call the Loiosh dance—futilely swinging her sword at him while he kept swooping in at her face then back out of range. He could do that all day.

The guy on the ground got his purse untied, though his fingers fumbled. I knelt and picked it up, the point of my rapier never moving from his throat. I spoke to my familiar.

"Get Rocza back. Let the other one go."

"She's on it, Boss."

She returned and landed next to my client's head and hissed.

"As long as you don't move, she won't bite," I said. He froze. I went to the woman, who was still flailing about, and now looking panicked. I said, "Drop it."

She glanced at Loiosh, then at me, then at her friend on the ground. "What about—"

"He won't hurt you if you drop your weapon. Neither will I."

Her sword hit the ground, and Loiosh returned to my shoulder.

"Your purse," I told her.

She had less trouble untying it than her friend. She held it out to me.

"Just drop it," I said.

She was very obliging.

"Now get out of here. If I see you again, I'll kill you. If you try to follow me, I *will* see you."

She sounded calm enough. "How did you—?"

"Wonder about it," I said.

"Not a bad day's work, Boss."

"Lucky you spotted them."

"Right. It was luck. Heh."

"May I stay and help my friend?"

"No," I said. "He'll be along presently. You can pick up your weapons once I'm out of sight. I won't hurt him."

He spoke for the first time. A very impressive and lengthy string of curses finishing with, "What do you call this?"

"A broken nose," I said. I gave him a friendly smile he may not have appreciated.

The woman gave me a glare, then just turned and walked away. I picked up the purse.

"Beware of Easterners with jhereg," I told the guy with the broken nose.

"———!" he said.

I nodded. "Even if things don't work out the way you planned, it's good when you can take something useful away from the experience."

I continued into the village, which had its requisite inn. It was an ugly thing, two stories high and misshapen, as if bits and pieces had been added on at random. The room I entered was big and full of Teckla, who smelled of manure and sweat, mixing with the smells of fresh bread, roasted kethna, tobacco smoke, dreamgrass, and now and then a whiff of the harsh pungency of opium, indicating there must be one or two nobles in here, among all the Teckla. Then I noticed that there were also a few merchants there. Odd. I wondered about it—even in rural inns, there generally isn't that much of a mix. The bar ran about half the length of the room, with ceramic and wooden mugs on shelves behind it. At one end of the bar was a large knife, just lying there—almost certainly the knife the innkeeper used to cut fruit to put in wine punch, but that's the sort of thing an assassin notices.

I got a lot of looks because I was human and had a jhereg on each shoulder, but none of the looks were threatening because I had a sword at my side and a jhereg on each shoulder. I acquired a glass of wine and a quiet corner. I'd ask about a room later.

Conversation went on around me; I ignored it.

"*Smells like real food, Boss.*"

"*Yep. Soon.*"

"*How long since we've had real food?*"

"*About a month. Soon.*"

"*How did we do?*"

I set the wine down and checked the purses, using my body to hide them from curious eyes. "*Not great, but, you know, it's pure profit. Strange place.*"

"*They're all talking to each other.*"

"*Yeah.*"

It really was interesting—you don't normally find an inn where merchants and peasants talk freely with each other, or noblemen and tradesmen; even in the East, where it was more common to see the mix of classes in the same inn, they didn't talk to each other much. I didn't even notice any special hostility between the two obvious aristocrats and the various Teckla. Odd. There was probably a story there.

Just because I was curious, I picked out a couple of merchants—both of them in the colors of the Tsalmoth—and bought them drinks. They gave me a suspicious look as I approached, but merchants are always aware they might be talking to a future customer, so they don't want to give offense.

"Pardon my intrusion," I said. "I'm Vlad."

They gave me their names, but I don't remember them; they sounded almost identical. Come to that, they looked pretty much the same, too—probably brothers. "I'm just curious," I told them. "I'm not used to inns where there is such a mix."

"A mix?" said the one whose name ended in the harder consonant.

"Teckla, merchants, noblemen, all in the same inn."

"Oh." He smiled a little. "We get along better around here than most places, probably."

I nodded. "It seems odd."

"It's because we all hate the navy."

"The navy?"

He nodded. That didn't explain anything—Whitemill was hundreds of miles from the nearest port.

It took a few more questions, but it finally emerged that, for whatever reason, the Empire had given control of the local canals to the Imperial navy, instead of whatever engineering corps usually handled such things. It was something that had happened long ago, when the Orca were higher in the Cycle and so could exert more economic pressure, and it had never been revoked even during the Interregnum.

"The whole region lives off those canals, mostly for watering the fields."

"And the navy doesn't maintain them?"

"They do well enough, I suppose, when they need to."

"I still don't—"

"The navy," he repeated. "They're all Orca."

"I know that."

"Orca," he repeated, as if I were missing something.

I glanced at one of the noblemen in the room, a woman having an animated conversation with the host; she wore the colors of the Tiassa. "So, the barons are Tiassa, but they need to deal with the Orca."

He nodded. "And the Orca want to soak every copper penny they can from the place."

"So everyone hates them more than they hate each other?"

He frowned. "We don't hate each other."

"Sorry," I said. "It's just a bit odd."

"You'd understand if you'd ever irrigated on a navy canal, or shipped goods on a navy barge."

"I already understand," I said. "I know Orca."

They both smiled, and offered to buy me a drink. I accepted. In case you don't know, the House of the Orca is the House of sailors and naval warriors, which is well enough, but it's mostly the House of bankers, and financiers. No one likes them; I don't even think Orca like other Orca. We traded stories of Orca we had known and hated; they made a few polite probes about my history and business, but didn't press when I steered the discussion elsewhere.

They filled me in on a few things I hadn't heard about, having been away from "civilization" for a while: an uprising of a few minor lordlings in the northwest, which would increase demand for spun wool; the recent repeal of the chimney tax within the House of the Tsalmoth, which was only a grain in a hectare; the recent decision "by Charlsom over there, fortune smile on his loins" to permit taverns to sell their own locally made brews without surcharge; and the proposed Imperial land-use loan, which would obviously be a catastrophe for the peasants without helping the landlords, or be a disaster for the landlords without helping the peasants, or else have no effect on anything. It was all from the point of view of the small merchant, which would interest me more if I were one. I nodded and smiled a lot while my mind wandered.

The conversation in the room was a chattering hum—no discernible words, just a constant noise of voices of differing pitches and tones, punctuated by laughs and coughs. It's always strange when you're hearing someone speak in a tongue you don't know, because names of people or places that you *do* know suddenly jump out. You hear, "blah blah blah Dragaera City blah blah," and for just an instant you think you understand that language after all.

It was just like that when amid the chittering and buzzing of meaningless noise I suddenly heard, clear as a whistle, the words "Sethra Lavode." I was instantly alert.

I shifted in my chair, but that didn't help—the speaker was at a table just behind the two Tsalmoth. I looked at my drinking companions and said, "Do you know what they're talking about?"

"Who?"

I gestured toward the table I'd overheard. "What they say startles me extremely, and I would admire to know if it's true."

Just so you don't get the wrong idea—may the gods keep me from ever conveying a false impression—I hadn't heard a thing except the words "Sethra Lavode."

They listened for a moment—being a bit closer to the

speaker—then nodded. "Oh, that. It's true enough. My cousin
is a post inspector, and told me while he was passing through
on his way to Gatehall from Adrilankha."

"Indeed," I said, looking impressed.

"Everyone's talking about it; I'm surprised you hadn't
heard."

"Are there any more details?"

"No. Just the arrest."

Arrest?

I said, "Forgive me, did I understand you correctly? Sethra
Lavode is arrested?"

He shook his head. "No, no. It is said that she has agreed
to be a witness."

"For?"

"The accused, my lord. Aliera e'Kieron."

"Aliera e'Kieron."

He nodded.

"Arrested."

He nodded again.

"For what, exactly?"

At that point, both of them spoke at once. It took a while
to get the story out, but apparently Aliera had tried to kill the
Empress, had loosed a demon in the House of the Dragon, and
had attempted to betray the Empire to an Eastern army. I got
the impression that this was a part of the story they weren't
sure of. But there seemed to be one thing they were sure of:
"The trial starts next month."

"Interesting indeed," I said. "How far are we from the River?"
In this part of the Empire, "the River" can only mean the Adrilankha River. My River.

"About two leagues. From here, there's no need to take a navy barge if you're going that way."

"And the nearest dock?"

"Upriver half a mile."

"My thanks," I said, and put a couple of orbs on the table. "Have another round on me."

I stood, turned on my heel, and crossed the room before they could start asking questions I didn't want to answer.

I found the host and arranged to get a room for the night.

Well, well. Aliera, arrested. Now, that was interesting. She must have done something pretty remarkable for the Empress—a good friend of hers—to have permitted that to happen. Or caused it to happen?

I lay on my back on the hard but clean bed the inn provided; conversation drifted up from below and the wind made the trees outside hiss as I thought things over.

My first reaction had been to return to Adrilankha and see if I could help her. I could get there fast. Anyone in Adrilankha would take more than a month to reach me here, barring a teleport or access to a really efficient post system. But I was only a few days from Adrilankha; rivers work like that.

Very little reflection was required to realize how stupid that idea was—even Loiosh hadn't felt the need to point it out. Adrilankha was the capital city, and the heart of the Empire, and the center of operations of a certain criminal organization that very much wanted me dead. I had spent several years now avoiding them—successfully, with one or two exceptions.

Returning would mean putting myself into their hands, an action for which Aliera herself would have nothing but scorn.

And, in fact, whatever sort of trouble Aliera was in, there was unlikely to be anything I could do about it anyway.

A stupid idea, to be sure.

Three days later I stepped off a boat onto North Market Pier Number Four in Adrilankha, smelling like fish and looking for trouble.

Even the Jhereg Wing would be safe—the thought of going there just to taunt them was only briefly tempting.

"*As stupid moves go, Boss, this one isn't bad. I mean, comparatively.*"

"*Glad to hear it.*"

"*I knew you'd be relieved.*"

Usually, if you're a professional and you're going to kill someone, it takes a while to set things up—you need to be sure of where to find your target, how you're going to take him, all the escape routes, and so on. Arriving unexpectedly in town like this, I figured my chances of making it safely to the Palace were pretty good. And if anyone did try anything, it would be a clumsy, last-minute effort that I ought to be able to deflect.

That, at any rate, was my thinking. And, right or wrong, I did make it; taking the Street of the Issola to what is called the Imperial Wing, though in fact it is not a wing, but the heart of the Palace, to which the other wings are attached. Once inside, I had to ask directions a few times, but eventually managed to walk quite nearly all the way around the Imperial Wing. In fact, I'd entered rather close to the Iorich Wing, but the Jhereg Wing was in between, and walking in front of it didn't feel like a smart move, so I took the long way.

The main entrance to the Iorich Wing from the Imperial Wing is through either of a pair of twin arches with no door. Above one arch is a representation of an empty hand, palm open like a porter expecting a gratuity; above the other is a hand holding an ax, like a porter mad at not getting one. These same symbols are on the opposite sides of the arch in the other order, so you can't escape the ax. This would, no doubt, be a powerful statement if I knew what the images were supposed to symbolize. High above both of the arches is a representation of an iorich, its toothy snout curving back as if looking over its low shoulder. Given what the ugly thing is famous for, that is another bit of symbolism that doesn't make sense to me. I could find out if I cared.

The Iorich like to make everything bigger than it has to be, I guess to make you feel smaller than you'd like to be. It was a long walk through a big, empty room where my footfalls echoed loudly. The walls were dark, only slightly lit by oddly shaped lamps hanging high overhead, and there were half a dozen marble statues—pure, white, gleaming marble, about twenty feet tall—depicting figures that I imagine were famous within the House.

Loiosh gave no signs of being impressed.

In front of me was a desk, elevated about two feet, with a square-shouldered middle-aged Dragaeran at it. Her straight hair glistened in the torchlight.

I went clack clack clack clack against the hard floor until I reached her; her eyes were slightly higher than mine. She glanced at the jhereg on my shoulders, and her lips tightened. She hesitated, I suppose trying to think if she could come up with a law against their being there. She finally gave up and said, "Name."

Her voice and demeanor—brisk and slightly bored—went with the surroundings the way lemon juice goes with cream; she sounded more like an Imperial clerk in charge of tax rolls than a magistrate of the House of justicers. I said, "I want information about a case."

"Name," she repeated.

"Aliera e'Kieron, House of the Dragon."

"Your name," she said, with the air of someone trying very hard to be patient in spite of provocation.

But you can't operate in the Jhereg without knowing some of the basics of the Imperial justice system; no one but an idiot breaks a law without knowing that he's doing it, and what he's risking, and the best ways to reduce the risk. "I don't choose to give it," I said. "I want public information on the case of Aliera e'Kieron, whose name has been entered under Imperial Articles of Indictment for Felonious Conduct." I paused. "Of course, if you wish, I can ask at the House of the Dragon, and explain that the House of the Iorich wasn't willing to—"

I stopped because she was glaring and writing; continuing the battle after you've won just wastes energy. She handed me a piece of paper; I didn't bother looking at it, because I don't know the symbols the House of the Iorich uses instead of the perfectly reasonable writing the rest of us get by with.

"Room of the Dolphin, see the clerk. He will answer your questions. Good day."

I walked down the hall. She hadn't even addressed me as my lord. Once. My feelings were hurt.

I'd been in the Halls of the Iorich often enough to believe I could find my way around, but not often enough to actually do so. I saw a few Iorich as I walked—clerks, men-at-arms, and perhaps one was a magistrate—but I didn't feel like risking a snub to ask any of them for directions. Nevertheless, after most of an hour, I managed to find the correct stairway to the cor-rect hallway to the correct room. The man behind the desk inside—very young, an apprentice of some sort, no doubt—glanced up as I came in, smiled, frowned, then looked puzzled about just what sort of attitude he was supposed to adopt.

Before he could decide I gave him the paper. He glanced at it, and said, "Of course," stood up, and vanished through a door on the far end of the room. He returned before I had time to decide if I should sit down at the chair opposite his desk. He had a fairly large sheaf of papers in his hand. The papers all had two holes on the top with pieces of white yarn running through them.

"Sit down, my lord," he said, and I did. "Aliera e'Kieron," he said.

I nodded.

"Arrested on the ninth day of the month of the Hawk of this year, charged with violation of Imperial Edict Folio ninety-one part thirty paragraphs one and two. Intent to Indict filed with Her Imperial Majesty the tenth day of the month of the Hawk of this year. Writ of felony placed before the Circle of Magistrates on—"

"Pardon me."

He looked like a draft horse pulled to a stop just short of the barn door, but he managed, "Yes, my lord?"

"Would you mind telling me what Folio ninety-one . . . that is, what the charges are? I mean, in plain speech?"

"Oh. Use of Elder Sorcery."

"Barlen's crack," I muttered. "Nice work, Aliera."

"Your pardon, my lord?"

"Nothing, nothing. I was talking to myself. Who accused her?"

"Her Majesty."

"Heh. Anything on how Her Majesty learned of the crime?"

"I'm not permitted to say, my lord."

"All right. Go on, please."

He did, but there was nothing useful in it, except that, yeah, she had been bound for judgment on a crime. A capital crime.

"Does she have an advocate?"

"She refused, my lord."

I nodded. "Of course she did. Any friends of the defendant presented themselves yet?"

"I'm not permitted to say, my lord."

I sighed. "Well, you may as well add me. Szurke, Count."

"House?"

"Imperial." I dug out the ring and showed it to him. He was very impressed and so on.

He made some notations, and pressed some seals onto a document, then said, "It is done, my lord. You wish to see the prisoner?"

"Yes."

"If the prisoner should agree, where can you be reached?"

"Castle Black," I said, hoping that was sufficient.

It was; he made a notation.

"Has she received any visitors so far?"

"I'm not permitted . . ." Then he shrugged and consulted another paper and said, "No." I guess that one doesn't matter so much.

I thanked him, and that concluded my business in the House of the Iorich.

And, having acquired the bare minimum of information—enough to know what I was dealing with—the next step was obvious: I stopped on the stairway, removed my amulet, and carefully made the teleport to the courtyard of Castle Black. I replaced the amulet around my neck and spent a moment taking in my surroundings. It had been years, but it still felt like home, in a different way than Adrilankha did. It's hard to explain.

I tapped the hilt of Lady Teldra, wondering if somewhere

down there she felt like she was home, too; but I didn't feel a response. I think.

I didn't approach the doors right away; I took a good look around. Around; not down. I knew what was down: a long drop and unforgiving stone. I wear an amulet that prevents sorcery from working on me, and sometime after I got it I came out here, to the courtyard, and it was only a day or two later that I realized I ought to have wondered whether the amulet would interfere with the spells that kept me up in the air. I mean, it was fine; whatever the nature of the courtyard, it doesn't require sorcery to act on me directly. But I really should have thought about that before walking onto it, you know?

There were pairs of guards stationed at various points along the walls. Always pairs: one fighter, one sorcerer. So far as I know, they've never had anything to do since the Interregnum, but they're always there. Cushy job, I suppose. But boring. Nice to know they still recognized me, though. At least, I assumed they recognized me, because otherwise they ought to have challenged me or something.

The walls were black; I could see the little veins of silver running through the ones nearest me. I turned, and the castle itself, also black, towered over me, the highest turrets were blurred and indistinct where they kissed the Enclouding. I lowered my eyes to the great double doors. How many times had I walked through them, to be greeted by Lady Teldra, followed by conversation deep or trivial, amusing or infuriating? Lady Teldra wouldn't greet me this time.

When I'd had my moment of nostalgia, I walked up to the doors, which opened for me in their usual grandiose, overdramatic way. I'm a sucker for that stuff, though, so I liked it. I stepped inside, and before me was a white-haired Dragaeran gentleman, in a frilly white shirt with green tapered pants. I stared at him. Rudely, I suppose, though I didn't think about it, and he didn't act as if it were rude. He simply bowed and said, "I am Skifra, and I welcome you to Castle Black. Am I correct in that I have the honor to address my lord Morrolan's excellent friend Lord Taltos?"

I returned his bow by way of assenting that he did, indeed, have that honor, such as it was.

He looked decidedly pleased and said, "If you would be so good as to follow me to the sitting room, I will inform His Lordship of your presence. May I get you wine?"

"That'd be great," I said, following him to another room I knew well.

I sat in a chair that was too big for me and drank a decent red wine that was slightly chilled, just the way I like it. That implied a great deal, which I set aside for later ruminating.

I expected him to return in five minutes or so to bring me to Morrolan, but in just about two minutes, he himself appeared: Morrolan e'Drien, Lord of Castle Black, bearer of Blackwand, and, well, stuff like that. I recognized his footsteps—walking quickly—before the door opened, and I stood up.

"Vlad," he said. "It's been a while. A couple of years, anyway." He gave Loiosh a quick smile; Loiosh fluffed himself on my shoulder and dipped his head in a sort of greeting. Morrolan said, "You heard about Aliera, then?"

I nodded. "I've been to the Iorich Wing, got my name added to the list—"

"List?"

"Friends of the defendant."

"What does that do?"

"Lets you see her, if she agrees."

"Oh, that's why . . . all right. Let's go up to the library."

I followed him up the wide stairway, got reacquainted with the paintings, then down the hall, past the pair of huge tomes chained to pedestals (an expression of Morrolan's sense of humor that I may explain some day) to another double door. Morrolan sure seems to like double doors a lot, for a skinny guy.

He shut the doors behind me, and we sat down in chairs that were like old friends, facing each other at an oblique angle, little tables by our right hands.

"It's good to see you again, Vlad." He poured himself something purplish-red from a cut-glass decanter. I still had my wine. "How have you been?"

"Same as always. Still kicking, still running."

"Sounds unpleasant."

"You get used to it."

"Any stories worth telling?"

I shook my head. "Tell me about Aliera." That's me: straight to business.

"Right," he said. He frowned into his wine. "I don't know exactly. She was engaged in some experiments, and the Phoenix Guard appeared, asking to see her. I showed them down to—"

"Wait. This was here?"

"Yes, that's right."

"They arrested her here?"

He nodded. "She lives here, you know."

"Uh, okay, go on."

"That's about all I know. They came in, got her, took her away."

"You let them?"

He cocked his head at me. "You expected me to launch a rebellion against the Empire?"

I considered that. "Yes," I said.

"I chose not to."

I dropped it. "What have you learned since?"

"Very little. I couldn't find out anything. They wouldn't let me in to see her."

"You need to go to the Iorich Wing and declare yourself a friend, then you can get some information, and if she approves it, you can get more, and you'll be permitted to see her."

"All right, I'll do that."

"Any idea why she refused an advocate?"

"None."

"Well, you're pretty damned helpful."

He smirked. "It's good to see you again, Vlad."

"Mind if I ask what you *have* done?"

"I've spoken with Norathar and Sethra."

"Oh," I said. Yes, the Dragon Heir and the Enchantress of Dzur Mountain would be good people to start with. "Uh, have they been keeping you informed?"

"As much as you'd expect."

"So: no."

"Right."

"She was arrested, ah, what was it? About two weeks ago?"

"A little more."

I nodded. "Okay, we need to find her an advocate."

"How do you know so much about this stuff, Vlad?"

I looked at him.

"Oh," he said. "All right, but didn't she refuse an advocate?"

"There may be a way to get one in to try to talk some sense into her."

"How?"

"I've no idea. But advocates are clever bastards. I'd have been Starred otherwise."

"Money isn't a problem," he said.

"No," I agreed. "It isn't."

He nodded. "Are you hungry?"

I realized I was, and said so.

"Let's go to the pantries and see what we can find."

We found some sausages in the style of some Eastern kingdom: oily and biting, tasting of rosemary. With it was crusty bread in long, thin loaves and a wonderfully sharp cheese. There was also a jug of red wine that was probably too young but still had some body. We ate standing up in Morrolan's pantry, passing the jug back and forth.

"Vlad, do you know what happens if she's convicted?"

"My understanding—which isn't perfect—is that either they execute her, or the Empress has to commute the sentence, which will raise havoc among the Houses."

Morrolan nodded.

We walked back to the library, brushing crumbs off ourselves. "What are you going to do?" he asked me.

"I don't know," I said. "But it will probably involve killing someone."

He chuckled. "It usually does."

"Would Sethra know anything about this by now?"

"Only if she's seen Aliera. I doubt she has."

"Maybe I should go and see her."

"Maybe."

"Or else go straight to finding the advocate."

He nodded and glanced at my hip. "How is Lady Teldra?"

I resisted the impulse to touch her. "I'm not sure how to answer that," I said.

"Has there been . . . contact?"

I considered. "Not as such. Feelings, sometimes, perhaps."

He nodded.

I said, "I know you two go back hundreds of years. I wish—"

"So do I."

"She was more than just seneschal to you, wasn't she?"

His jaw tightened a little. "I'm not sure how you mean that."

"Sorry. None of my—"

"Once she stood guard over my body for nearly a week, keeping it alive, while my mind and my soul traveled to Deathgate Falls and fought a battle over the Paths of the Dead. Keeping it alive was neither easy nor pleasant, under the circumstances."

"Um. Sounds like there's a story there."

He shrugged. "Ask the Empress; I've already said too much."

"I won't press it, then."

"Where are you going next?"

"I guess I'd better try to find Aliera an advocate, unless you want to."

"I'm willing, if you'll tell me how."

"I know what to look for, more or less. It's easier if I just do it."

"Unless," he pointed out, "you get killed trying."

"Yeah, that would slow it down. But if I stay in the Imperial Palace, I should be safe. And if I stay close to it, I'll stay close to safe."

"You know best."

I wanted to note the time and date he'd said that. "They already know I'm in town, because I took the amulet off to get here. So they'll know I'm in the Palace." I shrugged. "Let them gnash their teeth. I know how to slip away when I need to."

"Boss, you lie like an Issola."

"That's the nicest thing you've ever said to me."

"All right," said Morrolan. "I don't know the Iorich Wing. Where should I set you down?"

"Anywhere in the Palace they permit it that isn't the Dragon Wing or Jhereg Wing."

He nodded. "Ready?"

I removed the amulet, put it in its pouch, sealed the pouch, and nodded.

He gestured, and time passed during which I was nowhere, then I was somewhere else. I took the amulet out again, put it on, and looked around. Imperial Wing; good enough.

It took me a good hour to find my way out of the Palace, mostly because I wanted to leave through the Iorich Wing, so I could cross to the House of the Iorich as quickly as possible. Yes, there's a constant strain in knowing you're being hunted, but even that is something you can get used to. You take sensible precautions, and minimize risk, and don't let it get to you.

At least, that's the theory.

The House of the Iorich (as opposed to the Iorich Wing of the Palace—just so you don't get confused. I wouldn't want you to get confused) was distinguished by a high door with a gilt arch, over which stood the representation of the House; this one, unlike the one in the Wing of the Palace, looking forward. The door was open. The two guards, in the colors of

the Iorich, glanced at me but let me walk past without saying
anything.

An elderly Dragaeran in a simple gown of brown and white
approached me, gave her name (which I don't remember), and
asked how she could serve me. I told her I was in need of an
advocate, and she said, speaking in very low tones even though
no one else was around, that if I cared to tell her the general
nature of the problem, she could perhaps recommend someone.

"Thank you," I said. "That isn't necessary, if you'd be so
good as to tell me if Lady Ardwena is available."

Her face closed up like the shutters of a house in the East,
and she said, "Of course. Please come with me, and I'll show
you to a waiting room."

I did and she did, with no further words being exchanged.
I guess she knew what sort of clients Lady Ardwena took, and
she didn't approve. A blight on the House, I've no doubt.

The room was small and empty; it felt comfortable, though,
lit with a pair of ornate oil lamps. While we waited, I exchanged
remarks about the decor with Loiosh, who didn't have much to
say about it.

After about five minutes, she came in herself, stopping at
the door, looking at me, then stepping in and closing it. I stood
up and gave her a slight bow. "Lady Ardwena. It has been a few
years."

"I can do nothing for you," she said. There was a lot of
tension in her voice. I couldn't blame her, but neither was I
overwhelmed with sympathy.

"Just need some questions answered."

"I shouldn't even do that."

She wouldn't have put it that way if she'd intended not

to; she wouldn't even have seen me. I said, "It isn't even about me. My problems aren't legal."

"No," she said. "They aren't. Who is it about?"

"Aliera e'Kieron."

Her eyes widened a little. "You know her?"

Heh. And here I'd thought everyone knew that. "Yes. She needs an advocate. I need you to recommend one."

"I've heard she's refused advice."

"Yes, that makes it harder."

She nodded and fell silent for a bit. "I've heard of the matter, of course. Part thirty paragraphs one, two, and five, isn't it?"

"Just one and two."

She nodded. "They're moving on it quickly."

"Which means?"

"Which means that they don't like their case, or else they need it prosecuted for political reasons, and the issue isn't the issue, as it were."

"That's good to know."

She chewed on her lower lip and sat down. I sat down too and waited while she thought.

"You'll need someone who can handle a recalcitrant client, and someone who's done a lot of work with Folio ninety-one. Imperial Edicts are different from both Codified Traditions and Statutes. They're a bit like Ordinances except with the full force of the Imperium behind them, which makes them a bit of a niche. And then there's the fact that the Empire is moving so quickly . . . all right." She pulled out a stub of pencil and a tiny square of paper. "See him. If he won't do it, maybe he'll be able to recommend someone."

"Thanks," I said.

She stood up, nodded to me, and glided out. With the amount of money I'd given her over the years, I figured she owed me at least this much. She probably didn't agree, but was afraid that I was in a position to make life difficult for her if she didn't help me. And I was.

2

By "The State" we mean that body that holds the monopoly on the use of violence within a geographic region and has the power and authority to determine how much and in what manner and under what circumstances this monopoly will be delegated, authorized, or commissioned to other bodies or individuals. This power is expressed and interpreted through the body's various legal systems, coded or uncoded.

By this definition, (cf. Lanya), it is clear that to accept the existence of a State is to accept the monopoly on violence, and so too in reverse. The question, therefore, of the legitimacy of any act of violence by the State, whether deliberate or accidental, must first of all be determined according to:

1. The legitimacy of the State.
2. The legitimacy of the interests of the State in which the violence occurred.
3. The appropriateness or lack thereof of the particular acts of violence in serving those interests.

It is for this reason that, for example, any violence commit-
ted by a rebellious vassal is inherently illegitimate; any act of vi-
olence by agents of the State that are committed for personal
motivations are considered criminal misappropriation of author-
ity; and any act of violence that, in intent, fails to advance the
cause of the State is considered negligent.

The committee began its investigation into the events in
Tirma on this basis.

The name on the paper was Perisil. I'd never heard of him, but
then, the only Iorich I'd ever heard of were those who were
willing to take Jhereg as clients—a relatively low number.

I went and showed the name and got directions to a sub-
basement of the House, and from there to a narrow side passage that looked like an afterthought to the construction; it
was meaner and the ceiling was lower and the lighting not so
good. Here, unlike in the rest of the House, there were names
over the doors. I wondered if somehow having your name over
the door meant you were less important. In any case, it helped
me find the right one.

I clapped and waited. After a while, I clapped again. I still
heard nothing, but the door opened a little and a pair of odd
violet eyes were peering at me, then at Loiosh and Rocza, then
at me.

"Yes?" he said, or rather squeaked. His voice was high-
pitched and small; I couldn't imagine him arguing before the
Court. I mean, do you want the Justicer laughing at your advocate? Well, I don't know, maybe that would help.

"May I come in?"

He opened the door a bit more. He was only a little taller than Aliera, who was only a little taller than me. His shoulders were broad, and for a Dragaeran he'd have been called stocky. His dress was casual, to the point where the laces on his doublet were only loosely tied and his gloves were unevenly hanging on his belt. For an Iorich, that's casual, okay? He said, "An Easterner. If you're here on your own behalf, or one of your countrymen, I've never done anything with the Separation Laws, though I've looked through them of course."

The office behind him was tiny and square, mostly taken up by a wooden desk that looked old and well-used; it had grooves and scratches here and there, and it just barely left room for a couple of chairs that were ugly and metal. There were white spaces on the wall where some pictures or something had once hung, and there was some sort of framed official document hanging prominently above and behind his chair. I said, "You were recommended to me by Lady Ardwena. My name is Vladimir Taltos. I'm here on behalf of Aliera e'Kieron."

"Oh. Come in, then." He stepped out of my way. He looked at Loiosh and Rocza again. "Interesting pets you have."

"Thank him for me, Boss. I always love hearing my pets complimented."

I ignored Loiosh and stepped inside. "New office for you?" I said.

He nodded. "Just recently permitted into the House from an outside office." Then he stopped halfway into his chair. "How did you know that?"

He sat behind the desk. I sat in one of the chairs. It was ugly, but at least it was uncomfortable. "Aliera," I prompted.

"Lady Ardwena for Aliera e'Kieron," he repeated. "That's an interesting juxtaposition. But then, I think I've heard of you."

I made a sort of noise that could mean anything and let him talk. All the advocates I've ever met are perfectly willing to talk from Homeday to Northport. The best of them are willing to listen, too.

He nodded as if to some inner voice. "You have paperwork?"

"None," I said.

"Oh. Are you registered as a friend?"

"Yes, but not confirmed."

"Hmmm," he said. "She doesn't want to see her friends, and doesn't want an advocate."

"Well, you know Dragonlords."

"Not many, not well. I've never had one as a client."

"Dragonlords think there are two ways to solve any problem, and the first is killing somebody."

He nodded. "The second?"

"Most of them never need to come up with one."

He folded his arms and sat back. "Tough situation," he said. "Do you have money?"

"Yes."

He named a figure that was a substantial percentage of what I used to charge to kill someone. I borrowed his pen and ink and blotter and I wrote out a draft on my bank and passed it over. He studied it carefully, blew on it, then set it aside and nodded.

"Where can you be reached?"

"Castle Black."

"I know the place," he said. He steepled his fingers and

stared at nothing for a bit. "Am I correct that you don't know why she refuses an advocate or to see anyone?"

"I can speculate," I said, "knowing Aliera."

"She's outraged, offended, and more full of pride than her father was before he destroyed the world?"

"Oh, you know her?"

"Heard of her, of course."

"Dragons," I said.

"Indeed."

"Can you explain the laws that apply here?"

"There isn't much to explain. Elder Sorcery is forbidden by Imperial Edict."

"Yeah, what does that mean?"

"That it isn't a Codified Tradition. Codified Traditions are more fun."

"Fun?"

"For an advocate. With a traditional, we can always find interesting ways to reinterpret the tradition, or find an historical context for its creation that has changed, or question how it was codified. That sort of thing is always fun. Me, I work mostly with Edicts."

"Oh. Why?"

"I don't know. I fell into it, I suppose. It suits me, though. If I were a Dragon, I'd say it was because they're more of a challenge. In fact, I suppose what I enjoy isn't the interpretation of the law as much as establishing and arguing about the facts. Most of the law involves detail work and subtleties of interpretation. Edicts are yes or no, did or didn't."

In this case: did, I thought. "That this was an Edict means what, exactly?"

"It means it was explicitly declared by an Emperor at some

point. Like a Statute, only with the force of the Empire behind it. That one in particular is about as old as the Empire."

"What does it mean for us? In a practical sense."

"It means there's no way to attack the law itself; the only questions are: did she do it, and if so, how harsh should the sentence be."

"Can't get anywhere on the interpretation?"

"How can you when the Empress can just consult the Orb and ask?"

"Oh, right. Death is the maximum sentence?"

"Yes."

"You have to admit, Boss; it would be funny if Aliera ended up on the Star before you did."

"Yeah, I'll just laugh myself sick over that one, Loiosh."

"What is the minimum?"

"The minimum? I suppose the minimum would be the Empress saying, 'Don't do that anymore.'"

"I see. And what would you expect?"

"No way to tell. The Empress knows Aliera, doesn't she?"

"Yes."

He shook his head. "If they're friends, it will be harder for the Empress to be lenient."

I nodded. Politics.

He said, "It's going to be difficult if I can't get her cooperation, you know."

"I know. I think I can get you her cooperation, if I can manage to get in to see her."

He brushed his hair back. "I might be able to manage that."

"I'm listening."

"I'm not saying anything yet. Let me give it some thought."

I was good with that. He could do as much thinking as he

wanted. His voice didn't seem as odd after you'd been listening to it for a while.

After a moment, he said, as if to himself, "Yes, that should work."

"Hmmm?"

"One option is to petition, in your name, to have her declared incompetent to manage her affairs."

I laughed. "Oh, she'll love that!"

"No doubt."

"*I'll testify, Boss. I've been saying for years—*"

"*Shut up.*"

"Think they'll go for it?"

He frowned. "Go for it?"

"I mean, will you be able to convince the Empire that she's incompetent."

"Oh, of course not. That isn't the point. The point is to convince her to accept an advocate. If she won't in the dispute with the Empire, she might to prove she isn't mad. If not, it might convince her to be willing to see you, and give you a chance to talk her into accepting counsel."

"Ah. Yes, that might work. Or it might just make her more stubborn. She'll see through it, of course." I considered. "It's hard to know how she'll jump."

"Hmmm. There's another thing I might try first. It would be quicker, at any rate."

"If it's also less likely to get me killed, that would be good, too. What is it?"

"Procedural complaint to the Empire. If we start out attacking, we can always back off; if we start on the defensive, it's harder to change direction." He drummed his fingers on the desktop. Then he nodded. "Yes, I'll try that first. I should be able to get the petition written up and submitted in an hour. We might get results by the end of the day."

"They don't waste time."

"Not with this. For whatever reason, they're in a hurry with this case."

"Um, yeah," I said. "So it seems. Why is that?"

"Good question. If you want to do something useful, find out."

"What makes you think I'd be able to do that?"

"I recognized your name."

"Oh. I'm famous."

"If you wish."

"Can you tell me where to start looking?"

"You could ask the Empress."

"Okay."

His eyebrows rose a fraction of an inch. "I wasn't serious."

"Oh?"

"You know the Empress?"

"We've spoken."

"Well, if you think you can get her tell you anything, I won't stop you."

"All right," I said. "If that doesn't work?"

"Lord Delwick, of my House, might be able to tell you some things, if he's willing to talk to you. He's our Imperial Representative."

"Okay," I said. "A word of advice: Don't do anything to mess up his relationship with the Empire. The House hates that."

"So I've heard," he said.

"All right, I'll get started, then."

He opened up a desk drawer, dug around for a while, and

then handed me what looked like a copper coin with the Iorich insignia. "Show him this, and tell him I sent you."

I accepted it, put it in my pouch, and said, "I'll check back with you from time to time."

"Of course."

I stood and gave him a bow, which he acknowledged with gesture of his head, then I let myself out.

I made my way back to the entryway of the House without too much effort, assisted by Loiosh, who has a pretty good memory for twists and turns.

I sent him and Rocza out ahead of me to spot any assassins lurking in the area, was told there weren't any, and made a brisk walk across the way to the entrance of the Palace. I went as straight through as the twists of the Wing would permit, and out into the Imperial Wing.

Wherever you are in the Imperial Wing (all right, wherever I've been) you'll see pages and messengers scurrying around, all with the Phoenix badge, usually carrying a green folder, though sometimes it will be a gold one, and occasionally something other than a folder. I always resent them, because they give the impression they know their way around the place, which is obviously impossible. Doors, corridors, stairways are everywhere, and going off at absurd angles as if designed by a madman. You have no choice but to ask directions of someone, usually a guardsman, who will of course let you know exactly what they think of Easterners who can't find their way around.

It's annoying.

To the left, however, finding one of the rooms where the Empress is available to courtiers is one of the easier tasks, and after only a couple of minor humiliations I arrived outside that wide, open, chairless room called the Imperial Audience Cham-

ber or something like that, but informally known among the
Jhereg as Asskiss Alley.

There were big double doors there, with a pair of guards
outside of them, and a well-dressed man who could have been
a relative of Lady Teldra—when she was alive—standing at
his ease with a half smile on his face. I wanted to touch Lady
Teldra's hilt, but restrained myself. Instead, I placed myself before this worthy and bowed like I meant it.

"Vladimir Taltos, House Jhereg, and Count of Szurke, at
your service."

He returned my bow exactly. "Harnwood," he said, "House
of the Issola, at yours, my lord."

"I'm afraid I don't know the procedure"—he gave me an encouraging smile—"but I would have words with Her Majesty,
who may wish to see me."

If the request was surprising, he gave no indication. "Of
course, my lord. If you will come with me into the waiting room,
I will inquire."

He led me to an empty room painted yellow, with half a
dozen comfortable chairs, also yellow. They probably called it
the "yellow room." They're creative that way. He gave me another smile, a bow, and closed the door behind him.

I sat and waited, thinking about how long it had been since
I'd eaten.

I hate waiting.

I hate being hungry.

I shifted in the chair and chatted with Loiosh about our
previous encounter with Her Majesty—she had granted me an
Imperial title because of accidental services rendered. I suspect
she knew they were accidental, but felt like rewarding me for
her own reasons. I happened to know she had an Easterner as a

lover, maybe that had something to do with it. Loiosh made a few other suggestions for reasons, some of which were probably treasonous.

Or maybe not. I've heard that in some Eastern kingdoms it is a capital crime to fail to treat the king with proper respect, but I had no idea if that was true in the Empire. I imagined that I could ask Perisil, and get an answer much longer than I wanted that would come out to: sometimes. Imperial law seems to work like that.

This close to the Orb, I could easily feel my link to it, and knew when an hour had passed.

A little later, Harnwood returned with profuse apologies, a bottle of wine, some dried fruit, and word that Her Majesty begged me to be patient, because she did wish to speak with me. My heart quickened a bit when I heard that; isn't that odd? I'd known Morrolan e'Drien, and Sethra Lavode, and had even been face-to-face with Verra, the Demon Goddess, and yet I still felt a thrill go through me that this woman wanted to talk to me. Strange. I guess it shows what conditioning can do.

Harnwood left, and I drank the wine because I was thirsty and ate the fruit because it gave me something to do and because I was feeling half-starved. Loiosh ate some for the same reasons (dried fruit not being a favorite of his); Rocza seemed to have no problems with dried fruit.

Then I waited some more.

It was most of another hour before Harnwood came back, looking even more apologetic and saying, "She will see you now, Lord Szurke."

That was interesting. She would see Lord Szurke, not Lord Taltos. I didn't know what the significance of that was, but I was pretty sure there was significance. That's the trouble with the Court, you know: Everything is significant but they don't tell you exactly why, or how, or what it means until you're swimming in it. Maybe in my next life I'll be a Lyorn and be taught all that stuff or an Issola and know it instinctively. More likely not, though.

I stood up, discovering that sitting there for most of two hours had made my body stiff. I wondered if I was getting old.

I followed Harnwood out and down the hall, where we went past the door he'd been stationed outside of, then turned left, through a doorway, and into a much smaller hallway that ended in a flight of eight stairs—two few for it to be a stairway up to the next floor. I don't know; I never did figure that out. But at the top was a door that was standing open, and past it was a long, narrow room with a few stuffed chairs set haphazardly about. At the far end was Her Majesty, speaking quietly with a man in the colors of the Iorich and a woman in the colors of the Dragon. As I entered, all three glanced up at me, with uniform lacks of expression.

The Orb as it circled the Empress's head was a light green, which should have told me something about her mood, but it didn't. She turned to the two she'd been speaking with and said, "Leave us now. I wish to speak to this gentleman."

They gave her a deep bow, me a rather shallower one, backed up, and left by a door at the far end.

The Empress sat in a chair and motioned me to stand in front of her. I made an obeisance and waited, not entirely sure of the etiquette, and wishing I had Lady Teldra in the flesh, as it were, to tell me what I was supposed to do. Zerika didn't look as if I'd violated any sort of protocol. I reflected that the Empire did things rather more simply than these things were done in the East.

"Taltos Vladimir," she said, a smile flicking over her lips. She still looked impossibly young to be an Empress, but looks are deceiving. "What happened to your hand?"

I glanced at my left hand, missing the least finger. "A minor insect bite followed by a major infection," I said. I forced myself to not glance at the Orb while I said it; the Orb, I've been told, only detects falsehood when asked to do so, and even then it can sometimes be beaten, as I've reason to know.

She said, "You couldn't cure it with your arts?"

I touched the amulet hanging about my neck. "I'm not sure how much Your Majesty knows of—"

"Oh, of course," she said. "I had forgotten."

"It is kind of Your Majesty to remember at all."

"Yes. I am the personification of kindness, as well as mercy and justice, which as you know always match steps. What brings you back to the City, under the circumstances?"

Okay, well, she knew about the "circumstances." I was only surprised that she cared enough to, and I wondered why.

"Aliera is a friend of mine," I said.

"And mine," she snapped.

I almost jumped. It isn't good when the Empress is mad at you—ask anyone. I said, "Well, naturally, I wanted to see her."

She seemed to relax a little, and nodded.

"And help her if I can," I added. "I trust you have no objections?"

"That depends," she said carefully, "on just exactly what you mean by 'helping' her."

"I had in mind hiring an advocate, to start with."

She nodded. "I would have no objection to that, of course."

"Perhaps Your Majesty would be willing to tell me something."

"Perhaps."

"It may be my imagination, but it seems that the prosecution of Aliera is, ah, being expedited. If that's true, then—"

"It isn't," she said. She was terse. She was glaring. She was lying. It's something to make an Empress lie to you, isn't it?

I nodded. "As Your Majesty says."

She glared and I stared at a place on the wall above and behind her right ear. The Orb had turned a sort of orangish, reddish color. I waited. This isn't one of those situations where I need to explain why I kept my mouth shut.

At length, she gestured toward a chair. "Sit," she said.

"I thank Your Maj—"

"Oh, shut up."

I sat down. The chair was comfortable; I was not.

She let out a long breath. "Well," she said. "Now we have quite the situation here."

One thing I'd hoped to find a way to say to her was, "Look, you've known for years that Aliera and Morrolan dabbled in Elder Sorcery. Why is it such a big deal now all of a sudden?" I was now convinced there was going to be no way to ask it at all. The Orb circled her head, its color gradually fading back to a sick shade of green. It must be annoying to be unable to conceal your feelings.

"Was the Orb designed to display the Imperial mood, or is it a by-product of something else?"

She pretended not to hear the question. "Who have you hired as an advocate?"

"His name is Perisil."

"I don't know him. Will he manage to get you in to see her?"

"I hope so."

"Let her know that if she confesses, she'll be shown mercy."

I started to reply, then recast it in terms I hoped more suitable for the Imperial presence: "Is Your Majesty pleased to jest?"

She sighed. "No, but I see your point."

I was trying to imagine Aliera e'Kieron begging for mercy of anyone for any reason, and my mind just wouldn't accept it.

She said, "I should have mentioned it before, but I'm glad you're not—that is, I'm glad you're still alive."

"Me too. I mean, I thank Your Majesty."

"Who have you seen since you've back in town?"

"Morrolan, that's all."

"Has he, ah, said anything?"

"You mean, made disloyal remarks about his sovereign? No."

"I could put the Orb over you and make you repeat that."

"Must be nice to be able to do that whenever you want, Majesty."

"Not as nice as you'd think."

I cleared my throat. "With all due respect, Your Maj—"

"Oh, stuff your respect. What is it?"

"Someone in my position is hardly likely to overflow with sympathy for someone in yours."

"I wasn't asking for sympathy," said Her Majesty.

"No, I suppose not."

"And you know whose fault your predicament is."

"Yes. Can the same be said for yours?"

"Not without exploring metaphysics, which I haven't the patience for just now."

I smiled a little. "I can imagine Your Majesty in the library of Castle Black furiously arguing metaphysics with Morrolan."

"So can I," she said, granting me a brief smile.

It was like half the time I was being invited to talk with Zerika, and half the time to speak with the Empress. It was hard to keep up with.

I said, "It must be a difficult position."

"I said I wasn't asking for sympathy."

"Sorry."

She sighed. "Yes, it is. Between jailing a friend and violence in the—" She broke off and shook her head. "Well, I knew what I was getting into when I took the Orb."

Neither of us mentioned that at the time she had taken the Orb there was, quite literally, no one else to do it. I said, "You know I'm still willing to serve Your Majesty."

"Are you?"

"Yes."

"As long as it doesn't mean a disservice to your friends, as usual?" She sounded a little scornful.

"Yes," I said, not letting her know that her tone had stung a bit.

"I'm afraid," she said, "that this is an occasion when you're going to have to choose whom to help."

"Eh. Between my friends and the Empire? I'm sorry, that isn't that hard a choice. Can you give me enough of an idea of what's going on that I can at least understand why it has to be that way?"

After a moment, she said, "Do you know, Vlad, that from the best knowledge we have, it seems almost certain that at least five of the original sixteen tribes practiced human sacrifice?"

"I had not been aware—"

"There are many who assume that because we have evidence from the five, it is safe to make assumptions about the other eleven. I don't know if they're right, but I can't prove them wrong."

I cleared my throat, just as if I had something to say to that. She looked at me expectantly, so I had to come up with something. "Um, how did they choose the lucky person?"

"Different ways for different tribes. Captives in battle, selected for special honor, punishment, reward, auguries."

"When did it stop?"

"When the Empire was formed. It was made illegal. That was the first Imperial Edict."

"An act of kindness from your ancestor. Good way to start."

"Not kindness, so much. She'd spoken to the gods, and knew the gods were either indifferent or hostile to the practice. So call it practicality. I bring it up because—" She stopped, and looked blank for a moment, the Orb pulsing blue over her head. "I'm sorry, it seems I must go run an Empire."

I stood. "Thank you for seeing me." I made as good an obeisance as I could; which isn't too bad, I'm told.

"It is always a pleasure, Count Szurke."

I backed away a few steps (there is a correct number of steps, but I didn't know it), and turned away. She said, "Oh, and thank you, Vlad."

"For—?"

"The documents on making paper. I'm told they're valuable."

"Oh, right. I'd forgotten about—how did you know they came from me?"

She smiled. "Until now, I didn't."

The mention of making paper brought back a complex set of memories and partial memories that I didn't especially feel like dwelling on just then; but it was good of her to mention it. I gave her what I hoped was a friendly smile over my shoulder and took myself out of the room.

3

Q: *Please state your name, your House, and your city of residence.*

A: *Dornin e'Lanya, House of the Dragon, Brickerstown.*

Q: *Rank and position?*

A: *Sergeant, Imperial Army, Second Army, Fourth Legion, Company D.*

Q: *What were your orders on the second day of the month of the Lyorn of this year?*

A: *We were to escort a supply train from Norest to Swordrock. On that day, we were passing through Tirma, in the duchy of Carver.*

Q: *And what had you heard about Tirma?*

A: *We knew the entire duchy was in rebellion.*

Empress: *Did you know this officially, or through rumor?*

A: *It was common knowledge, Your Majesty.*

Q: *Answer Her Majesty's question, Sergeant.*

A: *We were never informed officially.*

Orb shows falsehood

Q: *Would you care to reconsider that answer, Sergeant Dornin?*

A: *No, my lord. That is my answer.*

Q: *Had anything unusual happened that day before you reached Tirma?*

A: *There were the usual problems with the wagon train, but no attacks or incidents.*

Q: *Describe what happened when you entered Tirma.*

A: *We were set on by a mob that was trying to take away the wagons, and we defended ourselves.*

Q: *While you were in Tirma, were you or your command involved in any fighting or violence that did not involve defending yourselves against an attack?*

A: *We were not.*

Orb shows falsehood

Q: *Would you care to reconsider your answer?*

A: *I would not.*

Q: *Are you aware of the penalties for lying beneath the Orb?*

A: *I am.*

I went back down the half-flight of stairs, down the hall, and stopped, trying to remember the name I'd been given.

"*Delwick.*"

"*I knew that.*"

"*Right.*"

"*Okay, I was about to remember.*"

"*Right.*"

"*Shut up.*"

I found my way back to where Harnwood still waited. He smiled as if he were glad to see me. I bowed as precisely as I could manage—not that he'd let me know if I missed my mark—and said, "Pardon me, do you know a Lord Delwick?"

"Of course, my lord. Shall I take you to where he is?"

"If you'd be so kind."

He would, in fact, be so kind. He exchanged a few words with the guard stationed by the door, and gestured with his hand that I was to fall into step with him. I did so. Having known Lady Teldra so long—in the flesh, I mean—I wasn't surprised that he made it seem effortless to shorten his strides to match my puny human ones.

I won't try to describe the turnings we took, nor the stairs we went up only to go down another. I will mention one extremely wide hallway with what looked like gold trimming over ivory, and hung with the psiprints of some of the oddest-looking people I've ever seen, all of them looking enough like Daymar to convince me they were Hawklords, and all of them staring out with the same expression: as if they were saying, "Just what manner of beast *are* you, anyway, and do you mind of if I study you for a while?"

We walked into a perfectly square room around the size of my old flat off Lower Kieron Road—it was a pretty big flat. The room was empty. Harnwood said, "This is where the various representatives sometimes gather to speak informally."

"Should I wait here?"

"No, we can find Lord Delwick's offices."

I was glad the room was empty. Meeting the Jhereg representative would have been awkward. We passed through it to a door at the other end, and stepped into a hallway. He nodded to the right. "That way, following it around to the right, you'll come back to the Imperial Audience Chamber, on the other side. Unfortunately, this is the fastest way without going through the Chamber, which is inappropriate."

"I understand," I lied.

He pretended to believe me and we turned left. There were a few doors on the right, and farther up the hallway split, but before that point he stopped outside one of the doors and clapped. There was the symbol of the Iorich above it. By then I hadn't eaten anything except a little dried fruit in about three years, and I was in a wretched mood. I resolved not to take it out on Lord Delwick.

"I can't wait—"

"Don't."

Rocza gave a little shiver that I'm pretty sure was laughter.

The door opened, and an elderly Dragaeran with severe eyebrows and thin lips was looking at us, with the smile of the diplomatist—that is, a smile that means nothing.

"Well met, Delwick."

"And you, Harnwood." He looked an inquiry at me.

"This is Lord Taltos, of House Jhereg, and he wishes a few words with you."

"Of course," he said. "Please come in and sit down." If he'd ever heard of me, he concealed it well.

Harnwood took his leave amid the usual polite noises and gestures all around, after which I accompanied Delwick into his room—or actually suite, because there were a couple of doors that presumably went to his private quarters or something. It was nice enough: a thick purple carpet of the sort that comes from Keresh or thereabouts, with complex interlocking patterns that took longer to make than a human usually lives. There was no desk, which somehow struck me as significant; there were just several stuffed chairs with tables next to them, as if to say, "We're only having a little chat here, nothing to worry about."

Heh.

He pointed to a chair, excused himself, and went through

one of the doors, returning in a moment with a plate of biscuits and cheese. I could have kissed him.

I said, "I hope you don't mind if I feed a bit to my friends here."

"Of course not, my lord."

I fed them, and myself, trying not to appear greedy, but also not worrying about it too much; there are times when the Dragaeran prejudices about humans can work for us. I didn't eat enough to be satisfied, but a few biscuits with even an excessively subtle (read: bland) cheese helped. He ate a few as well to keep company with me, as it were, while he waited for me to state my business.

I found the coin Perisil had given me, and showed it.

"Hmmm," he said. "All right." He looked up at me and nodded. "Very well." He sat back. "Tell me about it."

"Why is the prosecution of Aliera e'Kieron happening so quickly?"

He nodded a little. "I've wondered myself. So then, you have an advocate for her?"

"Perisil," I said.

"Hmmm. I'm afraid I don't recognize the name."

"He has a basement office."

"Where?"

"In the House."

"Ah, I see."

It seemed that the best advocates had quarters outside of the House. Maybe that should have shaken my confidence in Perisil, but I trusted his advice, and I'd liked him, and Loiosh hadn't made any especially nasty comments on him.

"I asked Her Majesty, and—"

"Pardon?"

"I asked Her Majesty about it, and she wouldn't answer."
Delwick caught himself and stopped staring. "I see."

"I hope my effort doesn't make your task more difficult."

He smiled politely. "We shall see," he said.

"So, you'll look into it?"

"Of course." He seemed genuinely startled that I'd even ask. Those little coins must have some serious authority. In which case, why did an advocate with offices in the basement of the House have one to throw around, or choose to use it on me?

Later. Note it, and set it aside.

"How shall I reach you?"

"Either through Perisil, or at Castle Black."

"Castle Black? Lord Mordran?"

"Morrolan."

"Of course. All right. You'll be hearing from me."

"Thank you," I said, standing. "Ah . . ."

"Yes?"

"Is there anywhere to eat here, in the Palace? I mean, for those of us who don't work here?"

He smiled. "Scores. The nearest is just out my door to the right, follow the jog to the right, down the stairs, first left."

"Thank you," I said, meaning it.

He nodded as if he couldn't tell the difference. I suppose if you hang around the Court long enough, you lose your ability to detect sincerity.

There was, indeed, food after a fashion; a room with space enough for a battalion held about four people, like a lonely jisweed on a rocky hill, and they were eating something dispensed by a tiny old Chreotha who seemed to be half asleep. I had unidentifiable soup that was too salty, yesterday's bread, and something that had once been roast beef. I had water because I didn't trust her wine. She charged too much. I couldn't figure why the place seemed so empty.

Loiosh didn't much like the stuff either, but he and Rocza ate it happily enough. Well, so did I, come to think of it. To be fair, it was, by this time, mid-afternoon; I imagined around lunchtime the place would be busier, and maybe the food fresher.

I finished up and left with a glare at the merchant—I won't call her a cook—that she missed entirely, and headed back to see my advocate. Aliera's advocate. The advocate.

At this point, I wish to make the observation that I had been spending the last several years wearing my feet out walking about the countryside, and I've known villages separated by mountain, river, and forest that weren't as far apart as a place within the Imperial Palace and another within the House of the Iorich located next to it. Loiosh says I'm speaking figuratively, and he may be right, but I wouldn't bet against the house on it.

I did get there eventually, and, wonder of wonders, he was still there, the door open, looking like he never moved. Maybe he didn't; maybe he had flunkies to do all his running around. I used to have flunkies to do all my running around. I liked it.

I walked in and before I could ask him anything he said, "It's all set up. Would you like to visit Aliera?"

Now that, as it happened, wasn't as easy a question as it might have sounded. But after hesitating only a moment I said, "Sure. The worst she can do is kill me."

That earned me an inquiring look which I ignored. "Are you coming along?" I asked him.

"No, you have to convince her to see me."

"Okay. How did you work it?"

"Her alleged refusal to see either a friend or an advocate could have indicated deliberate isolation on the part of the Empire with the cooperation of the Justicers."

I stared. "You think so?"

"I said it could."

"Oh. But you don't really think so?"

"I am most certainly not going to answer that, and don't ask it again."

"Oh. All right. But they believed it?"

"They believed I had grounds for an investigation."

"Ah. All right."

He nodded. "Now, go and see her."

"Um. Where? How?"

"Up one level, follow wrongwise until—here, I'll write out the directions; they're a bit involved."

They were. His scripting was painfully neat and precise, though he'd been fast enough writing it out. And I must have looked like an idiot, walking down the hall with two jhereg on my shoulders repeatedly stopping and reading the note and looking around. But those I passed were either as polite as Issola or as oblivious as Athyra, and eventually I got there: a pair of marble pillars guarded a pair of tall, wide doors engraved so splendidly with cavorting iorich that you might not notice the doors were bound in iron. You should go see them someday; cavorting iorich aren't something one sees depicted every day, and for good reason. Before them were four guards who looked like they had no sense of humor, and a corporal whose job it was to find out if you had good reason for wanting them open.

I convinced him by showing him that same coin I'd used

before, and there was a "clang" followed by invisible servants pulling invisible ropes and the doors opened for me. Morrolan worked things better.

It was a little odd to walk through those portals. For one thing, the other side was more what I was used to; I'd been there before, and a cold shiver went through me as I set foot on the plain stone floors. I'm not going to talk about the last time I was in the Iorich dungeons. And I'm certainly not going to talk about the time before that.

Just inside was a guard station, like a small hut with glass windows inside the wide corridor. There were a couple of couches there, I guess for them to sleep, and a table where the sergeant sat. There was a thick leather-bound book in front of him. He said, "Your business?"

"To see Aliera e'Kieron, by request of her advocate."

"Name?"

"Mine, or the advocate's?"

"Yours."

"Szurke."

"Seal?"

I dug it out and showed it to him. He nodded. "I was told you'd be by. You must either leave your weapons here, or sign and seal these documents and take an oath promising—"

"I know. I'll sign the documents and take the oath."

He nodded, and we went through the procedure that permitted me to keep Lady Teldra, whom I was not about to give up. When everything was finally done, he said, "Limper, show him to number eight."

The woman who stood up and gestured to me was a bit short and had a pale complexion and showed no signs of limping; no doubt there was a story there.

One thing about the dungeons is that unlike the rest of the
Iorich Wing, they were pretty simple: a big square of doors, guard
stations at all four corners, stairways in the middle. It might
involve a lot of walking, but you wouldn't get lost.

We took a stairway up. I'd never gone up from the main
level before. The first thing I noticed was that the cells, though
still made of the same iron-bound wood, were much farther
apart than the ones I'd had residence in. And they had clapper
ropes, for all love.

Limper used the rope, then dug out a key and used that
without waiting for a response. I guess they felt that the occu-
pants of these elite cells deserved warning about visitors, but
still didn't get a choice about whether they were admitted.
That made me feel a little better.

She opened the door and said, "You have an hour. If you
want to leave sooner, pull the knob attached to the inside of
the door." I stepped inside and the door closed behind me with
a thud. I heard the bolt slide into place while I looked around.

When I was growing up, the flat where my father and I lived
was a great deal smaller than the "cell" Aliera was in, and considerably less luxurious. The floor was thick Serioli carpet, with
wavy patterns and hard-angled lines all formed out of dots. The
furnishings were all of the same blond hardwood, and the light
was from a chandelier with enough candles to have illuminated
about fifty of the kind of cells I'd stayed in. I refer, of course,
only to the room I could see; there were at least two doors leading off to other rooms. Maybe one was a privy, and it was only a
two-room suite.

I didn't see Aliera at first; she was lounging on a long
couch that her plain, black military garb blended into; although I really ought to have seen the sparks shooting from

her eyes as she gave me the sort of kind, friendly, welcoming look I expected.

"What, by the thorns in Barlen's ass, do *you* want?"

"Can we just let that oath stay unexamined, Boss?"

"It's already gone, Loiosh."

It was, too; because while I was still searching for an answer, she said, "I didn't give you permission to visit."

"Your advocate arranged it."

"I don't have an advocate."

"Turns out you do."

"Indeed?" she said in a tone that would have put a layer of frost on Wynak's burning private parts.

"Some legal trick involved. I don't understand that stuff."

"And I have no say in the matter?"

"You had no say in being put here," I said, shrugging.

"Very well," she said. "Since they have taken Pathfinder from me, if he dares show his face, I shall have to see what I can do with my bare hands."

I nodded. "I knew you'd show sense."

She glared. "Do you know why I don't kill you right now?"

"Yes," I said. "Because to do so, you'd have to stand up. Once entering the Iorich dungeons, you are cut off from the Orb, and so you can't levitate, so I'd see how short you really are, and you couldn't take the humiliation. Going to offer me something to drink?" Just so you know, it had been years since she'd done that levitating bit; I just said it to annoy her.

She gestured with her head. "On the buffet. Help yourself."

I did, to a hard cider that was pretty good, though it wanted to be colder. I took a chair across from her and smiled pleasantly into her glare.

"So," I said. "What's new?"

Her response was more martial than ladylike.

"Yes," I said. "That part I sort of picked up on. But I was wondering about the details."

"Details." She said it like the word tasted bad.

"You were arrested," I said, "for the illegal study and practice—"

She had some suggestions about what I could do with my summary of her case.

I was coming to the conclusion that she wasn't in the best of moods for conversation. I sipped some cider, let it roll around on my tongue, and looked around the room. She even had windows. They had bars on them, but they were real windows. When I was in "Jhereg storage" I didn't have any windows. And they had done something that prevented psychic communication, though I'd still been able to talk to Loiosh, which put me in a better position than most.

"There is, I think, more going on here than just the violation of a law."

She stared at me.

I said, "You've been doing this for years, and everyone knows it. Why arrest you for it now? There has to be something political going on."

"You think?"

I said, "Just catching myself up out loud."

"Fine. Can you do it elsewhere? If there is anyone I want to see right now, it isn't you."

"Who is it?"

"Pathfinder."

"Oh. Well, yes." I could imagine one missing one's Great Weapon. I touched the hilt of Lady Teldra.

"Please leave," she said.

"Naw," I said.

She glared.

I said, "I need to get the details if I'm going to do anything about it. And I am going to do something about it."

"Why?" She pretty much spat the word.

"Don't be stupid," I said. "You know why. To gain the moral high ground on you. It's what I live for. Just the idea of you owing me—"

"Oh, shut up."

I did, and took the opportunity to ponder. I needed another way in. Once, years ago, I'd seen the room in Castle Black where the Necromancer lived, if it could be called a room. It could hardly be called a closet. There was space for her to stand, and that was it. I couldn't help but comment on how small it was, and she looked puzzled for a moment, then said, "Oh, but you only perceive three dimensions, don't you?" Yes, I'm afraid that's all I perceive. And my usual way of perceiving wasn't going to convince Aliera to tell me what was going on.

"What are they feeding you here?"

She looked at me.

I said, "When I was here, I got this sort of soup with a few bread crusts floating in it. I think they may have waved a chicken at it. I was just wondering if they were treating you any better."

"When were you here?"

"A few times. Not here, exactly. Same building, different suite. Mine wasn't so well appointed."

"What, that gives you moral superiority?"

"No, I get my moral superiority from having been guilty of what they arrested me for, and walking out free a bit later."

She sniffed.

I said, "Well, a kind of moral superiority anyway."

She muttered something about Jhereg. I imagine it wasn't complimentary.

"But then," I said, "you're guilty too. Technically, anyway. So I guess—"

"You know so much about it, don't you?"

I got one of those quick flashes of memory you get, this one of me lying on my back, unable to move, while bits and pieces of the world turned into something that ought not to exist. "Not so much," I said, "but more than I should."

"I'll agree with that."

"The point is, what would make the Empress suddenly decide that a law she was turning a blind eye to was now—"

"Ask her."

"She probably won't answer me," I said.

"And you think I will?"

"Why not?"

"I assume the question is rhetorical," said Aliera.

She looked away and I waited. I had some more cider. I love having a drink in my hand, because it gives me something to do while I'm waiting, and because I look really good holding it, shifting from foot to foot, like the waiter when the customer can't decide between the shrimp soufflé and the lamb Fenarian. Okay, maybe I don't look so good after all. I went over and sat down in a chair facing her, and took another sip. Much better.

"Yes," she said.

"Excuse me?"

"The question was rhetorical."

"Oh." Then, "Mine wasn't."

She settled back a little onto the couch. I let the silence continue to see if she'd finally say something. She did. "I don't know." She sounded quiet, reflective. It was unusual for her. I kept my mouth shut, sort of in honor of the novelty and to see if anything else would emerge.

"It isn't that simple," she said, as if I'd been the other party in whatever internal dialogue was going on.

"Explain, then."

"You keep wanting to make it friendship versus politics."

I nodded to indicate that I had no idea what she was talking about.

"But it's never that clear-cut. It's all about how bad this would be, and what are the chances of that happening, and how sure are you that this or that will or won't work."

I nodded again. Having Aliera e'Kieron in an expansive mood was too good a chance to mess up by speaking.

"But she wouldn't have done it unless—" She broke off and glared at me.

"Unless what?" I said.

"Just shut up."

"Don't feel like it," I said. "Will you talk to an advocate?"

"Why?"

"So they don't, I don't know, kill you or something?"

"You think I care about that?"

"I seem to recall you fighting once as if you did. Maybe you were faking it, though."

"You know damned well that's different."

"You know I've always had trouble seeing fine distinctions."

"You've always had trouble seeing anything that wasn't of immediate practical value."

"You say that like there's something wrong with it."

She made a sound of disgust.

"All right," I said. "Now probably isn't the time for philosophy. Will you talk to an advocate?"

"No," she said.

I took it as equivocal.

"Afraid you might be found innocent?"

She looked at me, then looked off. "Go away." Ambiguous.

"Sure. Meanwhile, what do you know or suspect that would have led to this, ah, situation, that you don't want revealed?"

"I'm not going to tell you anything, Vlad. Leave me alone."

It was hard to know how to react when she was being so hesitant about her wishes.

"You've been arrested for reasons of State," I said as if I were sure. "You may not know what they are, but you know that's what it is. And you're afraid that if you defend yourself it will interfere with whatever the Empress is doing."

"Drop dead."

"It must not have occurred to you that the Empress is counting on you to defend yourself, otherwise she'd never have used this device to accomplish whatever she's trying to accomplish."

She looked at me, and there was a flicker of interest in her eyes. "How would you know?"

"She told me. She all but told me, by what she wouldn't tell me."

"You spoke to her?"

"I can do that. I have an Imperial title, you know."

"And she said—"

"I got the feeling there were a lot of things going on she couldn't tell me."

"You got the feeling."

"Right."

"So you're guessing."

"Less than certainty, more than guesswork."

She made a general sound of disgust.

I waited. Dragonlords are much too stubborn to be convinced of anything by argument, so the trick to dealing with them is to avoid saying something that will get you killed until they come around to your opinion on their own. This is more true of Aliera than most.

She said, "If Her Majesty had not wished for my conviction, she wouldn't have begun the arrest proceedings."

"Uh huh," I said.

Those were the last words spoken for some few minutes. Spoken aloud, I mean; Loiosh spoke a bit into my mind, mostly making observations about Aliera's character. I'd heard them before. I'd said them before.

"I wish to reemphasize the one important thing," I said eventually.

"What. Is. That?"

"If you don't have an advocate, it'll be pretty obvious to everyone that you're deliberately sacrificing yourself. If you are deliberately sacrificing yourself, that is liable to undo a great deal of what the Empress is trying to accomplish."

She stared at me. I think she knew I was just trying to maneuver her into doing what I wanted; the trouble was that it was a valid argument. Eventually she said, "Is the advocate any good?"

"How would I know?" I said. "Probably not."

She glared. "All right. I'll see him."

"I'll let him know."

"Get out of here."

That time I did.

4

Lady Otria e'Terics reported that, while no weapons were found on the scene, save those in use by the Imperial army and so marked, and three personal, unmarked weapons claimed by same, there were several implements in or near the cottage that could have been utilized as weapons. See list Appendix 12. Upon being asked if there was evidence that they had been so utilized, Lady Otria e'Terics declined to answer. See Deposition 9.

There's an inn called Dancer's Rest not far from the Iorich Wing. It's one of those places where they figure if they fill the courtyard with marble statues and fountains and flowers that are blooming off-season, they can charge two orbs a night for a nine-copper room. It works, I guess. At least, I paid it. Some of the statues were pretty. And, you know, when you've been away from civilization for a while, you value a nine-copper room at any price.

It had the other advantage that, by Jhereg custom, anyone staying there was considered at home. In theory, I should be safe there. In practice, since one of the things the Jhereg wanted me for was breaking a rule like that, I probably shouldn't bet my soul on it.

It cost another orb to have food sent up to my room, which had a window from which I could see the upper reaches of the Iorich and the Chreotha Wings, the first with its signature bell tower, the latter with its massive wall of bas-relief jungle plants. I could see them well, because the window was glass. That's the sort of thing you get for two orbs a night.

The bed was considerably softer than the ground I'd gotten used to sleeping on, and there was even enough room to turn with my arms stretched out. That's the thing about rooms near the Palace: They're small; probably designed to make the Palace seem bigger, I don't know.

"You ever planning to fall asleep, Boss?"

"The walls are too thick. It's too quiet. I'm used to things chittering and rustling all night."

He didn't answer, and somewhere in there I fell asleep and had a confusing dream about thick walls that were in between me and something I wanted, I don't remember what, and I kept trying to dig through them with the dull edge of a knife. Why the dull edge? How should I know; I was only a spectator.

I woke late the next morning, feeling pretty good. Loiosh and Rocza scouted the area, decided it was safe, and I went out looking for klava. Found some. Drank it. Was happy. I also picked up a warm sweet bun stuffed with kethna, and it was good too. Then, with Loiosh and Rocza taking precautions for me, I made my way back to the Iorich Wing.

The advocate's door was closed and there was a note pinned to it with the initial V in tight, careful script. I took down the note and unfolded it to read, "Running an errand; wait in my office."

I shrugged and reached for the door handle, and Loiosh said, *"Boss!"*

I froze. *"What is it?"*

"I don't know."

My hand brushed Lady Teldra's hilt, but I didn't draw. Pulling a Morganti weapon in the House of the Iorich is the sort of thing that gets you talked about, and I wasn't going to do it if I didn't have to.

"Something about that note bothers me."

"If you tell me you've suddenly turned into a handwriting expert—"

He didn't answer; I could feel him thinking, or at least doing something with his mind, probing or sensing in a way that I couldn't feel. I waited. I hoped no one walked by, because I'd either kill him or feel like an idiot for standing outside of this door not moving. I studied the note again. Was it the same handwriting I'd seen from Perisil? Pretty close. I started to pull out the directions he'd written out for me to compare the writing, but Loiosh spoke before I could.

"There's someone inside."

"Okay."

"It isn't him."

"Okay. Anyone else around?"

"A few of the other offices have people in them."

"Send Rocza ahead."

She left my shoulder almost before the words were out of my metaphorical mouth. I turned and walked back the way I'd come—not too fast, not too slow, trying to stay alert for any sound, any flicker of movement. It's the sort of experience that wakes up every particle of your body. If it weren't for the thrill of the thing, I'd just as soon skip it completely.

"She says it's clear ahead, Boss."

The hallway was much, much longer than it had been two minutes before when I was going the other way, and my footsteps were much louder. Two Justicers were walking slowly toward me, deep in conversation, and I gave them an extra look even though I could tell they weren't Jhereg from the frankly curious glance they gave me. I could feel Loiosh watching them until they were well past.

I reached the stairway at the far end of the hallway with Rocza still scouting ahead. On the main floor I could relax a little; there were uniformed armsmen there, and a few more people as well as more open space; it was a bad place for an assassin to make a move.

The same elderly woman was in the same place near the door. Next to her was a Chreotha with a cart selling food of some sort. I bought a hot and flaky pastry filled with garlicky potato. I stood off to the side eating and thinking.

I fed the remainders to the jhereg; people around pretended not to notice. Lady Teldra would have been proud of them.

I brushed crumbs off my fingers.

"Okay, Boss. Now where?"

"Somewhere safe."

"Yeah, like I said."

"This is pretty safe, but I think after standing here six or seven hours I'll start to feel silly."

"When has that—"

"Of course, it might be fun to stand here until the assassin gives up and leaves, and then give him a big smile as he goes by."

"Sure, Boss. Whatever floats your castle."

"The other idea is not to do that." I reviewed a list of more

practical possibilities, then approached the woman behind the desk with a short bow. "Is there a common waiting area?"

She frowned. "If you wish to see an advocate, they each have offices."

"Yes," I said. "I'd rather wait elsewhere, if you don't mind."

She looked like she wanted to ask why, but only gestured to her right, saying, "Fourth door on the right. It should be open."

"Can a note be delivered to Lord Perisil?"

She frowned again. "Would that be High Counsel Perisil?"

"Yes," I said, while the ghost of Lady Teldra probably tsked at me for not knowing the proper title and at her for correcting me.

The clerk was kind enough to let me use a piece of coarse paper and a cheap pencil. I wrote a short note and handed it over, not even bothering to fold it. "I do not know the customs of your House," I said. "I trust this will go to his hand, and nowhere else?"

"That is correct," she said, a bit contemptuously. She probably hated her job, sitting there hour after hour sending people one way or another. I wondered how long she'd been doing it. Since the Interregnum ended, to look at her.

She took the note and put it casually on her desk under what looked like a piece of polished stone. I turned away from her slowly, scanning the room: A few people, mostly Iorich, were passing by on business of their own. The jhereg got some curious glances.

The place she'd directed me to was big and comfortable, mostly done in a pale blue that was probably calculated to make me feel something or other.

"*You know, Boss, for someone who hates waiting—*"

"*Oh, shut up.*"

Not that he wasn't right. I found a chair against a wall because all of the chairs were against a wall. I stretched my legs
out, closed my eyes, and tried to relax. Somewhere below me,
there was a Jhereg expecting me to walk into Perisil's office so
I could be killed. Was Perisil in on it? Unlikely. The Jhereg
don't like to use advocates for illegal stuff; and besides, if he'd
been in on it the note wouldn't have looked funny.

Here's the thing: Anyone can be shined. That's just how it
is. If you want someone bad enough, you can get him. But if
he knows you're after him, he can pretty much keep out of
trouble as long as he stays alert. Which makes the question
simple: How long can someone stay alert, always watching al-
leyways, aware of anyone who is carefully not looking at you,
keeping an eye out for a good place to make a move. How long
can you keep that up?

For most people, the answer is: hours, maybe a day or two.

But it turns out that you can do it a lot longer if you have
a pair of jhereg taking shifts for you.

Did that mean I was safe? Not hardly. Sooner or later they
were bound to get me. But thanks to Loiosh and Rocza, I had
a pretty reasonable chance of making it later rather than
sooner as long as I didn't do too many stupid things.

I know what you're thinking, and you're wrong; I've gone
for months without doing anything stupid. Did I just survive
this time because the assassin got sloppy? Maybe. I'd like to
think that if it were me I'd have been more careful with the
note. Perhaps not, though. No one can do everything perfectly;
mistakes happen. But we're assassins: when we make mistakes,
people live.

From time to time someone would come into the room,
wait for a while, be met by someone, and leave. I guess I was

there for a couple of hours before Perisil came in. He nodded to me, and said, "You could have waited in my office."

I stood up, nodded, and followed him back down the stairs. We didn't see anyone in the long hallway. He walked in, took a seat behind his desk, and gave me a questioning look. I decided it was a safe bet that if there'd been an assassin standing there holding a knife, he'd have reacted somehow, so I went in after him and took a seat.

"Want to explain?" he said.

"Explain what?"

"Never mind, then."

"You saw Aliera?"

"Just got back. She's very, ah, proud," he said.

"If you aren't stating the obvious, then I'm missing the point."

"I'm stating the obvious."

"All right."

"Mostly." He sat down behind the desk as if he'd just been through a battle. It was a very familiar motion, although when I sat down like that, the battle had usually been more physical.

"Want to tell me about it?" I said.

"I got her to agree to let me defend her."

"Well done."

"But she won't cooperate in the endeavor."

"That would be a problem."

"Yes."

"So, what are you going to do?"

"Think about it."

"I've tried that with Aliera."

"Not much luck?"

"She isn't subject to what passes for logical thought in most people."

He nodded. "I'll see what I can come up with. Have you learned anything?"

"The Empress was hit with some sort of disaster that reflects badly on her."

"With whom?"

"Knowing the Empress, probably history. She's never seemed to care much about public opinion."

"Can you be more specific?"

"Not very. Not yet."

"You think it might be Tirma?"

"Maybe. Hard to say, since this is the first I've ever heard of Tirma."

"Oh. That's right, you've been out of the city, haven't you?"

"Yes. I only heard about Aliera's arrest by a fluke."

"Tirma is a village in the far northwest. There was some unrest there, and a request for Imperial troops. No one knows what happened, but some peasants were slaughtered."

"Innocent ones?"

"Some say."

"I'll bet Kelly has a lot to say on the subject."

"Who?"

"Never mind. How does arresting Aliera help? A distraction?"

"Maybe."

He looked like he was thinking, so I let him alone. After a minute or two he said, "The bigger question is, how does Aliera think it helps?"

"Yeah," I said. "Assuming all our speculations are right."

"We have to find out for sure."

"You're telling me that's my job."

"I'm saying I expect your help."

I grunted. "I guess that's fair."

He nodded.

I suppose I could have told him that the Jhereg already knew I was back in town, and it wouldn't be safe for me to go sniffing around places. But then what? I mean, it had to be done.

"Sure, Boss. But do you have to be the one to do it?"

"Seems like."

"Why?"

"No one else is."

"Right, Boss. Why?"

"Oh."

". . . and until then, I'm not going to be able to—"

"Sorry, I was distracted. Start over?"

He gave me an odd look. "I was saying that I need something I can take to a Justicer."

"What do you mean, take to a Justicer?"

"I mean sending a Petition of Release, or make a case for Dishonorable Prosecution."

"Dishonorable Prosecution? They have that?"

"It's in the books."

"How many times has it been brought?"

"Successfully?"

"At all."

"Twenty-seven."

"Successfully?"

"Never."

"You'd bring that against the Empress?"

"Against the Empire, but, in effect, yes."

"Forget it. Aliera will never permit it."

He nodded as if he'd come to the same conclusion. "Probably true, but I want to have it there anyway."

"Whatever you think," I said.

"What I think is that this is very odd."

"Seems like it to me, too. The Empress prosecuting a friend isn't—"

"No, that's not what's odd; Emperors do what they have to do, and being a friend to an Emperor sometimes means losing your head. It's always been like that."

"All right, then. What's odd?"

"The law they're prosecuting her with. It isn't intended to be used against high nobles whose House is near the top of the Cycle."

"Ah, you'll have to explain that."

"What's to explain?"

"Some laws apply to high nobles, and some not?"

"How else?"

"Um. I don't know. I hadn't thought about it."

"To prosecute a noble under the Code, you have to get a majority vote of the princes. The princes aren't going to vote against a noble when the House is powerful without a more compelling case than this is."

"So this is a waste of time?"

"No, no—you misunderstand. That's under the Code. This is an Imperial Edict, which means the Empress and the High Justicer make the decision. That's why they can get a conviction."

"Well then, what's—"

"But using the Edicts against a noble, at a time when you couldn't get a conviction, is going to raise quite a stink among the princes. The High Justicer has to know that, and so does the Empress."

"Would they let that interfere with justice?"

"Are you being funny?"

"Yes."

"Eh. I guess it was a little funny at that. But, you know, there is making the law, and enforcing the law, and interpreting the law, and they all mix up together, and it's people who do those things, and the people all mix up together. You can't separate them."

"It'd be interesting to try."

He waved it aside. "The point is, this will create lots of bad feelings among those who matter. And bad feelings are bad statesmanship, and the Empress isn't known for bad statesmanship."

"Um. Okay, I think I get the idea. What's your conclusion?"

"My conclusion is that I want to know what's going on. I'll look at it from my end, you look at it from yours."

"All right."

"Do you know how you're going to start?"

"Of course not."

He nodded like he'd have been surprised to get any other answer. "Are you open to suggestions?"

"Sure."

"Stay away from the Empress."

"That part is easy. I don't have that much call to see her, you know. But that only tells me what not to do."

"I'm sure we can find more things for you not to do if we put our minds to it."

"*See, Boss? He* does *have a sense of humor.*"

"*Such as it is.*" Aloud, I said, "You need something that will provide a legal angle for Aliera."

He nodded.

"Yeah, well, I know about as much about the law as you know about—that is, I don't know much about the law."

"You don't need to. Find out why they're prosecuting Aliera, and be able to prove it."

"Prove it. What does that mean, exactly?"

"Find people who saw or heard things, and will swear to it beneath the Orb."

"Oh, and where would I—oh."

"Right. But stay away from the Empress."

"Great. And what will you be doing?"

"Same as you, only to different people. And I'll be reviewing the laws, and looking through decisions and case histories. You aren't going to be too useful for that part."

"I imagine not." I stood and headed out.

Let me explain again something I've already mentioned: The way an assassin operates involves picking a time and a place, setting up whatever is necessary (which usually means making sure you have a good edge on your knife), and striking. If for some reason things go wrong—like, say, the guy gets suspicious about the handwriting of a note—then you go back and start over. All of which means that no one was going to be making a move on me for a day at least. Which means I should have been able to relax as I left the waiting room and headed toward the Palace.

Yeah, well, you try it sometime and see how relaxed you are.

Loiosh was pretty tense too, either because he sensed that

I was, or because he knew what was going on. It's pretty crazy, that feeling of walking through a big, wide corridor, your boots echoing, almost no one in sight, thinking you're safe, but feeling anything but. I stopped just inside the door to cross the wide pavement to the Iorich Wing, and let Loiosh and Rocza explore carefully. The trees that dotted the pavement were too thin for anyone to hide behind, but I studied them anyway.

I kept an even walking pace across the long, long, long paved promenade between the House of the Iorich and the Palace.

"Boss, no one is going to make a move in the middle of the day, out in the open, in front of the Imperial Palace."

"Who are you trying to convince?"

"Me, of course."

"Just checking."

"But you have to figure you're being watched."

"I know."

I got inside, and started toward the Imperial Wing. I had the idea that it would be fun to count the number of disdainful looks I got on the way, but I forgot to actually do it. I'm still not sure how I got lost; I thought I had the route memorized. I wasn't even aware of having gone wrong until I stepped into a large open area I hadn't realized existed, and heard the drone of voices and saw strange and wondrous things: a shoemaker's shop, a tailor's, a wine seller's, a sorcerer's supply, a silversmith. The ceiling, if you can call it that, was high and domed, and somehow the dome's silvery white color made it seem even higher.

"Boss, there's a whole town here."

"I think I should have gone up that flight of stairs I went down."

"Or maybe down the one you went up?"

"*This is a whole city.*"

"*There's probably an inn with better food than that place yesterday.*"

"*I can always count on you to get right to the important stuff.*"

"*The important stuff is finding your way back to where you want to be.*"

"*The important stuff is not to get killed. This is a good place to shine someone up.*"

"Oh," he said. And, "*It is, isn't it?*"

"*It's still too soon for them to have set anything up, but—*"

"*We're watching, Boss.*"

I tried to be inconspicuous—which I'm not bad at, by the way, even with a pair of jhereg on my shoulders—and looked for someone to ask directions of.

A girl who was too young to work for the Jhereg came along, carrying a box full of something that steamed. Probably someone's lunch that I was going to make cold.

"I beg your pardon, lady," I said. Teckla especially like being called "lady" when they're too young to be. "Can you tell me how to get out of here?"

She stopped. "Out of where?"

"To the Palace."

"You're in the Palace, sir." Her tone said she thought I was deranged or else stupid.

"The Imperial Wing."

"Oh." She gestured with her chin. "That way until you see the three pillars, then left to the wide stairway, and up. You'll be right there."

"You have my thanks."

There were streets, buildings, pushcarts with food, and I

think I even saw a beggar. What I didn't see were three pillars, until I finally noticed what looked like an inn in miniature—chairs and tables set in a small courtyard near a long bar—that spread beneath a hanging sign showing three pillars. Yeah, all right.

After that it was easy enough to find the stairway (I climbed a lot of stairs, but not as many as it seemed I should have climbed to get above that domed ceiling; there's some weird geometry with that place), and a bit later I found a page in Tiassa livery who was kind enough to point me in the right direction. Ten minutes or so later I was once more in an area that looked familiar—for the symbols of the Imperial Phoenix that marked every door, if for no other reason.

It was the middle of the day, and it was busy—Phoenix Guards looking impassive, advisers looking serious, adjutants looking important, courtiers looking courtly, and all of them moving past me like I was standing in the middle of a stream that flowed around me as if I were of no interest, and it might sweep me off if it felt inclined. I looked for someone who wasn't in a hurry, because rushing down a hallway filled with teeming functionaries isn't the best way to have a conversation.

After about fifteen minutes, I gave up and started drifting along in what I was pretty sure was the direction of the throne room.

"*Not to make you nervous or anything, Boss, but someone who could nail you here, right in the Imperial Wing, would earn himself quite the reputation.*"

"Yeah."

The hallways of the Imperial Wing near the throne room are wide and tall and copper-colored, and you can't imagine there being a time of day or night when they aren't full of people scurrying about looking important. Here and there were wide archways or narrow doors, and from time to time someone will vanish into one or pop out and enter the flow. I didn't go out of my way to call attention to myself, but I didn't try to fit in, either, because that would have involved becoming part of the constant movement, and I wanted to take some time to just observe.

Eventually I found a place I recognized—I'd eaten there yesterday. I didn't care to make that mistake again, but a number of others weren't so particular: this time the place was doing a pretty good business. There was a low, steady hum of voices punctuated by metal trays and utensils.

I stood off the side for a while and just watched. On the other side, all alone at a table, there was a Dragaeran of middle years—say a thousand or so—who had the pale complexion and round face of the House of the Teckla. I studied him for a moment; he was drinking slowly, and seemed relaxed and maybe lost in thought. I approached and said, "Mind if I join you?"

He jumped a bit and started to rise, took in my mustache, the jhereg on my shoulders, and my sword. He hesitated and frowned; I gestured to him to remain sitting to make it easy for him. Teckla are never exactly sure whether they are above or below a nobleman who happens to be an Easterner—we throw off all of their calculations just by existing.

"By all means, my l . . . ah, sir."

"Thanks," I pulled up a chair. "I'll buy you another of whatever you have there, if you don't mind. What does the yellow armband signify?"

He had light brown hair peeking out from under a hat that

was too tall and not wide enough to look anything but absurd. He glanced at the armband as if he didn't realize it was there, then said, "Oh, I'm a message-runner."

"For whom?"

"For hire, sir. Did you wish a message sent somewhere within the Palace? If it is outside the Palace itself, I have to charge more, because I pass it on to—"

"No, no. I was just curious about what it meant."

He nodded, held up his mug, and gestured in the direction of a young Chreotha who seemed to be working for the older woman who was still there, only now much more awake.

"I'm Vlad," I said. "Baronet of this, Imperial Count of that, but skip all that." He wouldn't, of course. He'd be incapable of skipping it.

"I'm Poncer," he said.

"Well met."

He gave Loiosh and Rocza a look, but then his drink arrived—it smelled like the sort of dark beer that makes me hate beer—and that distracted him.

"What can I do for you, sir?" he asked after a swallow.

"Tell me what you know."

"Sir?"

I smiled. "Do you need to be anywhere for the next couple of hours?"

"Well, I should look for work—"

"How much do you earn?"

"Three pennies within the Imperial Wing. If I have to—"

I gave him an imperial.

He stared at it, then at me, then back to it, then he took it and put into a pouch at his side.

I now had his attention.

5

The orders from the Warlord to General Lady Fardra e'Baritt were not put in specific terms (see Appendix 2), but did include the phrase "minimal damage to property and non-combatants in the region is a priority second only to suppression of the disorders." One question before this committee, then, is to consider what "minimal" means in this context, and who is a non-combatant, and who can reasonably be assumed to be a non-combatant by individual soldiers of various ranks and responsibilities in high-risk areas.

"You see people," I told him.

"My lord?"

I'm not completely sure how much the titles and how much the imperial had to do with me becoming "my lord." I said, "I'm trying to learn my way around this place, and who's who, so I don't make a fool of myself when I meet strangers."

He nodded as if it were a great idea, and he was just the man for the job.

"Who do you want to know about first?" He had a serious, business-like expression. I avoided laughing in his face because it would have been unproductive, not to mention rude.

"Who is close to Her Majesty?"

"Close?" he said, as if I'd mentioned something scandalous.

"Who does she listen to?"

"Oh," he said, and looked thoughtful again. "Well, first, there's Lady Mifaant."

"Who is she?"

"An Issola. She doesn't have, ah, an office or anything. I mean, there's no name for it. But she's Her Majesty's, um, I don't know the word. The person the Empress goes to when something is bothering her."

"Confidant? Best friend?"

Something about that bothered him—like, I don't know, maybe the Empress isn't supposed to have friends—but he finally gave a hesitant nod.

"Who else?"

"Nerulan, of course. Her physicker."

I nodded.

"And her, well—" He hesitated, and turned a little red.

"Hmmm?"

"You know."

"I don't, actually. Unless you mean she has a lover."

He nodded once, watching me carefully, as if for a clue as to what sort of expression he should have.

"Who is he? Or she?"

"He. He's, um, he's . . ." His voice trailed off and looked a little desperate.

"An Easterner?" I said. In fact, I knew very well, but the less I admitted to knowing, the more he'd tell me.

He nodded.

"Yeah," I said. "I'd heard rumors. What's his name?"

"Laszló," he said. I nodded. Poncer dropped his voice and said, "He's a witch."

"Well," I said. "Interesting."

And it was.

"He's been alive for, well, longer than they're supposed to live, anyway." He looked at me, reddened again, and became very interested in his drink.

I gave him what I calculated to be a friendly, reassuring chuckle. "What does he look like?"

He frowned. "Like you," he said. "His skin is your color, and he has hair growing like you have, above his lip. More hair, though, and curlier."

"I take it he's usually surrounded by courtiers?"

"They try," he said.

"Yeah, they would."

"He tries to stay away from them, though."

"I don't blame him. So, how do I manage to talk to him?"

"Um," he said. I think the question startled him. Gossip was one thing; actually using the gossip seemed to make him uncomfortable. I waited.

"I don't know," he said. "I can't think of any way."

I waited some more.

"It won't help," he said, "but there are rumors . . ."

"Yes?"

"There are rumors that he knows the Enchantress of Dzur Mountain."

I didn't have to pretend to look startled.

"Easy, Boss. 'Rumors,' remember?"

"But still—"

"And if she knew him, why didn't she ever mention it?"

"Oh, come on, Loiosh. She's Sethra."

"That's good to know," I told Poncer. "Who else sees the Empress? Does she have a Prime Minister?"

"No," he said. "Well, some say she does, but it's secret."

"She must have advisers she consults regularly."

"The Warlord, for anything about the army. And the Lady of the Chairs for anything to do with the Council of Princes. And then for finances and stuff—"

"The Warlord."

He nodded.

"I thought the Warlord was under arrest."

"The new Warlord."

"Who is the new Warlord?"

"Her Highness Norathar," he said.

I stared at him. After a moment, I said, "I thought she was Dragon Heir."

"She's both."

"Interesting. And they see each other often?"

"I don't know."

"Who is Lady of the Chairs?"

"Lord Avissa."

"House?"

"Issola. The Lady of the Chairs is always an Issola."

"Oh. Of course." I almost touched the hilt of Lady Teldra, but I didn't want to make Poncer any more nervous than I had to.

We talked a little longer about inconsequential things,

and I bought him another beer, dodged a few polite questions, and took my leave. I'm much better at getting information from Teckla than I used to be, thanks to a ghost and a knife, in that order. Long story, never mind.

Norathar and Sethra. Yeah, I shouldn't be surprised that two of the Empress's secret confidants were people I knew. Aliera herself was a third, for that matter. I had surrounded myself with those types by a complex process that had started years ago when a minor button-man started skimming from me. And no, I'm not about to give you any more details. Get over it.

I thought about walking to the Dragon Wing and seeing if I could have a long chat with Norathar e'Lanya, the Warlord and Dragon Heir. Once, she'd been a Jhereg assassin. She'd worked with the Easterner who became my wife.

My son would be about eight now. The last time I'd seen him, he'd been four. A lot goes on in those four years. By now—

No.

I stood still in a hallway deep in the heart of the Palace that controlled the mighty Empire of Dragaerans, letting humanity (to use the term loosely) flow around me, and tried to convince myself to attend to business. Seeing Cawti and my son would make me miserable and put them in danger. So, naturally, it was exactly what I wanted to do.

Cawti had named him Vlad Norathar.

I suddenly had the feeling that if I met with Norathar—I mean, the Warlord—I'd smack her on the side of the head. Probably best not to talk to her just now.

"Boss?"

"Mmmm?"

"We should visit Sethra."

"I know."

"You don't want to?"

"Partly that. Partly, I don't want the whole Jhereg knowing I went there. Castle Black is one thing, but Dzur Mountain—"

"You think you'd be in danger in Dzur Mountain?"

"No, not danger. I just don't feel comfortable having the Jhereg know I'm there; at least right away."

"Oh."

"Maybe there's a way . . . okay, let's do it."

"Uh, how, Boss?"

"How what? How do we get there? I have a clever and devious plan."

"Oh, great."

I worked my way around to the Athyra Wing and, eventually, out into the world. It was bright out there, making me think of the East where there's no overcast to protect you from the Furnace. I blinked and waited for my eyes to adjust.

The Athyra Wing is usually pretty quiet and today was no exception; that meant that just in case there were any assassins who'd been following me waiting for an opportunity, I'd see them—pardon me, Loiosh would see them in plenty of time. I set out on the Street of the Athyra, turning to pass the obsidian monolith (oh, yes, we're so impressive) of the House of the Athyra on my right, continuing just a few score of yards beyond it to Mawg Way. "Mawg," I was once told, means "merchant" in some disused language that goes back to before there were any such things as merchants. That makes you wonder, you know? I mean, "mawg." An ugly word. Where did they get "merchant" out of that? Maybe there are people who study things like that. If so, they're probably Athyra.

A few doors down, on the left side, was a windowless cottage built of round stones. It had a thick door bound in iron strips; the door was standing open. Above the doorway was a particularly detailed sign in which an Athyra was flying over a map of the Empire.

"Boss, you aren't serious."

"Why not?"

"Ever heard of the Left Hand of the Jhereg, Boss? You know, the sorceresses?"

"Sounds familiar."

"Boss, the Left Hand doesn't like you. And even if they did, the Jhereg could hire one of them to watch places like this. As soon as you teleport, a sorcerer can . . . what are you laughing about?"

"Just watch me, Loiosh."

I went in. The entry room was just big enough, and held a door opposite. A young lady of the House of the Athyra sat in a wooden chair facing the door, looking serious and mystical and very business-like: she may as well have had "apprentice" stenciled on her forehead.

She looked me over, decided on just how noble I was (I was an Easterner, but I dared to wear a sword openly), and inclined her head slightly. "Yes, sir?"

"How much is a teleport?"

"One imperial, to a known location."

"How much to have the sorcerer come to me?"

"My lord? Oh, you mean to teleport from somewhere else? Two imperials, if it's within the city."

"And how much to have it done surreptitiously, and untraceably? And add in a short-term spell to make me sorcerously invisible."

"How short-term?"

"A minute. Half a minute."

"Ten."

"That's fine. My name is Vladimir Taltos, I'll be going to Dzur Mountain, and I wish to have a sorcerer meet me in the Temple of Verra on Waterhill in South Adrilankha."

Her nose wrinkled and she hesitated, looking for an excuse to say no. Eventually she said, "I'll have to ask."

"I'll wait here," I said.

She gave me a suspicious look before going through the door. It isn't like there was anything in the room to steal. She returned a moment later, asked for my name again. This time she wrote it on a small slab of some sort, and nodded. "She will meet you."

"Want the money now?"

"If you please."

I put two five-imperial coins into her hand and sketched a bow. I opened the door, standing far enough to the side not to be open to anything unpleasant that might shoot through it, but not so far as to make it obvious what I was doing. Loiosh flew out; I'd have loved to see the look on the apprentice's face, but my back was to her. Loiosh said it was safe, so I stepped out onto the street.

Crowded streets make it harder to set something up reliably, but easier to get the drop on your target, and easier to get away safely afterward. Empty streets, of course, have the opposite problems. I compromised and took a mix of both, making my way to the Chain Bridge and so across to South Adrilankha.

"So, Loiosh, you get it?"

"I know what you're thinking—the Jhereg won't go after you in a temple."

"Right."

"But you still have to get to the temple."

"I have complete confidence in you."

One thing that cannot be done psychically is mutter, but Loiosh took a pretty good run at it.

There are scores of shrines to Verra in the city, and several temples to her in South Adrilankha. The one I'd chosen was a low stonework affair, set back from the road, with a flagstone walk flanked by scrawny trees. Moreover, it was in a neighborhood with a lot of space between the houses. Put it all together, and there were no good places for assassins to hide. Even Loiosh grudgingly agreed, after a few minutes flying around, that I could go ahead and venture up to the doors—after that, he made no guarantees.

Opening the door was scary. I didn't care how stupid I looked; I listened, stood to the side, and was moving when I flung it open.

No one was there. Yeah, I looked stupid. I might have gotten some funny glances from people passing on the street, but I didn't wait around to see, I just stepped inside.

It was a single room, with a black altar opposite the door, about ten paces from me. I knew from memory that there were small holes cut into the altar for candles, though I couldn't see them from here. Beyond that, the place was utterly bare. The priest here believed that one should bring nothing to the Goddess but the desire to serve, or something like that. I don't remember exactly how he'd put it; it was years ago. Services here were held two or three times a week, I forget the times and dates, and on the obvious feast days.

I positioned myself behind the altar and waited for the sorcerer—or an assassin, if I'd misjudged the Jhereg. Sorry, don't mean to be mysterious. There are rules to how we operate: you don't kill someone in front of his family, you don't mess with him in his home, you don't touch him in a temple or at a shrine.

The thing is, all of these rules have, at one time or another, been violated; one reason I was in trouble with the Jhereg was for violating one of them. I'd had a bad day that day. The point is, I was calculating on them following the rules, at least this time, and for a while. If I was wrong, things were liable to get exciting.

I got to be nervous for about twenty minutes before the sorceress showed up. No assassins came with her. Score one for me. She had the dark complexion of the Athyra but her hair was such a light brown it was almost blond, producing a slightly startling effect. There was a vague look in her eyes that was common if not universal among Athyra.

She gave the place a half-interested and disdainful look, then nodded at me. "Lord Taltos?" she said.

I nodded.

"Dzur Mountain," she said. "Untraceable, with a brief lingering cloud."

I nodded again.

She looked like she might be considering offering me advice on going there, but she must have decided not to, and just said, "Are you ready?"

I pulled the amulet from around my neck and put it away, thus, no doubt, alerting a dozen or so Jhereg sorcerers. "Ready," I said.

She didn't even gesture, as far as I could see; for an instant the room seemed about to spin, but then it went through a familiar slow fade, going through all the colors from white to almost-white; interminable seconds went by when I was in two places at once, and I could feel myself pushing air out of the way. In that time, it suddenly hit me that she might have been bribed, and be delivering me to an assassin. In that empty, lingering time-space, I became so convinced of it that I was already reaching for a dagger when the world settled down to a familiar place on the lower slopes of Dzur Mountain.

My first reaction was relief, my second was annoyance. Yeah, this place was familiar—I knew how to reach Sethra's home from this spot: it involved climbing more stairs than ought to exist in the world. I wondered if the sorceress had brought me to this entrance deliberately. I still wonder.

I replaced the amulet then entered through a wooden door that wasn't nearly as flimsy as it appeared. You don't clap when entering Dzur Mountain—depending on which door you use, at any rate. I've wondered about that, and I think it's because in some way the mountain itself isn't her home, only the parts of it that she claimed as her residence; and so I passed through the first door into the mountain, and started climbing stairs. It seemed much louder this time, my feet on the stone stairway made echoes and echoes of echoes; my memory was doing the same thing.

You don't need to hear about it; it was a long, long way up. Partway up, I passed the place where Morrolan and I had almost slaughtered each other; it bothered me a little that I couldn't identify the exact spot.

Eventually I reached the top, clapped, and opened the door without waiting for a reply. Her residence doesn't seem all that big once you're aware of the size of the mountain; but then there's probably a lot I haven't seen. And, at her age, I imagine she needs lots of space to store stuff she's accumulated.

I wandered a bit, hoping to run into her, or her servant, or someone. The halls—dark stone here, pale wood there—all echoed strangely and gave me the sudden feeling that Dzur Mountain was deserted. It wasn't, actually—I came across her in one of the smaller sitting rooms that she put here and there. She was drinking a glass of wine and reading a thick, heavy book with a cover I couldn't see. She wore a black garment that seemed to wrap around her, pinned with a gold or copper bracelet at the left arm, and looping through a jeweled necklace high on her chest, with another loop on her right hip with similar jewels. She said, "Hello, Vlad," without looking up. I took that as a cue to stand there like an idiot, so I did, and presently she marked the book with something that looked like it had silver tracings on it and gave me a nod. "I've been expecting you."

"It takes a while for word to reach the outlands. That's a nice dress you're wearing. Are those sapphires on the necklace?"

"A gift from the Necromancer. Have a seat. Tukko will bring you wine."

I sat in a chair that faced her at a slight angle. "And I will drink it. Good. We have a plan."

A courtesy smile came and went.

Tukko showed up with wine and a scowl. The wine was less offensive; a strongly flavored red that should have had some heavily spiced meat to go with it, but I didn't complain. I sipped, nodded, and said, "So, what can you tell me?"

"I was going to ask you that."

"Heh. I just came in from out of town."

"Yes, and found an advocate, got Aliera to accept him—which ought to rate you as a master sorcerer—and you've been snooping around the Imperial Palace since then. So—what can you tell me?" She smiled sweetly.

I stared at her, remembering things about her I sometimes forget. Then I said, "If you were trying to impress me, it worked."

"Permit me my small pleasures."

"I'd never think of denying them to you," I said. "All right. In brief, the Empress seems to be prosecuting Aliera to distract attention from some massacre in some little town no one cares about. The mystery is that she picked Aliera, who I've always figured was a close friend. The charge, as far as I can tell, is nonsense."

She nodded slowly. "It isn't as if the Empress hasn't known about Aliera's studies for years."

"Right."

"When you spoke to Her Majesty, what was the Orb doing?"

"Eh? Floating over her head."

"I mean, what color was it?"

"Green at first. Orange when I annoyed her. It turned blue around the end of the conversation. She said she had to go do something."

"What shade of blue?"

"Um, shade?"

"Did it seem cold, icy?"

"Sorry, I don't have that good a memory for colors."

"All right," she said.

"Can you explain—?"

"Not really. Just trying to learn everything I can. I wish I'd been there."

"Yes. That brings up another interesting point." I cleared my throat. "Why weren't you?"

"Beg pardon?"

"That's what I really wanted to ask you. Why is this my job?"

She frowned. "No one is forcing you—"

"That's not my point. Aliera has friends coming out her—Aliera has a lot of friends. Most of them are more influential than an ex-Jhereg Easterner on the run. What's going on here?"

She looked away from me. When everything in Sethra's home is very quiet, there is a soft, continuous sound, as of air slowly moving down a tunnel. It seemed to me I'd noticed it or almost noticed it before.

Finally she said, "You've spent a day or two with the Justicers now. What do you think?"

That didn't seem to have anything to do with my question, but I've known Sethra long enough to know that not every change of subject is a change of subject.

"They're pretty obsessive," I said.

"About what?"

"About the law, and its quirky little ins and outs."

"And what do you think about the law?"

"Most of my thoughts about the law involve ways to circumvent it," I said.

She smiled. "I always knew you had the makings of an Emperor."

"Eh?"

She waved it aside. "What are all those laws for?"

"Oh, come on, Sethra. I know better than to try to answer a question like that, from you of all people."

"Fair point." She frowned and fell into thought for a moment. Then she said, "Some people think the law is about protection—you have the Imperial Guard and the local constabulary to make sure the innocents are protected. Others think it is about justice—making sure no one can do anything

bad without getting what he deserves. Still others see it as re-
venge: giving peace to the victim by hurting the perpetrator."

She stopped. I waited.

"The House of the Iorich is near the bottom of the Cycle
right now," she said.

I nodded. I always forgot about that stuff. Well, I mean,
obviously since I'm unlikely to live long enough to see the
Cycle move even once, whereas a Dragaeran might live to see
it shift two or three times. And then there's Sethra; we won't
talk about her.

"Okay, I trust that ties into this somehow?"

She nodded. "The Iorich is the House of justice."

"Yes, I know. The courts, the advocates, the law-scribes,
all of that."

She shook her head. "That isn't justice; that's the law."

"If you're telling me that the law has nothing to do with
justice, you aren't giving me any new information."

"What I'm telling you is that sometimes it does."

"Um. That would be when the Iorich are near the top of
the Cycle?"

She nodded.

"Okay. And what happens the rest of the time?"

"What passes for justice is the result of machinations among
the nobles."

"That sounded like it should have made sense."

She chuckled and Tukko appeared with a small glass of
something clear. She threw it down like a soldier and nodded.
"I know what you mean."

"Maybe you could—"

"The Empire perpetuates itself. It protects the nobles who

support it, and the machinery of state it needs to keep itself going. Anyone who threatens those things gets ground up."

"Except during an Iorich reign?"

She nodded.

"The Iorich reign must be an interesting time."

"Follows the Jhereg, you know."

"Oh, right. So they have plenty to keep themselves busy."

She nodded.

"So then," I said. "What did Aliera do that threatened the Empire?"

"Nothing," she said.

"Nothing?"

"Wrong place at the wrong time, if you want to call it that. Or, she was convenient. Or something."

"Sethra, are you drunk?"

"A little."

Okay. Well. This was a new one for me. I wasn't exactly sure how to deal with it. The most powerful sorceress in the world: sloshed. Aren't there laws against that sort of thing?

"Sethra, are you saying that to defend Aliera is to attack the Empire?"

"I thought that was obvious."

Maybe I should get drunk, too.

"And that's why none of Aliera's friends will step in?"

"She's pretty much forbidden it."

"Morrolan must be about ready to burst."

"He's not doing well."

I nodded. "So that's where I come in. But, okay, I still don't see why the Empress chose Aliera to do this to."

"Who would you suggest?"

"Sethra, there must be hundreds, thousands of people who

are violating some law that can be used to distract attention from whatever the Empress wants people not to notice."

"Not really," she said. She drew her finger through a spot in the air in front of her, and a small slash of white light remained. "Aliera is widely known, even among the Teckla, as witness the fact that you heard about it from wherever you were." She made another slash next to the first. "She is widely known to be a friend of the Empress." She made a third slash—I need to learn how to do that. "It's common knowledge that the Empire turns a blind eye to her activities. Who else can all that be said of?"

I felt myself scowling. "Yeah, all right. So it's on me. How do I do it?"

"I understand the advocate you found is very good. Rely on him."

"He is?"

"Within his specialty."

"That's good to know. He's got me—you know what he's got me doing."

"Yes. It seems wise."

"I'm going to have to speak to Norathar."

"Oh," she said. Then, "Oh."

"Yeah."

"All right," she said after a moment. "I'll arrange it."

"Thank you."

I drank some more wine without tasting it. We sat there until the comfortable silence became uncomfortable. Then I said, "Sethra, who else are you?"

"Hmmm?"

"I mean, you must have other, ah, identities, besides—"

"Oh. No one you've ever met. Or heard of, I imagine."

"It must be difficult."

"Sometimes. Sometimes it's the only fun I ever have."

I nodded. I wanted to ask her about some of the other people she was, but it was pretty obvious she didn't want to talk about it, so I finished my wine and fell silent.

A little later she said, "Norathar has agreed to see you."

"When?"

"Now, if it's convenient."

"Convenient," I said. "Heh. All right. Later, I'd like . . ."

She frowned. "What?"

"Nothing. I'm going to see Norathar. After that, I think I'd like some food."

She looked away. "Valabar's is watched constantly."

"So I'd assumed. I was thinking about somewhere safer. Like, say, the Punctured Lung."

"I'm afraid I don't know it," she said.

"Sorry, Jhereg slang. The Punctured Jug."

"Ah. Yes, by Clover Ring."

"It's Jhereg owned, so it's safe. Niscan used to eat there when half the city was walking around with embalming oil for him."

She nodded. "As long as it's safe. I wouldn't want anything to happen to you."

"Kind of you to say." I stood up and nodded.

"I'll do the teleport," she said.

How do you ask the Enchantress of Dzur Mountain if she's too drunk to manage a teleport safely? Answer: You don't.

"Thanks," I told her.

Interlude: Memory

It came back sharp and clear, all the edges distinct, the colors vivid, even the sounds echoing in my ears. I had stood there, looking at where she lived then, and unable to speak. I had just finished proving I wasn't a hero. Kragar came along that time, to provide moral support or something, but had waited a bit down the street so I could meet the boy by myself first.

She invited me in.

"Where is—?"

"It's his nap time."

"Oh."

"He'll be up again in a bit."

We sat and talked about nothing for a while. Then there was a sound in the next room like a cat whose tail has been stepped on, and my heart did a thing.

"I'll be right back," said Cawti.

Across from me was psiprint of Noish-pa, looking haughty and forbidding, which shows you how false psiprints can be. It was a long two or three minutes before she returned.

A toddler toddled behind her. He wore short pants and a

gray frock, and his dark hair was neatly brushed. His eyes were huge and reminded me of Cawti's. She said, "Vlad, this is your father."

The boy stared at me for a moment, then turned and pressed himself against Cawti's legs. She gave me an apologetic smile. "He's bashful around strangers," she said. I nodded. "Just ignore him," she said. "He'll come around."

Ignore him. Yeah. "All right," I said.

"Come on, Vlad. Shall we find your turtle?"

He nodded into her knees. She took his hand and led him over to a long, reddish wooden box under the window. I knew that box; it had once held weapons. Now, it seems, it held a cloth turtle stuffed with I know not what.

I expected him to hug it, but he didn't; he walked into a corner, sat down, and began studying it. Cawti sat on the edge of a short couch I didn't recognize and picked up her glass. We watched him.

"What's he doing?" I asked in a low tone.

"Figuring out how it's put together," she said.

"Oh. Is it that difficult?"

"It's a sort of puzzle. The cloth folds over in certain ways to make a turtle, and if you unfold it right you get something else. The first one was a lyorn, the second a dayocat. I don't know what this one is. I guess we'll find out."

I smiled. "He solved the first two?"

"Quick."

I smiled more. "Where did you find the toy?"

"A little girl makes them, and brings them around. I don't know why, but she seems harmless."

"A little girl? Does she have a name?"

"Devera."

I nodded.

"Do you know her?" she asked.

"Um. Yes and no. But you're right; she wouldn't hurt him."

That seemed to satisfy Cawti. We watched my son a little more. If he was aware that we were watching him, he chose to ignore it. It was hard to talk about him as if he weren't there. Probably a bad idea, too.

Vlad Norathar walked over to his mother and presented her with an object. "That's very good," she said. "Do you know what it is?"

"It's a horse," he explained.

She nodded. "Show your father."

He turned and gave me an evaluating look; I wished I could have decided what expression to have on my face. I settled on trying to look interested but not demanding, and it must have worked because he marched over and showed me the horse.

"That's very good," I said. "But the turtle must be pretty crunched inside it."

He frowned and considered that. "You're silly," he explained.

I'd never been called silly before; I wasn't sure how I felt about it. Good, I think.

He tucked the horse's ears back in and out a few times, satisfying himself that he had the secret, then he went over and sat on the box and set about turning it into a turtle again. Cawti and I watched him.

"He's very bright," I said.

She smiled.

We watched Vlad Norathar a little longer. With no warning, he turned to me and said, "I have a hawk."

"I'd like to see it," I said.

He dug in the box and came out with a porcelain figure about a foot high, and very lifelike. He walked over and handed it to me without hesitation. I studied it carefully. At last I said, "This is the bird that is called a vahndoor in the language of our ancestors."

He studied me. "Are you being silly?"

"Not this time," I said. "There are lots of languages. People speak different."

"Why?"

"Now that is a fine question. Maybe because they invented talking in different places, or else moved away from each other so far that they started talking differently. In this language, the one we're speaking, there is only one word for all sorts of birds of prey. In Fenarian, each sort of bird has its own name."

"Does each bird have its own name too?"

"If someone names it."

"Don't they name themselves?"

"No, they don't. Well, maybe they do, come to think of it. I'm not sure."

"What sort of bird is that?"

"Okay, now I'm insulted."

"It isn't a bird, it's a jhereg. A sort of flying reptile that eats dead things and makes sarcastic comments."

"What does that mean?"

Me and my big mouth.

"It means sometimes he says things he doesn't mean because he thinks they're funny."

"He talks?"

"Into my mind."

"What's he saying now?"

"He isn't saying anything just this minute."

"Does he like me?"

"How would I know? I haven't tasted him."

"Don't."

"Sorry, Boss."

"You can touch him if you wish."

"What is that, punishment?"

"Yes."

He shook his head furiously, his eyes wide. I smiled. "It's all right." I went back to studying his hawk. I handed it back to him. He took it and brought it over to Cawti, and spent some time studying Rocza, perched on her shoulder. After a moment, Rocza stretched her neck out toward him and lowered her head. He hesitated, then reached out a finger and touched her head as if it were a hot stove. When she didn't move, he stroked the top of her head once.

"I'm trying to figure out if I should be jealous," said Loiosh.

"Let me know when you've decided."

"I want one of my own," announced Vlad Norathar.

I looked at Cawti, who looked back at me and shrugged. "These are very special animals," she said. "You have to study a long time to be able to have one."

He looked stubborn.

"If you want one," she continued, "we'll start you on the training."

He looked at her and nodded once, then went back to his box of toys. Was he too young to start training as a witch? Maybe. It wasn't my decision.

"You're looking good," I said.

"Thank you."

Vlad Norathar turned around from the box and said, "Why aren't you living with us?"

I met his eyes, which was more difficult than a lot of other eyes I've had to meet. "There are people who want to kill me. If I stay here, they'll find me."

"Oh," he said. He considered it carefully. "Why don't you kill them instead?"

I stroked the hilt of Lady Teldra inside my cloak and said, "You know, I've asked myself that same question."

Cawti said, "You can't always solve problems by killing someone. In fact, as your father can testify, most of the time killing someone just makes things worse."

"That," I said, "is unfortunately true. But, hey, it's a living."

"Your father is teasing," said Cawti.

I nodded. "I do that sometimes."

"Why?" said Vlad Norathar.

"Another good question," I said.

"I could answer it," said Cawti. "But I shan't."

"Probably best."

He looked puzzled for a moment, but let it go—a trait that he'd certainly find very useful later in life. He said, "Why do they want to kill you?"

I started to say something about breaking the rules, but Cawti cut me off with, "He was saving my life." Was there an edge of bitterness when she said it, or was it purely my imagination?

"He did?"

"Yes," she said.

"They want to kill him for that?"

"Yes."

Vlad Norathar said, "That isn't fair."

"No," said Cawti. "It isn't."

I resisted the urge to make some trite remark about how life wasn't fair, and instead let the kid think about it.

He pulled a lyorn out of the box, held it in one hand with the horse in the other and studied them carefully. Then he put the horse down and began playing with the lyorn's horn, pushing it in and out. It seemed to me he was still thinking about our conversation, but maybe that was my imagination.

I said, "Kragar would like to meet him, too."

She frowned. "I have no objection, but another time would be better."

"All right."

I stood up. "I should be going."

Cawti nodded. "Say good-bye to your father, Vlad."

He got bashful again and hid his face. Cawti gave me an apologetic smile and the two of them walked me to the door. Rocza rubbed Cawti's face then flew over to my left shoulder.

I turned and walked back to where Kragar waited.

6

Lukka, I just had a talk with Nurik, and it was made pretty clear that we're supposed to dump this all on the lowest ranks we think we can get away with. I told him if he wanted that sort of game played, he'd have to get someone else to run the thing, because I won't go there. If I resign, you're the obvious choice to take over, so think hard about how you'll handle this. I know what sort of pressures N. can bring, so if you go with it, I'll stay mute, but it's worth considering. I know Papacat and the new Warlord do not favor any such arrangement, and you should remember that HM is, so far as I know, not in on it either; I think she wants the investigation to be forthright, mostly because she wants to know if it's all her fault. I'd tell her if I knew. Maybe in another week, if I'm still running this thing. But if you want a career, you can't ignore N., you know it and I know it. Anyway, give it some thought.

—Private note in the handwriting of Desaniek
(not authenticated)

I ducked into the doorway in front of me without waiting to
figure out where it went. I was in a narrow hallway with a flight
of stairs at the end. I went up without stopping, swallowing
the acidic panic that comes with only having one direction to
go when you know someone is after you. If Sethra had been
sober, she'd have thought of that, dammit.

There was a door at the end of the hallway. I opened it
without clapping, my right hand brushing the hilt of Lady Teldra.

The Warlord seemed to have been napping; her head
snapped forward and she stared at me. If she'd gone for a
weapon, which wouldn't have been all that unthinkable, there
would suddenly have been a lot more people than the Jhereg
looking for me—or else no one at all.

She blinked a couple of times as I caught the door and
shut my breath, or whatever I did.

"Vlad," she said.

I stood there, trying to neither pant nor shake. "Hi there,"
I said.

Her office was tiny; just enough room for her, a chair, and
a small table. There was another door to her left.

"I must have dozed off," she said. "Sorry."

"It's nothing. As you see, I came in anyway."

"Shall we find somewhere more comfortable to talk?"

"I don't mind standing. Thanks for seeing me, by the way."

She nodded and looked up at me—an unusual experience
for both of us. "Last I heard," I said, "you were Dragon Heir. I
guess congratulations are in order."

She gave something that could have been a laugh. "I
guess."

"Are you addressed as Warlord, or as Your Highness now?"

"Depends on the subject."

"Is there a story there? I mean, in how it is that you happened to become Warlord?"

"Not one I'm inclined to talk about."

"Is your becoming Warlord related?"

"To what?"

"Eh, I thought you knew why I was here."

"Sethra said you wanted to see me about Aliera."

"Yes."

"To that."

"What is it you wanted to see me about exactly?"

"Aliera's situation."

She hadn't answered my question. Just wanted to let you know I caught that. Can't get one past me.

"I'm not sure how much I can tell you," she said.

"Lack of knowledge, or are there things you aren't permitted to say?"

"Both. And maybe things I could say but choose not to."

"Yeah," I said. "Well, I'll ask, you tell me what you can."

"It isn't that I don't care about Aliera," she said.

I nodded, feeling suddenly uncomfortable. It wasn't like Norathar to feel she had to justify herself to me. I leaned against a wall, trying to look relaxed. When she didn't say anything, I cleared my throat and said, "In my own way, I have some understanding of duty."

She nodded, staring past me.

"So, what happened?"

She blinked and seemed to come back from wherever she was.

"Aliera was caught practicing Elder Sorcery, which is illegal. For good reason, by the way. It was used to destroy the Empire. By Aliera's father. The Empire frowns on being destroyed. It tends not to like things that can do that."

"Yeah, I know. That adds a certain—uh. Wait. How much of this is because of her father?"

"I don't know. That's probably what made her the perfect—I mean, that may be why . . ."

She trailed off.

I should have thought of that sooner.

"And how does she—I mean the Empress—feel about it?"

"Beg pardon?"

"She's Aliera's friend. How does she—?"

"You know I can't give you personal details about Her Majesty."

Since it was exactly the personal details I was looking for, it was a little sad to hear that. "All right," I said. "Did you hear about Aliera's arrest before it happened?"

"I don't understand." She was giving me a suspicious look, as if I might be mocking her but she wasn't sure.

"Oh," I said. "You were given the order."

She nodded.

"I don't know how these things work, but that seems unusual. I mean, arresting criminals isn't what I think of as the Warlord's job."

"It usually isn't," she said. Her lips were pressed tightly together.

"But—?"

"With someone like Aliera, I can't see it happening any other way. She wasn't going to dispatch a, a constable to do it."

"It would be disrespectful to her position."

She nodded. I need to work harder on communicating irony.

I said, "Who carried out the arrest?"

"I did."

I grunted. "Must have been fun."

She gave me a look.

"Sorry," I said. "Was she surprised?"

"Is this necessary?"

"I want to know if she had any warning."

"Oh. Yes, she was surprised. She thought I was joking. She said—"

The wall over her head was blank, a pasty color. She should put something there. I resolved not to tell her that.

"Sorry," she said.

"How long was it from the time you were given the order until the arrest?"

"Ten minutes."

"Had you expected the order?"

She studied me carefully. "No," she said. "I was told I was now Warlord, and ordered to arrest Aliera, and to deliver the communication relieving her of her position."

I tried to imagine that scene, but I couldn't do it. I was glad I hadn't been there to see it.

"Had you expected something like this to happen?"

"What do you mean?"

"Aliera was arrested to distract attention from something the Empress doesn't want people thinking about. Had you expected—"

"That's your theory," she said, as if refuting it.

"Uh, yeah. That's my theory. Had you been expecting Zerika—"

"Her Majesty."

"—Her Majesty to do something like this?"

"I don't concede your premise," she said.

"Um. Okay." I looked around the room. Maybe one of the walls had secret writing that would tell me how to pull the information I needed from Norathar. Nope, guess not. "I'd have thought the Warlord would have a bigger office."

"This isn't the office, it's more of a private retreat. The office is through there." She indicated the door to her left.

"Is this a temporary position for you?"

An eyebrow went up. "Well, it certainly won't last longer than the next Dragon Reign."

"I meant more temporary than that."

"I don't know."

"How did it happen in the first place?"

"How did what happen?"

"The incident that started it all. You're the Warlord now, you must have access to—"

"I can't discuss that."

"I don't mean the details."

"Then what? Getting philosophical on me?"

"Sarcasm aside, yes."

"Are you serious?"

"Yes."

"How does it happen? I'm told you served in the army, in wartime, in the line."

"Briefly."

"In combat."

"Briefly."

"And you need to ask how something like that happens?"

"I'm not sure what you mean."

She shook her head. "Pay no mind. If that's all, Lord Szurke, I'm rather busy."

I wondered if "Lord Szurke" were intended as a cut, and if so what the insult was supposed to be. "I'll try to be brief," I said.

She did the lip thing again. "Very well."

"If I can't ask about the Empress, I'll ask about you."

"Hmmm?"

"What are you hoping will happen?"

"I have no hope." Nor much inflection in her voice, either.

"Things were easier in the Jhereg, weren't they?"

She looked up at me, eyes narrowed; then she shrugged. "Different, anyway."

"Generally, the only ones who get it are those who deserve it."

"And not all of them," she said.

"Fair point."

"What else?"

I hesitated. "Does it seem odd to you that this law is being used against someone in Aliera's position?"

She shrugged. "There's been talk about that at Court. I don't pay much attention."

"So you can't explain it?"

"If I have any guesses, I don't care to share them with you."

"Norathar, are we enemies all of a sudden?"

"I serve the Empire. That means I serve the Empress."

"You didn't answer my question."

Her fingers rolled on the tabletop. "No," she said. "We aren't enemies."

"Good, then—"

"We're opponents."

"Um," I explained. "I'm trying to get Aliera out of this mess. Aren't you her friend?"

"If you can find a way to do that without unacceptable consequences, I'll be glad to work with you."

"That's exactly what I'm hoping you'll help me find."

"I know."

"Norathar, you aren't giving me a lot of help here."

"Is there a reason why I should?"

"I don't know. Old times' sake? I mean, my son is named after you."

She looked down and drew a circle with her finger on the table. I did the same thing, back when I had a desk; it was a little strange seeing her do it. She said, "Cawti would like to see you."

After a bit, I managed, "Are you sure?"

"No," she said. "But she said so."

"When?"

"Yesterday."

"She knows I'm in town?"

"Evidently."

After a bit she said, "Will you see her?"

"Yes," I said. "If I can do so without getting her killed."

"I think she can look after herself, don't you?"

"You think so? Against the Jhereg? If they decide to take after her to get at me? Not to mention the Bitch Patrol, who developed a sudden interest in her activities a few years ago, and who don't like me much."

"They guaranteed to leave her alone. And they've done so."

I nodded. "So far."

She scowled. "If they don't—"

"What will you do? Bring the House of the Dragon against them? Or the Empire?"

"I'll bring me against them."

I nodded. "And the Jhereg quakes in fear."

"You, least of all, should mock me."

I clenched my teeth and nodded again. "I'll go see her," I said.

That marked the end of the interview. I gave her a bow that I tried to make devoid of irony and started to leave the way I came, only she stopped me.

"Use the other door. You can get into the Palace that way; the way you're going leads outside."

"Thanks," I said. "Nice to know you haven't forgotten some things."

"There are things you don't forget," said Her Highness.

I went out the way she indicated, got lost in the Dragon Wing, got lost in the Palace, and eventually made my way onto the streets of the City, where I hailed the fourth closed footcab to come by, and gave directions to the Punctured Jug in the Summergate section of Adrilankha. Loiosh and Rocza flew above the cab, watching and complaining.

This was a place I'd been to a few times. I'd heard a few different stories about who actually owned it. It was variously put as (1) belonging to everyone on the Council, operating through shells; (2) belonging to a guy with no ties to the Organization, but lots of pull at Court; or (3) owned jointly by the Council, so there'd always be a safe meeting place. Whichever;

it was one of a dozen or so places in the City where you could eat without worrying about unpleasantness, no matter who was after you.

Of course, walking out the door afterward was your problem.

There's an L-shaped bar running the length of the wall to the right and continuing to the far wall. The rest of the room is filled with chairs and a score of tables almost big enough for two people, all of which have four chairs in front of them; you usually end up holding your plate on your lap and keeping just your drink on the table. A row of small windows high on the wall lets in a token amount of light. The rest is provided by two massive candelabra behind the bar, and I imagine those who work there acquire a good number of head-bumps as well as a few odd burns until they get to know the place.

It was the middle of the day and not very crowded; about a third of the tables were occupied, mostly with the Chreotha and Jhegaala tradesmen that you'd think comprised most of the population of the City if your eyes pass over the innumerable Teckla. A hooded woman in dark clothing, with nothing to indicate her House, sat alone at a table near the door. I sat down opposite her; Rocza turned around on my shoulder to watch the door.

"Hello, Kiera. I hope you weren't waiting long."

She raised her head and her lips quirked. "What are you drinking?"

"Here? Something white and inoffensive. I don't trust them."

"You're a snob."

"Yes. But I'll pay; this is my meeting. Are we eating?"

"Nothing for me."

That was a shame. This was one of the few Dragaeran

places that had good food—a specialty called "cure" which involved meat covered in a spicy-sweet sauce. Other places made it, but here they'd been using the same oven for more than eight hundred years; it's hard to compete with something like that. But it was my meeting, and she wasn't eating, so neither would I. Lady Teldra would have approved.

Kiera got the attention of a middle-aged Teckla with extraordinarily thick eyebrows and a slack mouth, who tightened up his mouth long enough to nod at the order. A guy with almost no chin and wearing Jhereg colors came in and took a seat where he could ostentatiously watch me. I ignored him; Kiera kept an eye on him without discernible expression. *"Is he the only Jhereg in the place, Loiosh?"*

"At the moment. Give it two minutes. They'll be coming in the windows."

"I don't doubt it a bit."

The wine arrived; it was as inoffensive as the Teckla who delivered it.

Kiera nodded her thanks. "It's been years," she lied. "I trust I find you well?"

"My ass is smaller and my feet are flatter, but I'm all right other than that."

"And your purse? Is that flatter and smaller as well?"

"No, it's all right. I still have most of what I got for Laris."

She looked mildly startled. In this light, her eyes seemed almost gray, and her complexion nearly as dark as mine. She always seemed a little smaller than she was. "When I heard you wanted to meet me, I assumed you wanted something stolen. Is it information, then?"

"No, you were right. Well, both, really. I want something stolen. But not for recompense."

"Ah. Of course." She looked interested. "Tell me more."

"How long has it been since you broke into the Imperial Palace?"

"Oh," she said. She fell silent, her eyes lidded. Then, "Are you sure you want a thief, and not a spy?"

"I want a spy," I said. "But I don't know any I can use right now."

"They're different skills, you know."

"I know."

She nodded. "Go on, then."

"There must be wonderful amounts of paperwork associated with Aliera's prosecution."

"Boxes, I'm sure. Stealing them will be less of a problem than transporting them. Not to mention that someone will notice they're missing."

"I don't need all of them. Just one."

"Which?"

"That's the kicker. I don't know."

She gave me the eyebrow and waited for me to continue.

"Somewhere," I said, "among the earliest papers associated with the case—maybe the very earliest—I'm hoping there will be something that will tell us how it started. I want to know who thought of arresting Aliera, or how the idea came up, or how hard it was to talk the Empress into it, and who objected and why, and—"

"Why should such a thing exist?"

"Because—okay, look: I won't claim to know the Empress. We aren't buddies. But I've met her, talked to her, and been there when Aliera and Morrolan and Sethra talked about her."

She nodded. "Go on."

"It wouldn't have crossed her mind to solve her problem by ordering the arrest of a friend. I don't think it would have crossed her mind to solve her problem by ordering an arrest."

Kiera chewed her lip, then nodded. "I can see that. All right."

"So someone else came up with the idea. I want to know who it was."

"You think that will be in one of the papers in her case files?"

"I'm hoping to find something to point me in the right direction. I'm not expecting a complete answer, just a hint about where to look."

"You *do* want a spy."

"Yes. Know any?"

"A few. But this sounds like a challenge. I'd like to try it."

"Good! How much?"

"Two thousand. What, too much?"

"No, no. Just startled me. But for what I'm asking, pretty reasonable." I pulled out bank draft and a pencil, wrote a little, and handed it to her.

"I suppose you're in a hurry?"

"Hard to say. Aliera's in prison, so maybe she is."

She nodded. "I'll see what I can do. I'm looking forward to this." She grinned the unique Kiera grin that brought back some memories and drove out certain others.

We drank our wine quietly; there was a low hum of conversation around us. The door opened again behind me, and an inoffensive-looking fellow in Jhereg colors came in and took a table against the far wall. He leaned against the wall, stretched out his legs, and looked at me.

"Think the Jhereg knows I'm here?"

"Possibly," she said. "Do you have a plan for getting out?"

"Not a plan as such. I mean, I can run a lot faster than you'd think."

"Somehow, I don't think you'd have come here if that was the best you had."

I shrugged. "I can always teleport to Castle Black. It isn't officially safe, but the Jhereg isn't going to mess with a Dragon."

She nodded. "But they'll know where you are, and they'll be watching for when you leave."

"Yeah. I've gotten kind of used to that, though."

"If you'd prefer, I have another idea."

"Let's hear it."

She told me. I laughed. Loiosh laughed.

I removed Lady Teldra's sheath from my belt and slipped it into my cloak. "Do it," I said.

She was quiet for a moment while she psychically spoke with a mutual friend, or maybe acquaintance. At one point she looked at me and said, "Where do you want to end up?"

I considered a few things, then told her. She nodded and again got that blank look. Eventually she focused on me and said, "It's all set." Then we drank wine and got a bit caught up on little things that couldn't matter to anyone else.

Presently, the door opened behind me. Kiera focused over my shoulder and I turned my head. They were both women, nearly identical in appearance, both wearing the black and silver of the House of the Dragon and the gold uniform half-cloak of the Phoenix Guards.

They took two steps forward until they were directly behind me, and one of them said, "Count Vladimir Taltos of Szurke? Please surrender your weapon and come with us."

I could feel everyone in the restaurant staring at us. I didn't look, but I could imagine the carefully expressionless faces of the two Jhereg. I gave the guards a big smile.

"Of course," I said. I removed my sword belt and passed it back to them, then stood up slowly, my hands well clear of my body.

"It was a pleasure, Kiera. Until next time."

"Be well, Vlad."

I turned and gave my captors a nod. "I'm at your service."

They escorted me out, one on either side, and directly into a prison coach. The driver and another guard were already in position. Loiosh and Rocza launched themselves from my shoulders, which the guards pretended not to notice; I guess they'd been informed that something like that might happen. I didn't spot any assassins, but I wasn't looking that hard, either. The guards climbed in, one next to me, the other opposite. The door closed, and the lock snicked, and there was the shifting of the coach as the sideman took his position next to the driver. Then the coach started moving and the Dragonlord opposite me handed me my weapon back.

"I trust that went as requested?"

"Yes," I said. "My thanks."

She shrugged. "Orders are orders. I don't need to understand them."

That was my invitation to explain what this was all about; I declined.

We rattled off. I couldn't see where we were, but Loiosh kept me informed. Not speaking with my "captors" became uncomfortable, so I leaned my head back and closed my eyes. That lasted until the first jolt cracked the back of my head against the hard wood of the coach. After that I stared straight ahead, and just waited.

I didn't need Loiosh to tell me when we arrived at Innocent's Gate, as we call it in the Jhereg—the sudden dip into the lower floors where they bring prisoners. We stopped, and there were a few words exchanged in low tones, and then we started forward again—something I'd never done.

"*Going through a tunnel, Boss. Okay, now we're in a kind of courtyard. They sure have a lot of those coaches for prisoners. Stables, too.*"

"*Yeah, I can smell them.*"

"*Out of the tunnel, and, okay, you're heading away from the Palace.*"

"*In the right direction, as agreed?*"

"*Yes.*"

"*Good, then.*"

Or maybe not. I had mixed feelings about the whole thing.

The two guardsmen in the carriage with me seemed a lot more comfortable not talking than I was. We clanked through the streets; it's always strange to ride in one of those, because you know everyone is staring at you, but you also know they can't see inside the coach.

Eventually we reached our destination. One of them tapped the ceiling—two, then one. The reply came back, three slow taps. The coach bounced more, there was a clanking, and the door opened, letting light in and me out. My legs were stiff.

I looked around and felt a moment of panic; I didn't recognize the place. It was a little cottage in a neighborhood full of two-story rooming houses. I noticed a small niball racquet, in front of it, on the narrow walkway between the street and the front door.

The carriage pulled away. Loiosh's feet tightened briefly on my shoulder.

I took three steps forward, started to clap, and noticed a rope hanging from the eaves. I pulled it and heard the faint clackety-clunk from within. I was feeling something similar, but never mind. The door opened.

"I've been expecting you, Vladimir," said Cawti. "Please come in."

7

Q: *State your name, your House, and your city of residence.*

A: *Bryn, of Lockhead, Your Worship.*

Q: *House?*

A: *I'm not certain, Your Worship.*

Q: *Not . . . You may address me as my lord. How is it you don't know your House?*

A: *I was born into the House of the Teckla, my lord, but I enlisted in the army, and—*

Q: *You are still of the Teckla, son.*

A: *Thank you, my lord. Teckla.*

Q: *How did you come to enlist?*

A: *For the honor of the Empire, my lord, and to serve Her Majesty.*

Q: *That's very good, son. Why else?*

A: *My lord?*

Q: *Who convinced you to join the army?*

A: *The recruiter, my lord. He offered three imperials to anyone who'd enlist.*

Q: *That's a lot of gold, isn't it, son?*

A: I'd never seen, that is, yes my lord.

Q: What would you do for that much gold?

A: My lord? I don't understand.

Q: You've explained that this is a lot of gold to you.

A: Oh, yes!

Q: It would seem that for money like that, you would have been willing to do things you otherwise wouldn't.

A: All I had to do was follow—

Q: Nevertheless, Bryn, isn't it true that there are things you would have been willing to do for three imperials that might have seemed wrong before you took such payment?

A: I guess.

Q: Can you describe what happened on the first Marketday of Lyorn of this year?

A: Yes, my lord. Deppi said we'd gotten orders to—

Q: Just answer the question, son. Describe what happened.

A: We were going through a sort of hamlet about a mile west of Seerpoint, when—

Q: What do you mean when you say "a sort of hamlet"?

A: About four or five cottages and a post stable, my lord.

Q: Was it four or five cottages, Bryn?

A: (Hesitation) Five, I think.

Q: Very well. Observe that it is important we be exact in all details. The Empire insists on no less.

A: Yes, my lord.

Q: Continue, then. Did this hamlet have a name?

A: Tirma, my lord. It was called Tirma.

Q: Very well. And what happened there?

A: The Stuffies were—

Q: Stuffies?

A: Your pardon, my lord. The, ah, the enemy.

Q: Go on.

A: They were hidden behind a stone wall on one side, and a row of jacklenut bushes on the other.

Q: And what happened?

A: It was a 'stoun, my lord. There must have been—

Q: Pardon me, son. A "'stoun"?

A: Um, a surprise? An ambuscade?

Q: I see. Go on.

A: They killed Jaf. He was on point, and at least three of them jumped him. They cut him to pieces, you know? Just hacked away, even after he was dead. We couldn't get to him.

Q: That must have made you angry.

A: Yes, my lord.

Q: Very angry.

A: Yes, my lord.

Q: So, what happened then?

Her eyes were just the same, though maybe they looked a little bigger than I remembered them. I stood looking at her.

"Nice place," I managed.

A quick smile. "You haven't even seen it yet."

"From the outside."

She stood aside and I walked in.

"It's nice in here. I like the hearth being near the kitchen, so you can use it for cooking."

"Not much of a kitchen, really."

"You have water."

"When the pump works. When it doesn't, there's a well in back."

"You share a room with, with the boy?"

"Yes. One other room."

"I remember that chair."

"Sit in it. I'll get you something."

I didn't really want to sit in it, but I did. It seemed to remember me. Rocza flew over and landed on Cawti's shoulder, rubbed against her cheek. I felt the most bizarre flash of jealousy I can recall, then chuckled at myself. Here and there, on counters and mantelpieces, were things I remembered: the small white vase, the lant, the winneasaurus bookends. Other things I didn't recognize: a jar of a such a pure violet color that it was almost painful, a frame drum with attached beater, the books between the bookends.

She found a bottle and opened it. She was much better with the tongs and feather than she had been before; I'd always opened the bottles.

She poured a couple of glasses and brought them back, sat down opposite me. By turning my head, I could see outside, where there was a little garden; I couldn't tell what was growing, but I guessed a mix of bright-blooming flowers and vegetables.

I raised my glass to her. "You've become very domestic."

She nodded. "Necessity."

"Yeah, that'll do it."

Rocza remained on her shoulder, nuzzling and getting reacquainted.

I said, "Where is Vlad Norathar?"

"Out playing; I expect him back soon."

I nodded. "He has friends?"

"A few. And the little girl, Devera, comes by from time to time."

"Good," I said.

I wanted to ask if she missed me, only I didn't want to ask. I said, "Do you see much of Norathar these days?"

"Yes," she said. "She's pretty much the boy's other parent."

I nodded. "How's that working out?"

"Well. We haven't gotten to the political conflicts yet." She smiled a little. I tried to smile back, but I think it came out more of a grimace.

"This business with Aliera," I said. "It must be hard on her."

"I suppose."

"I mean Norathar."

"Oh. Yes, it is."

"How is it she was picked to be Warlord?"

"I don't know; it isn't something I'm comfortable talking about with her."

"I guess."

"And if it were, I don't think she'd want me talking about it with you."

I nodded and drank some wine.

I said, "I trust everything is settled in South Adrilankha."

"I'm not involved, if that's what you mean. Things are as they were, there. No better."

"Are you still giving reading lessons?"

"Twice a week, until lately."

I nodded.

Various questions formed in my mind: "Do you miss me at all?" "Is it hard to raise him without me here?" "Does he ever ask about me, and if he does, what do you tell him?" I didn't give them voice.

"Do you like the wine?" she asked.

"You know I do."

"Just trying to make conversation."

"And avoid talking."

"Yes," she said. "That too."

I let out a breath. "Sorry. I didn't intend to be difficult. I just wanted to see you. And the boy."

She nodded. "And see if you could find out anything that might help your current project."

I nodded. There was something about how she said "project" that I could have explored if I'd felt like it, but I didn't.

She said, "If there was something I could tell you that would help, I would."

"I know."

Cawti said, "What has happened since you were here last?"

I laughed. "Could you answer that question?"

"Probably not," she said, gifting me with a small smile. "Any lovers?"

"One," I said. "A Dragaeran, oddly enough."

"Interesting. I'm surprised. How did that work out?"

"That's hard to answer. I guess it still hasn't, quite. You?"

"Lovers? A couple, but not really lovers as you and I understand the word."

I nodded. "Also, I had a few things out with the Demon Goddess."

"Oh, really? Settled to your satisfaction?"

"No, but I learned yet more things to make me uncomfortable. On account of I didn't have enough uncomfortable information, I suppose."

"I see. Do I want details?"

That was a hard question. "No," I finally said.

"I'll trust your judgment." She hesitated. "Can you beat them?"

"The Jhereg? No. Not in the long run. They're going to get me eventually. You know how it works, Cawti."

"I do. I wasn't sure you were willing to face it."

"They'd have gotten me already if I weren't."

She hesitated again. "I suppose you've thought about the way to make sure they can't use a Morganti weapon on you."

I nodded. "Suicide? Of course. I can't do that. It isn't in me."

"So, what do you do instead?"

"You pack as much living as you can in between delaying the inevitable."

"I guess that's all you can do."

"Unless, of course, I can fix it."

Her eyes flashed. "How?"

"I'm not sure, yet. I have some ideas."

"Anything you can tell me about?"

"Not yet."

"I'll be interested, when you can."

"Yeah, me too."

At which point, Vlad Norathar came bursting in the door, obviously about to say something important, then looked at me, stopped, and stood motionless. I don't know what I expected; I know that a child changes from four years old to eight; but he had so little in common with my memory that it was startling. His face had thinned, his eyes weren't so amazingly large, though they were still bright. His hair, though not black, had become a much darker brown, and was long and curled just a little. And he'd become lanky where he had been chubby.

I stood up. "Well met, Vlad Norathar," I told him.

Cawti said, "Shut the door, Vlad. Do you remember your father? If not, do you remember your manners? Either will do, for now."

The boy shut his mouth, looked at me, then at Loiosh and Rocza, and said, "I remember. Well met, sir. I've been studying the Art, as you suggested."

I remembered making no such suggestion, but I said, "I'm gratified to hear it." I turned to Cawti. "Is he doing well?"

"Yes, very well, when he chooses to apply himself."

He came more fully into the house. "I'm pleased they haven't killed you yet."

"Thank you, so am I, and you have a good a memory."

"You make an impression," said Cawti, with an expression that was a hard to decipher. Then she addressed Vlad Norathar and said, "You should get cleaned up."

He nodded, and sketched me a bow, and went through to the other room.

"He's quite the boy," I said.

She smiled. "Yes, he is."

"He should meet his great-grandfather."

"I'm planning a trip this summer."

"Good."

"Any chance you can be there, meet us?"

"Maybe. If it seems safe."

She nodded.

Vlad Norathar came out again. He didn't look any tidier, but his mother gave a nod of approval. He walked over and stood in front of me. "Sir," he said. "May I touch the Jhereg?"

"Loiosh?"

"What, I have a choice?"

"This time."

"Sure, all right."

"Go ahead," I said. Loiosh bent his neck down and suffered his head to be scratched.

"He's so cold," said the boy.

"In every way," I agreed.

"Heh."

He looked momentarily puzzled, then he said, "I remember you."

"Good," I said. "I'd hate for you to forget."

"I won't," he said, looking very serious.

Cawti cleared her throat. "Vladimir, would you care to sup with us?"

"Another time, if I can," I said. "There are things I need to do." I stood up and solemnly bowed to my son. "Until I see you next, be well."

"And you, sir."

"It was good seeing you again, Vladimir," said Cawti.

"You too."

"I miss you."

I think I must have said something there, and then I was walking away from the house. I heard the door close. "Thud," it said.

"*No one. You'd think they'd have this place watched all the time.*"

"*Who? What?*"

"*The Jhereg, Boss. You know, the ones trying to kill you?*"

"*Oh, right. Them.*"

"*You okay, Boss?*"

"*Compared to what? Compared to how I'd be if there'd been assassins waiting outside her house, I'm doing fine.*"

"*Boss, why wasn't her house being watched?*"

"*Economics. If they're going to watch here, there are at least ten other places to watch. That's more than thirty people they have to pay to stand around and not earn, on the chance that I'll show up. They want me bad, but I don't think they want me that bad.*"

"What if you're wrong?"

"Then they were here and I didn't see them. Or they weren't here for some other reason. What's the point in what-ifs, Loiosh?"

"To get answers."

"How?"

"Gee, Boss. Do you know anyone in the Jhereg who might be willing to talk to you?"

"Kragar."

"Kragar."

"So, how do we get there without telling the whole Jhereg where we are? Any suggestions for that, O wise one?"

He made a couple of sarcastic ones. I trusted him and Rocza to keep a careful watch for me; I let my mind wander to see if it happened to stumble over a clue or something. I was making my way toward the Stone Bridge when Loiosh said, "Let's steer clear of Five Markets, Boss. It's too easy to miss something." It was a good plan, and I was happy to go along with it. My mind, instead of looking for clues, sent me down the best alternate route, which was along the Flintway. Farther down, past where I was going, the Flintway would run into Malak Circle, and from there it was just a step to my old area.

So I continued until I reached the long, winding Flintway, which meandered from the Chain Bridge to what had once been the Flintwood Estates, far out of town. It was an uncomfortably narrow street, with rooming houses of three and four stories looming over you and channels cut into odd places for drainage. It changed its name three or four times during the walk, but to locals it was always the Flintway. I walked past a woodworker's shop. The door to the shop was flanked by the doors to two rooming houses. In one of them, there had once lived the mistress of a s'yang-stone banker who had thought he could make some extra cash by feeding information to his boss's competitor. I'd gotten him as he emerged from visiting his mistress. Yep, that same odd mark in the grain of the door, like someone had partially squashed a pear.

A little farther down it joined Malak Circle. From there I cut left; my feet knew the way. I felt an odd little jolt as I reached my destination. I stepped inside, exchanged nods with the guy keeping the peace for the players, and gestured up-stairs. He gave me an odd look as he nodded, like he might suspect who I was but wasn't sure. I made my way up the nar-row stairs.

I didn't recognize the secretary; he seemed rather small, friendly, ingenuous, and was probably very dangerous. He asked if he might be of some service to me.

"Is Kragar around? That is, assuming you'd notice."

He smiled as if it were a shared joke, just between us. "I'm afraid he's stepped out. If you'd care to wait?" He gestured to a chair.

"Sure," I said.

I sat down and stretched out, memories of this old place flooding back. Funny, I'd never noticed the smell before: a mix from the herbalist shop across the street, the baker down the way, and the musky smell of ancient furniture. Kragar should get around to getting new furniture one of these days. It was comfortable, though.

"What's your name?" I asked.

He looked up, and smiled. "Yenth," he said, or something like that.

"A pleasure," I told him. "I'm Vlad."

"Yes, I know," he said pleasantly. "The jhereg on your shoulders were kind of a clue."

"You could make a lot of money by letting certain persons know I'm here."

He nodded, still looking friendly. "I know that, too. But the boss might not be so happy with me."

"He might not," I agreed.

It was very strange hearing Kragar referred to as "the boss."

"Is it all right if I wait in his office?"

He frowned. "Mind if I ask why?"

I gave him an honest answer.

"Ah," he said, laughing. "I can see that. Will you make it good for me with the boss, if needed?"

"Yeah, I think I can do that. Want some money to make it official that you were bribed?"

He chuckled. "No, thanks. That might lead to questions I wouldn't care to answer."

"Fair enough," I said, and moved into what once had been my office, with my desk, a new chair where mine had once been, and the same ugly view from my window. Sometimes I'd had that window boarded up, other times I kept it open so Loiosh could use it. I took another chair and shoved it into a corner next to the coat rack and waited, thinking invisible thoughts.

The door opened, he came in and sat behind the desk, opened a drawer, and pulled out a ledger. "Hey there," I said, and I swear he almost screamed.

He settled down and stared at me. "Vlad!"

"Hey, Kragar. You know, I've been wanting to do that to you for more years than I can remember. If the Jhereg gets me now, my last thought will be of the pleasure I've just had." I smiled.

"I think I'll kill you before the Jhereg gets to it. How did you get past Yenth?"

"I bribed him."

"How much did it take?"

"No cash, he just wanted in on the vicarious pleasure of seeing you jump."

"I'll kill you both."

"Don't blame you."

"But first I'm going let my heart rate slow down to something below the imminent death level."

"When that happens, you can maybe tell me a few things."

"Maybe. I'll think about it. What do you want to know?"

"What's up with Aliera?"

"She's been arrested."

"I know that. Why?"

"Practicing pre-Empire sorcery."

"I know that," I said. "Why?"

"Because the Empress needs to distract attention from the mess in Tirma."

"And there was no other way to do that than arrest a friend of hers?"

"How should I know? The Empress hasn't been taking me into her confidence lately."

"How about the Jhereg?"

"Hmmm?"

"Do you know how they plan to get me?"

"You don't know?"

"Well, I've had the thought that this whole thing with Aliera was concocted just to get me back here, but that seems a bit paranoid even for me."

"Yeah, that may be going over the edge."

"For one thing, how do they get the Empress to cooperate?"

"Right."

"Unless—"

"Hmmm?"

"Kragar, have you heard any whispers or rumors of something big being up with the Jhereg in combination with another House, or more than one?"

He looked at me. I said, "That look tells me that the answer is yes."

"How did you—?"

"What is it?"

"I asked first. How did you know?"

"I didn't know. In fact, I assumed I was wrong. But if this is all a means of getting me back here, then the key element is to convince the Empress to do what they want."

"Okay, I can see that."

"The Jhereg is at the bottom of the Cycle. They aren't in any position to influence the Imperium, unless—"

"—they work with another House, maybe even two or three."

"Right. Which means they have to have something to offer, which means—"

"Something big. Got it. I keep forgetting how devious you are."

"Me? I'm not the one who came up with it, whatever it is. Which reminds me, what is it?"

"Now that I can answer," said Kragar, "I have no idea."

8

Yes, certainly I'm willing to cooperate with your committee, but I have no idea what you imagine I can tell you. As you know, I had no position in the Imperial army at the time of incident, and no knowledge of it beyond rumor and what I was told by friends, none of whom were directly involved either. If your question concerns military matters in general, certainly I will give you my opinions, but it would seem there are others more qualified. In general, such "testimony" as you want from me I can give right now: If you put soldiers in a position where the enemy is the populace, you must expect them to treat the populace as the enemy. This does not require knowledge of the higher reaches of the sorcerous arts to devine.

Nevertheless, as I said, I am willing to speak to your committee at any time that my duties do not require my presence elsewhere. A message sent to me through the House of the Dragon will reach me quickly, and a message sent to the Office of the Warlord, Dragon Wing, Imperial Palace, will reach me instantly.

—Norathar (authenticated)

"What did you hear, and where did you hear it?"

"I didn't exactly hear anything, but there have been a few Orca—"

"Orca!"

"—who have been exceptionally polite of late."

"Um."

"It bugged me enough that I set someone to find out what was up, and all I learned was that there are orders from some of their House not to offend us." Given how easily the Orca offend everyone, and how habitual it seems with them to do so, that certainly was significant—of something.

"Um," I said again.

"Maybe you think that's normal—"

"Heh. Yeah, okay. Something is up."

"I'm still not sure of your conclusion, though."

"You mean, that it's all directed at me?"

"Right. Something that big—"

"I know. I may be a part of it, or maybe they just took the opportunity. But I'm going to follow up my guess that somewhere between the Jhereg and the Orca, and maybe another House too, someone is putting pressure on the Empress."

"If we could find out who, or how—"

"Kiera is working on that for me."

An eyebrow went up, then he nodded. He kept looking at me.

I said, "What is it?"

"What's what?"

"That look you're giving me."

"Oh, sorry."

"Um. Well?"

He hesitated. "You're older," he finally said.

"Yeah, that happens."

"I know. Just, faster than I'd thought it would."

"That's two of us."

"Sorry."

"No problem; I needed cheering up anyway. Besides, I don't think old age is what's going to get me."

"It is if it slows you down."

"You are just full of cheer, aren't you?"

"Lord Cheerful, that's what they call me."

"All right, Lord Cheerful. I guess it wouldn't hurt to find out who is trying to do what. I take it you're on that?"

"I'm not hopeful, Vlad. This obviously goes all the way up to the Jhereg Council. They aren't easy to crack."

"Go in through the Orca."

He nodded. "All right. I'll take a run at it. What are you going to be doing?"

"I'm not exactly sure. Give me a few minutes to think about it."

"Take all the time you need." He sat back in his chair. I had to admit, he looked like he belonged there.

"Supercilious," I said. "That's the word I'm looking for."

"Thanks," he said. "I had a good teacher."

There was nothing to say to that, so I stared out what used to be my window. Sometimes I'd found the answer to a problem on the wall of the building across the way. It didn't work this time; I guess I had to be sitting behind the desk.

"Hungry?" he said.

"Come to think of it, yeah."

"Should I round up bodyguards or should I send out for something?"

"Send out. I don't trust your secretary; I think he'd take a bribe."

"What are you hungry for?"

"Pretty much anything."

He yelled for Yenth and instructed him to have lunch brought in. "And get yourself some moldy cheese and vinegar," he added. Yenth left with a smirk he must have learned from Kragar.

"How are things here?"

"Not like I expected."

"Oh?"

"You have to keep pushing. If you aren't pushing, you're being pushed."

"That's true, I guess."

"It gets, uh, tiring."

"If you want a break, we can swap places."

"If we swapped places, neither of us would have a problem: you'd enjoy pushing, and the Jhereg would never notice me."

"Good point."

Presently, Yenth came back and delivered a big box containing pastries from a vendor I remembered with longing, as well as a bottle of wine, a selection of fruit, and a bucket of flavored ice from the local sorcery shop. I hadn't had the flavored ice in years—I smiled when I saw it and wondered why I never treated myself to stuff like that anymore. Yenth held up a steaming pastry and said, "Moldy cheese and vinegar. They made it special for me."

"Get out of here," said Kragar.

I bit into a pastry and burned my mouth. Chicken, maize, tubers, and a thick gravy that was sweeter than I'd have made it but still good. Kragar gestured, and the wine tongs began to glow red.

"You've been practicing."

"Only the easy stuff." He opened the wine and poured us each a glass. It was very dark and strongly flavored. We ate in silence, each with our own thoughts. Loiosh shifted on my shoulder; Rocza hissed softly at him.

"What do you know about Norathar's appointment as Warlord?"

Kragar looked up. "Vlad, you think I pay attention to Court politics?"

"I think you pay attention to everything."

"What do you want to know?"

"I'm not sure. She was acting funny."

"You saw her?"

"Yes. I got the feeling there was something odd about the appointment."

"It isn't the first time the Heir has been Warlord during a Phoenix Reign, but it hasn't happened much."

"Yeah. Why not?"

"Two reasons: The second is continuity—the more Court officials who are continued over between reigns, the smoother the transition is."

"Right. Makes sense. And the first?"

He looked at me.

"Oh," I said. "Yeah. Sort of begging for a coup, isn't it?"

He nodded. "What was funny about how Norathar was acting?"

"Eh. Like she wanted to tell me things, but didn't. Like she was on both sides at once."

"Just what about that seems anything other than predictable?"

"I know, I know. But there was something else to it."

He shrugged. "Like, maybe she knew what was going on, and wanted to tell you, but had, oh, I don't know, sworn an oath that prevented it, or something like that, maybe?"

I called him something my grandfather wouldn't have approved of. "Want to spend some more time showing how smart you are?"

"Sure."

"What is it she wanted to tell me?"

He waved his hands over the desk, like a jongleur in the market about to make something vanish "with no trace of sorcery whatsoever!" He said, "Mmmm . . . the spirits are being obstinate. I must cajole them. Have you some token I may give to them so they—"

I made a few suggestions about what sort of token I had and what he and his spirits could do with it.

He said, "It's no secret that you're trying to help Aliera. Norathar has information that would be useful. She can't give it to you. What's the big mystery?"

"There are two: The first is, what does she know that she can't tell me? The second is, how can I find it out? Got an answer for either of those, O Mystic One?"

"You could have Daymar do a mind-probe." He smirked.

"The information wouldn't do me much good if I were ground up into Vlad-meal after getting it."

"Everything has to be perfect for you."

"I'm just that kind of guy."

"So, what's the next step?"

"I wait and see what Kiera can tell me. After that, I'll see. Kill someone, I suppose."

"You're so romantic. That's why you get all the girls."

"It's such a trial figuring out where to put them." I stood up and started pacing.

"It's good to see you again," said Kragar.

I stopped, looked at him, wondered if he was being sarcastic, if I really missed being where he was, and if he'd yet gotten a good enough offer to sell me out. "Thanks," I said. "You too."

"Your food's getting cold."

I got busy with the food again, feeding some to Loiosh and Rocza. When I get distracted from eating, it's a pretty good sign that things have gotten difficult. When Loiosh and Rozca fail to remind me, it's an even better sign.

I finished the pastry, drank some wine, and said, "I'll tell you what I can't figure out: It's too small."

"Small?"

"For the Empress. The way I've been reading it, the Empress got into a mess because some soldiers no one knows anything about killed a few Teckla no one cares anything about. So she arranged this prosecution of Aliera to distract attention, and Aliera is being a good soldier and letting herself be sacrificed."

"Well, she *was* the Warlord when it happened, so maybe she feels she deserves it."

"True, but beside the point. I'm saying Zerika wouldn't do that just to save herself from some unpleasantness. Even from a lot of unpleasantness."

"I don't know her."

"I do, sort of."

"Okay, Vlad. Say you're right. What does it mean?"

"It means there is more at stake than what happens to Zerika. For her to do something like that, she has to be preventing something much worse than anything that can happen to her personally."

"Like what?"

I spread my hands.

"Okay," he said. "Well, you now know what you don't know. See how much progress you've made?"

"Could you do something for me?"

"If it involves a mind-probe of the Empress, no. Otherwise, probably."

I reached over and found a blank piece of paper on his desk, right where I used to keep them. I wrote a name on it and passed it over to him. He looked at it and did a thing with his eyebrows. "Left Hand?"

"Yeah. I have an itch that tells me they're in on this. I'd love to be wrong, but if I'm right, she's probably in it. Find out what you can about her."

"I already know more than I'd like to."

"Start with that, then."

"Madam Triesco is one of the high figures in the Left Hand. She's probably richer than the Empress. She answers to Caola, and I don't think Caola would dirty her hands with this directly. When someone sells a trinket to influence the roll of the stones, Triesco is getting some of it. If it doesn't actually do anything, she's getting more. Every malicious imitation spell in town, some of it goes to her. Whenever there's an unauthorized clairvoyance spell cast, she's getting a piece. When—"

"Hey. Are we safe?"

"Hmmm?"

"Could someone be watching or listening to us? How good are your protections?"

"They're the same ones you had, Vlad. Three tied to two, double-filled and locked. Cast for twenty years, remember? Checked four times a year."

"All right. Anyway, yeah, I know she's big."

"What else do you want to . . . oh."

I shook my head. "Don't jump to conclusions. I just need to know things. I'm not ready to start indiscriminately putting shines right and left."

"All right. But you'll let me know before you do, so I can be somewhere else?"

"I'll send a special courier."

"Thanks."

"You'll check on her for me?"

"Just like the old days."

"Except now you have people to do the legwork for you."

"Yeah, except for that, it's just like the old days."

"And you're more sarcastic than you used to be."

"Right."

"Which I didn't think was possible."

"When you stop being surprised, you've stopped living."

"All right, all right. Can I get an escort back to the Imperial Palace?"

He called for Yenth, and said a couple of names I didn't recognize. I didn't recognize their faces, either, when they showed up. Kragar gave them instructions that didn't leave any room for doubt about the condition I was to arrive in, or what would happen to them if I so much as stubbed my toe; they appeared to notice.

"Thanks, Kragar. I'll be in touch."

He gave me a salute, and my escort escorted me back down the stairs, out the door, and onto the sweet-sour smell of the part of the City I knew best. I'd have liked to have relaxed more and enjoyed the walk, but I was too busy thinking.

I made it back to the Palace, the Iorich Wing, and the over-priced inn, giving my escorts a couple of orbs to drink my continued good health. The room was empty, the bed was soft, I was tired.

I woke up with that ugly feeling you always get when you sleep in your clothes—years on the run hadn't inured me to it. I checked the Orb and found the time, tried to figure how long I'd been asleep, and realized I had no idea what time it had been when I'd lain down. Was it light out? I couldn't remember. It was disorienting and annoying.

"*You've been out about six hours, Boss.*"

"*Okay. Was everything solved while I slept?*"

"*Almost everything. Just a bit of cleanup left.*"

"*Good, then.*"

I hauled myself out and took myself to the public baths nearest the Iorich Wing; over-priced like the rest of the area, full of marble and sorcerously created hot springs. I wrapped my things in my cloak, which I kept next to my hand, and had an attendant have everything else cleaned while I soaked for a long time. It helped.

I dried myself off, picked up my cloak, slipped a hand onto Lady Teldra's hilt, and went over to the attendant to pick up my clothes. I over-tipped, because I'm just that kind of guy. There was enough privacy near the privies that I could replace the surprises about my person—the few I still carried: dagger for each sleeve, throwing knife in a boot, garrote in the collar of the cloak, a couple of darts inside it, and so on. Then I strapped on my sword belt, with the rapier hanging from it in front of Lady Teldra, and the cloak covering the whole thing. There. Ready to face the world again. Assassins? Bring 'em on.

No, actually, don't. Skip that. Just kidding.

"Breakfast?"

"I'm not hungry."

"Liar."

"Okay, breakfast."

I negotiated my way back to the Palace, figuring to grab something there and hoping to run into Poncer again. The dining area was much busier now, and those I'd noticed before were gone. I found a vendor selling fresh, hot potato bread with an orange-flavored mustard, about which you shouldn't laugh until you've tried it. Loiosh and Rocza had theirs without mustard; I explained that the looks they kept getting were because of that, but I don't think they bought it. There was no sign of Poncer.

I returned to the House of the Iorich and made my way to the advocate's office. His door was open and there were no ambiguous notes on it, so I clapped and went in.

He glanced up from the tome he was reading, his finger guiding him, and said, "Lord Taltos."

"High Counsel."

He gestured to a chair. "What have you found out?"

"That was going to be my question," I said.

He grunted and waited.

I sighed. "I'm not sure how much to tell you."

He shrugged. "Don't tell me anything you want kept secret. I'm not about to withhold information I'm compelled to disclose."

"I was afraid you'd say something like that."

"You can keep it hypothetical, if you want."

"Hypothetically, what would happen if you were questioned about this conversation?"

"Hypothetically, I'd give evasive answers."

"And then?"

"Hypothetically, either or both of us could find ourselves at the long end of a short slide."

"Right. What if there were no hypothetical situations?"

"Eh?"

"Never mind. I don't think telling you my current theory is a good idea."

"I can't argue, but it makes my work harder."

"I know. What have you learned?"

"They're skipping several steps."

"Like what?"

"Seals on depositions, verification of psiprint maps, character vetting of witnesses—"

"So, that means they want to rush this through?"

"No, it isn't that simple." He frowned. "I've been reading some histories of prosecutions with political motives."

"And?"

"They come in various forms, but they usually fall into two classes: the ones they try to rush through, so it's over before there can be any outcry, and those that make certain all the formalities and niceties are observed, ah, scrupulously, so it can stand up to any examining among the nobles who may question it."

"And the public?"

"Hmm? Oh, you were jesting."

"So, this is the former?"

"Yes. And that's what's puzzling me."

"Go on."

"There's no point in rushing through it when everything is already known, being talked about in every theater, written about in stock sheets."

"I see your point. So, why are they doing it?"

"Just what I was wondering."

"Any theories?"

He shook his head. "Could what you're not telling me account for it?"

"I don't see how. But I don't know enough to have an intelligent opinion."

"I do, but I don't have the information you have." He didn't sound like he was making an accusation, just stating facts.

"I don't have information," I told him. "Just theories."

He grunted. "Is there anything you *can* tell me?"

"I can ask you something. What's up with the new Warlord?"

"Norathar? She's also Dragon Heir. Unusual, though not unheard-of."

"So I'm told. What does it mean?"

"You mean, aside from believing her the best choice?"

"Was she? Why? Her experience in the Jhereg?"

His eyebrows rose. "I heard something about that. Is it true?"

I shrugged. "What makes her the best choice?"

He spread his hands. "I know nothing about what makes a good Warlord. I was just assuming the choice was based on merit."

"Is that how things work in the Iorich?"

"Yes. Well, no. Not entirely." He frowned. "It's complicated."

"Involving patronage, family, wealth—"

"Let's stay with the problem, shall we? If you're right, and there is something odd about Norathar's appointment as Warlord, then that's something we should look into."

"We?"

"You."

"How would I go about doing that?"

"I'd start with speaking to Norathar."

"I did. Didn't get much."

He grunted. "Do you have other sources?"

"I used to. I've been on the run for a while."

"Can you—?"

"Maybe." I'd already asked Kragar. I could also ask Morrolan, but I found the idea distasteful; there was still the matter of Lady Teldra between us. I realized Perisil wasn't talking. I cleared my throat. "There are avenues I can pursue," I said.

He nodded. "Pursue them."

"I will. What will you be doing?"

"Studying legal history, and trying to pick up on gossip."

"Gossip?"

"We talk to each other, you know."

"You mean, the Imperial legal staff will tell you—"

"No, no. Nothing like that." He shuddered, as if the idea were abhorrent at some deep level. "No, but they'll sometimes make oblique remarks to friends, and friends have friends, and I have friends who are friends of friends."

"So, we're talking precise information here."

"No," he said, ignoring my tone. "But possibly useful information."

"All right."

He frowned. "I'm not the enemy."

"I know that. If you were the enemy I'd, ah, I'd not have come here."

"I'm saying that if we're going to manage an acquittal for Aliera, both of you are going to have to trust me, at least a little."

"But you just told me that I didn't dare tell you anything I didn't want the Empire knowing about."

He nodded. "That makes it hard, I know."

"But you're saying I should tell you anyway?"

He hesitated. "No. I wouldn't care to take responsibility for that. When I said that if I were compelled, I'd reveal anything you told me, I meant it."

"Well then?"

He sighed and shook his head. "Just keep in mind what I said. This isn't going to be easy, and you're both going to have to trust me."

"Okay," I said. "I'll keep it in mind."

"Where are you going to start?"

"Back in the Palace. Dragon Wing—my favorite place. Listen to gossip, see if I hear anything that will help."

He nodded. "Best of luck."

I stood up. "Thanks."

"I'll be here."

As I turned away, he was already studying his book again.

9

─────────────────────────

In this appendix, we will be addressing some of the tangential rumors that have been spread among various sections of the Court and the nobility relating to the incident. In particular, we will look at theories of influence by outside parties on the events, and on the effect of narcotics, psychedelics, depressants, stimulants, and hallucinogens that may or may not have been in use by any of those involved.

The committee wishes to observe that it addresses these issues under protest: it is our opinion that for the Empire or its representatives to respond to rumor and innuendo from unreliable sources sets a precedent that can, in the long run, have no effect but to give credence to and encourage such rumor and innuendo. That said, we now examine the substance. . . .

Unfortunately, their surprise and timing were perfect; not even Loiosh could warn me. Fortunately, they didn't want to kill me. These facts were related: the Jhereg would not come after you in the Imperial Palace, and certainly not in the Dragon Wing.

There were four of them. It was just like old times. They wore the stupid gold half-cloak of the Phoenix Guards, and they were big and strong, as Dragonlords usually are. Two came up behind me, two came out of a door I was passing and stepped in front of me. I thought about Lady Teldra—how could I not?—but of course I didn't draw her. Using Morganti weapons on Dragonlords makes you very unpopular, and even drawing her in the Imperial Palace would have caught the attention of several hundred trained fighters, all of whom would have seen it as in horribly poor taste.

Besides, it would be wrong to destroy people's souls when all they want to do is give you a good beating, and you know how I am always guided by trying to do the right thing.

Heh.

Look, do you mind if I skip the details? Yeah, I remember them; but if I say them out loud, they'll always be vivid for me, because that's how my memory works. And, really, what do you need to know that can't be told in general?

There they were, two of them in front of me, and Loiosh told me about the two in back, and I knew what was going to happen, because I'd been through it before.

"Keep Rocza out of this."

What Loiosh replied doesn't readily translate, but in any case he got Rocza out of the way. He and I had been through this kind of thing a few times, back when I was running my area. He knew by now that I didn't want to hear any sympathetic words, or anything else; it was just a matter of waiting until it was over.

It always happens so fast, you know? The times I've been jumped and managed to avoid it, I'd been out of the situation almost before I knew I was in it. This time, before I really knew what was happening, they'd pushed me into the room and were going to work. I had time to decide what not to do, as I said, but that was about it.

They didn't draw any weapons—just used their fists and their boots. And they could have made it much worse than they did, if they'd wanted to: They cracked a rib, but other than that didn't break any bones. They also didn't say anything—I assumed they took it for granted I knew what it was about.

Eventually they got my arms pinned, though I did them some harm first. A lot of harm, if you remember how much stronger than an Easterner a Dragaeran is. I remember being really annoyed that I had no access to any of the magic, Eastern or Dragaeran, that would help me recover quickly, whereas they'd have their bruises seen to in an hour or so and be feeling fine. It didn't seem fair, you know?

When they were finished I let them have the satisfaction of seeing me lie there, curled up on the floor, while they walked away. I might have been able to stand up, but if they'd taken it as a signal to start again, I wasn't sure I'd have the self-control to keep things non-lethal.

"Just like the old days, eh?"

"You all right, Boss?"

"In every important sense, yeah."

I stood up, which took a long time, and wasn't any fun; I had to use the wall for support and push up against it, then when I made it up I leaned against it. Nice wall. Good wall. That wall was my new best friend.

Breathing hurt. So did a few other things, though not as much as they were going to. And I was shaking, of course; I always shake after I've been through something exciting, no matter how I feel about it.

"*Any idea what it was about?*"

"*One idea. If I'm right, then it may have been worth it just to find out.*"

"*Someday, Boss, let's talk about ways for you to learn things that don't involve people kicking you.*"

"*Good plan.*"

I was glad to be in the room—which may have been an unused coat closet or something—instead of out in the hall, because I didn't want anyone coming along and asking questions. Or, worse, being sympathetic. Loiosh was carefully not sympathetic; he knows me.

I wanted to get somewhere to bind up my rib. Ever have a cracked rib? Avoid it if you can. Walking hurts. Breathing hurts. Don't cough. And for the love of your favorite deity, don't even *think* about sneezing. And if you make me laugh I'll kill you. Later.

When I'd caught my painful breath a bit, I pushed away from my friend the wall and wished I hadn't.

"*Where to now, Boss?*"

"*I'm not sure. I can't decide if I ought to wait a day or two until the bruises are nice and purple.*"

"*Wait for . . . ?*"

"*Nah, too much is going on to waste a day on cosmetics. This way.*"

I strolled back into the hallway, and then ambled around the corner, after which I sauntered. Anything to look like walking didn't hurt as much as it did. Which was okay; it didn't hurt nearly as much as it would tomorrow. As I walked, my heart rate returned to normal. My tongue played with a tooth that was wobbly, but I didn't think I'd lose it; punches to the face are the easiest to slip, if you don't mind your neck snapping a little.

The few people I passed—Dragonlords—glanced at me and then looked away, carefully unconcerned. After what seemed like a long, long time, I made it to the long, narrow stair I was looking for. It seemed very, very long indeed, just now. I started up it, using the time to plan. I knew what I wanted to do, I just had to figure out the nuances. The planning distracted me; it wasn't too bad.

This time I clapped outside of the office. I heard a brusque "Enter," and did so, suddenly realizing that she might not have been in, and I'd have made that climb for nothing. It would be smart if I thought of those things ahead of time, wouldn't it?

She glanced up as I came in, and said, "What is—" then stopped and looked at me closely.

"I'd been thinking," I said, "of waiting a day so you could see the results in all their splendor."

"That eye is going to swell shut," she said.

"I imagine it will."

"It can't have been the Jhereg, or you'd be dead."

"It wasn't the Jhereg."

"Do you know who?"

"Yes."

She frowned. "Are we playing a game here?"

"I don't know. That's what I came up here to find out."

"If you have a question, Vlad, just ask."

"Did you send them?"

She looked shocked. I think she was shocked, which she shouldn't have been, whether she was guilty or not. She went through some facial contortions, then said, "What kind of game are you playing?"

The kind where I lose if you know the rules. "No game. I just want to know if they were yours."

"They were Dragons?"

"Oh, yes. Phoenix Guards."

"And you think I sent them?"

"It had crossed my mind. So I'd thought I'd ask if you did. And, if so, why you didn't, I don't know, drop me a note instead."

"I didn't send them," she said.

"All right."

"And I think you know that," she added.

"I—"

"Which makes me wonder what you're trying to do by accusing me."

"I didn't accuse you."

"All right. Asking me."

She was studying me carefully, suspiciously.

I shrugged, which was a mistake. "What am I supposed to think? I start asking nosy questions about you, and the next thing I know—"

"What questions have you been asking about me?"

"Your suddenly being made Warlord, of course. Why it happened, what's behind it. You wouldn't tell me, so—"

"There's nothing to tell."

I gave her a brief discussion of fertilizer. She seemed unimpressed with my agricultural expertise. "Believe what you like," she said. It was good to have permission, but I resisted telling her so.

"Either way," I said. "If it was intended by you or someone else to make me stop looking into this, it isn't going to work."

"I don't care—"

"Not to mention that if there were nothing to it, why would anyone beat me up over it?"

"Are you sure that's what it was about?"

"Seems like a good guess."

"But you don't actually know."

I made a disgusted sound.

She started to say something, stopped, inhaled, and let it out slowly. "Very well. We'll assume you're right."

"Thanks."

She ignored the sarcasm. "I had no part in it," she stated.

"All right." She still looked suspicious, as if she didn't believe I genuinely thought she might be involved. She's a Dragon; that doesn't automatically mean she's an idiot. Besides, she'd spent years in the Jhereg. I said, "Then they acted without your knowledge. Why? What is it every Dragonlord knows that they don't want a humble Easterner to find out?"

"How should I know?"

I looked at her. I'm not an idiot either.

She sighed. "There are things I'm not permitted to tell you."

"I figured that part out. What I'm working at is, I'll bet there are things you could tell me if you wanted to. Things that might help Aliera. Things that might explain why I just got a tooth loosened. Things that—"

"Shut up."

I did so, and waited.

She looked past me; I gave her time to think.

"It isn't easy," she said. "My loyalties are divided. I don't think there are any right answers."

I nodded.

"All right. I'll tell you this much. Her Majesty is not very happy about all of this."

"Norathar. Warlord. Your Highness. Whatever I'm supposed to call you. I picked up on that."

She nodded, her eyes still focused past me; I had the feeling that I wasn't there. "Her friendship with Morrolan goes way back, you know."

"Morrolan? How does Morrolan enter into this?"

She focused on me, a puzzled look on her face. Then she said, "I keep forgetting how much you don't know."

"So. fill me in on some of it?"

"You want a history lesson?"

"No. I don't. I really, really don't. I think I'd rather have another beating. But if I need one to understand what's going on, then I'll just sit here and take it."

She made an effort at a smile. "I think we can skip it, for now."

See? My goddess loves me. "Okay, what do I need to know. That you can tell me."

She hesitated, then it came out quickly. "When she asked me to be Warlord, she extracted a couple of promises. One I'm breaking now, by talking to you. The other is that Aliera is to escape."

"Escape," I repeated.

She nodded.

"I trust Aliera doesn't know about this?"

"That is correct."

I sighed. "Well. And the Empress is, you say, a *reborn* Phoenix?"

Her eyes narrowed. "Just what is that supposed—"

"Sorry. That was out of line. Being stupid doesn't mean being decadent."

She said, very precisely, "I do not consider Her Majesty to be stupid."

"No, I guess she isn't. In fact, this shows how smart she is."

"What are you talking about?"

"A stupid person can make only certain, limited types of errors; the mistakes open to a clever fellow are far broader. But to the one who knows how smart he is compared to everyone else, the possibilities for true idiocy are boundless."

"Vlad—"

"Norathar. Never, ever, will Aliera go along with this. To escape is to admit guilt. Think about it."

She started to argue, stopped, frowned. I let her work it through. It shouldn't have taken that long.

"You're right," she said.

"Yeah."

"I have to speak with Her Majesty."

"Good thinking. Had a whole plan, didn't you?"

She nodded. I was tempted to smirk, but she might have killed me. Besides, it wasn't all that funny.

"All right," I said. "I'll get out of your way. This clears up a few things, but unfortunately, doesn't help me. But at least I'm convinced you didn't order those Dragonlords to attack me."

"How do you know they were Dragonlords?"

"Huh? Well, for starters, if they were Jhereg they'd have killed me."

"And if they were Orca?"

I stared at her. She flushed; something I could never have imagined her doing.

"*Well done, Boss!*"

"*Every once in a while, you get a break.*"

I let her sit there for a moment and reflect on the difficulty of unsaying something. Then I said, "Don't feel too bad. I'd been pretty sure of it, anyway."

She cursed softly under her breath.

"I feel your pain," I said.

"You will soon," she said.

"So, feel like filling in the missing piece?"

She glared. "And if I don't?"

That took me a moment, then I got it and shook my head. "No, no. I'm not going to tell anyone anything about what you did or did not tell me. I'm asking you to fill in the pieces I'm missing. If you don't, I'll find out another way; that's all."

She bit her lip, then nodded. "What exactly do you want to know?"

"I know the Jhereg and the Orca are working together. On what, exactly? And how are they forcing the Empress to cooperate?"

"All right." She took a deep breath. "It goes back to before the Interregnum."

I almost made a remark about how I'd been promised no history, but there are times not to be clever.

"The Jhereg had come up with a big moneymaking scheme that they never got to pull off because the world blew up before they could try it. And maybe for other reasons, too, I don't know. Anyway, the Left Hand got wind of it a few years ago, started collaborating with the Right Hand and the Orca, and have been trying to put it back."

"And what is 'it'?"

"Narcotics, hallucinogens, psychedelics, disassociatives—"

"Norathar, I don't know most of those words."

"All right. Opium. Logfungus. Dreamgrass. Laughwort. Koelsh leaf. Poppy extract."

"What about them?"

"What if they were suddenly illegal?"

"Huh?

"What if—"

"I heard you, I'm just trying to wrap my head around it."

"What would happen?"

"I don't know. Um, well, it would drive the prices through the roof."

"And who would sell it?"

"The Jhereg, of course. Yikes. What a scam! And the Orca?"

"They'd supply it."

"And the Left Hand?"

"Facilitating deliv—I hadn't said anything about the Left Hand."

"It was my own theory. Go on."

"Facilitating delivery and hiding and selling spells to detect Imperial agents, the way they do now with gambling games."

"I didn't know they did that; I never used them."

"They do. And there is liable to be Iorich involvement too—bribes for mild sentences, and so on."

"Iorich do that?"

"Funny guy."

I shook my head. "This is huge. How are they convincing the Empress to go for it?"

"The massacre at Tirma."

"Huh?"

"Word is about to leak out that it happened because the sergeant was using a combination of koelsh leaves and poppy."

"Oh. Hmmm. Public outcry?"

The Warlord nodded.

"Is it true? Was he?"

"No."

"Then why can't he be made to testify to that?"

"In fact, once this becomes public, that is exactly what will happen."

"Well, and?"

"And who will believe it? It will be seen by the nobles and the middle classes as a means of distracting attention from the lucrative trade in brain chemicals."

"How does arresting Aliera help?"

"If Aliera is arrested on an obviously bogus charge, it will add weight to the idea that the massacre in Tirma came from orders on high. It will look like the Empress blames Aliera, but knows she can't get a conviction on the actual charge, because—"

"Because it must be approved by the Council of Princes, who wouldn't approve it, so the conviction must be on an Edict, which bypasses peer approval."

"Well, very good, Vlad. I had no idea you were so well acquainted with the law."

"I've managed to pick up a few pieces here and there," I said modestly.

"So, now you know, and now I've betrayed an oath by telling you."

"Yeah. And now I know what's going on, and why, but I'm not sure it helps me."

"On the contrary," she said, her eyes narrowing. "It potentially helps you a great deal."

"How is that?"

"If you reveal what I've told you—"

"Oh, come on, Norathar. You know I won't do that."

She grunted. "There's another thing it gets you, then: an ally."

"You?"

"Yes. Anything I can do without betraying Her Majesty."

"Hmmm. That may be a bit like, 'I'll run any errand you want that doesn't require me to stand up.' Still, I appreciate the offer, and I'll keep it in mind."

"Do that," she said.

So there I was: I'd uncovered what was hidden, I'd found the big secret, I'd turned over the key rock, and now I just had the minor, unimportant little detail of figuring out what to do about it. Splendid. I tried to recall some of the vocabulary I'd picked up during my brief stint as a foot soldier, but you have to keep up with those skills or you lose them.

So, back to the beginning. I'd have to wait for Kiera to get some confirmations, and wait for Kragar to learn a few details about the Left Hand. In the meantime—

"Vlad?"

"Hmmm?"

"I asked if there was anything else."

"Oh, sorry. No. Thank you."

She nodded and I took my leave. If the fates loved me, I'd make it back to my room alive, and Kiera would be waiting there. I did, and she wasn't—make of that what you will.

I unloaded a few pounds of hardware next to the bed, and stretched out on it. It felt wonderful for about ten seconds, then I gradually became aware of each bruise. Once, long before and in a different part of the world, I'd removed my amulets to perform a simple spell to get rid of some aches and pains. It had proved a mistake for two reasons: It almost got me killed, and it had given Loiosh a chance to say I told you so. I was willing to risk the first, but I'd rather hurt than take a chance on the second.

I didn't fall asleep, but to take my mind off how much I

hurt, I spent some time wishing someone would bring me something to eat. Loiosh picked up on the thought, and made an offer of sorts which I rejected; I wasn't that hungry.

"*Boss, do we have a plan?*"

"We will."

"*Oh, good. I feel so much better when we have a plan.*"

"In that case, maybe you come up with one this time. One that doesn't involve a dead teckla."

"*Division of labor, Boss. That's what makes this work, you know.*"

"Yeah, I keep forgetting that. Division of labor. I come up with the plans, and you laugh at them."

"*Exactly.*"

I closed my eyes, the better to concentrate on everything that hurt. No, I don't know why I do these things; stop asking.

After a while, I heard a clap at the door and at almost the same moment Loiosh said, "*It's Kiera.*"

Now, there was good news at a good time. "Please bring your sneaky and most welcome self inside," I called out.

The door opened and she came in, looking worried. "I heard you were beaten," she said.

"How did you hear that? Are there more of you than I know about?"

She gave me a reproachful look.

"Sorry," I said.

She sat down on the edge of the bed and looked me over carefully. Loiosh flew over to her, and she absently scratched under his chin while she studied me. "They did a pretty thorough job, it seems," she said judiciously.

"I guess. Want to tell me what you learned?"

"Just what you expected me to."

My heart skipped a beat. Yes, I'd expected it. But I hadn't really, well, *expected* it. "Details?"

"Minutes of a meeting called by Her Majesty to discuss the massacre in Tirma."

"And?"

"The list of those present include the representative of the Jhereg."

"Is that usual for something like this?"

"No."

"All right. And the representative said?"

"Nothing that was recorded."

"Then—?"

"Did they hit you in the head a lot?"

"Yes, as a matter of fact."

She made a disgusted sound. "Work it out anyway."

"They wouldn't have had the Jhereg representative there, except to hear something, or to inform the Empress of something."

"Yes."

"And either way, it means the Jhereg has their hand in this."

"Which you knew."

"Suspected, then later had confirmed by—uh, I shouldn't say."

"All right. Why?"

"Why what?"

"Why is the Jhereg involved."

"Two reasons. I can't talk about one, and I don't need to talk about the other."

"You don't need to? What do you mean?"

"Kiera, have you been beaten too, lately?"

Her eyes narrowed as she concentrated, then she said, "Oh. You think it's all about you?"

"I always think it's all about me. When I'm wrong I look stupid; when I'm right, I'm still alive to keep looking stupid."

"It's a little hard to believe," she said.

"Why?"

"Engineering a massacre of peasants, embroiling the Empress in—"

"No, no. I don't think that was about me. That just gave them the opportunity."

"Ah. You mean, not the problem, but the solution."

"Yes."

"The Jhereg knew that if Aliera was in trouble, you'd find out and come back and they could get to you. They were doing something else involving the Empress, and just grabbed the opportunity to pull you into it."

"Pretty much. You know the Jhereg. Does that seem far-fetched?"

"No," she said with no hesitation.

"It doesn't to me, either."

"Do you have an idea of how to deal with it?"

"One. Tell the Empress."

"Vlad, do you know what happens if you do that?"

"Something pretty unpleasant for the Jhereg. Do I care?"

"What about for the Empire?"

"Do I care about that?"

"And for Zerika?"

"Like she cared how unpleasant it was for Aliera?"

"She did, you know."

"Stop, Kiera, before you move me to tears. Oh, wait, no,

that's the pain from the beating I got for asking questions about how much she cared."

"I don't think that's why you got beaten."

"No, neither do I. I think it was because it's considered rude for Easterners who are also Jhereg to go asking questions about the Warlord."

"Maybe."

"You have another idea?"

"No, just a feeling."

"A feeling."

"The beating. It doesn't feel right." I started to make an obvious remark but she cut me off. "No, listen, Vlad. I'm serious. Try to reconstruct the sequence in your head."

"It isn't that hard. I was asking questions about Norathar, and—"

"Of whom?"

"Eh? Well, Norathar, first of all. And Cawti. And a servant in the Palace, who first told me Norathar was now Warlord."

She nodded. "Go on."

"Isn't that enough?"

"Is it? Where did these Dragonlords hear about it?"

"I assume from the Teckla. Or, indirectly from the Teckla."

"That's what's bothering me."

"You didn't even know about it."

She didn't deign to answer that. "Imagine how they heard it."

"The Teckla gossips to one of his friends, the Dragonlord overhears it—"

"When is the last time you knew of a Dragon listening to a Teckla's gossip?"

I shrugged, which sent pain shooting from my rib to the

opposite shoulder. "Okay, then the Teckla mentions it to some-one who someone will listen. Snake up a rope, as they say."

"When did you speak to the Teckla?"

"Yesterday."

"So, how long did this all take?"

"Kiera, how long *does* it take?"

"I'm not saying it's impossible. I'm just suspicious."

"What do you think happened instead?"

"I would very much like to know."

"If you're offering to look into it for me, you know I'm not going to turn you down."

She sat on the edge of the bed, cross-legged, which was only strange when I thought about it later. "I'm not sure," she said at last. "The fact is, I don't want to look into it, I want to figure it out."

"I know that one."

"So, any ideas?"

"Yeah, give up. At least, it's never worked for me."

"Vlad—"

"Look, I still think it was just what it seemed to be. How can I figure out what I don't think happened?"

"Work with me."

I sighed. "All right, let's assume you're right. In the first place, if the beating wasn't a message not to investigate the Warlord, then the message didn't come across very well, because I have no idea what it might be about."

"I think we can assume they weren't telling you not to help Aliera."

"That sounds pretty safe."

"So, what else have you been doing that might have of-fended someone?"

"Hiding from the Jhereg. And you know how much Dragons hate that."

"Heh." Then she said, "No, wait a minute."

"Kiera, if Dragonlords start caring about Jhereg business—"

"Vlad, what made you think they were Dragons?"

I sighed. "Everybody is asking me that. Mostly because if they were Jhereg, I'd be dead. And if they were Orca, I'd have won."

"Orca? What do Orca have to do with this?"

I waved it away. "If they weren't Dragonlords, who do you think they were?"

"I think they were Jhereg."

"Then why didn't they—"

"Because they weren't hired to kill you, just to beat you."

"By whom?"

"The Left Hand," she said.

10

Q: *Please state your name and house.*

A: *Efrin, Teckla.*

Q: *Where do you live?*

A: *Nowhere. I used to live in Tirma.*

Q: *Address the Court as "my lord." You say you live nowhere, how is that possible?*

A: *My home was burned down on the same day my wife, my son, and my daughters were murdered by butchers in uniform.*

Q: *The witness is reminded to address the Court as "my lord." How is it you weren't there when it happened?*

A: *I was taking the mule and the kethna to Nuvin's, to keep them safe from the monsters.*

Q: *The witness is reminded for the last time to address the Court with respect, and speak of the Imperial soldiers—*

A: *Imperial monsters.*

[witness is removed]

"All right," I said at last. "Tell me about it."

"How much do you know about the Left Hand of the Jhereg, Vlad?"

"Last time we spoke, about as much as you, and you knew nothing."

"That was several years ago. You made me curious. I've been learning things."

"Then maybe it's time to fill me in on what you've learned?"

"I could tell you, but then I'd have—"

"That isn't funny."

"Yes it is."

"Uh, all right. It is. But tell me anyway."

She nodded. "You know how they started?"

"I've heard stories. Sorceresses expelled from different Houses for illegal sorcery banding together, that sort of thing."

She nodded. "From me, as I recall. Well, they're pretty much true, as far as I can tell. And, yes, they're involved in illegal magic; everyone knows that, and it's even true."

"Rare for something everyone knows," I suggested.

"But they're also—I don't know how to say this without insulting your culture, Vlad."

"I have a pretty thick skin."

"They have customs like an Eastern cult."

"Um. I'm less insulted than I am confused."

"Eastern magic—at least, in reputation—is secretive, yes?"

I thought about my grandfather and started to object, then remembered the other witches I'd encountered, and grunted an agreement.

"The Left Hand is like that, complete with oaths of silence and obedience and rituals of membership."

"Huh. Doesn't sound very businesslike."

"That was my thought, too."

"If the Jhereg tried to operate that way, they'd be laughed—"

"We used to."

"What?"

"Before the Interregnum."

"You're kidding."

"Nope." She extended her hand and crossed her middle fingers and intoned, "For the breath of this life I bind myself to protect my protectors, to provide for my providers, to—"

"You're kidding!"

She shook her head. "Not too many laughed about it, as it happened."

"Good thing I wasn't around then. I'd have laughed, and chances are they wouldn't have cared for that."

"Chances are," she agreed.

"All right, so they wallow in childlike superstition in between making people unrevivifiable and eavesdropping on private conversations. What else?"

"All sorts of arcane rules."

"Rules. The kind that are good for business, or the kind that interfere with business?"

"Some of one, some of the other, and some that depend."

"Dammit, don't be coy."

"I'm giving you what information I have; you have to decide what's useful and what isn't. Isn't that what you always do?"

"Uh. I guess. So, the beating?"

"The Left Hand doesn't want you interfering with their machinations."

"Then why not kill me?"

She shook her head. "You aren't their problem. You're the Right Hand's problem."

"But—"

"And don't make the mistake of thinking they're all one cohesive whole, Vlad. Individuals, factions—some might have wanted to take you out for the bounty, others don't care about that, just want this interfering Easterner out of the way. But the big thing is this: the Jhereg—our Jhereg, the Right Hand—wants it Morganti. Having a few people dress up as Dragonlords to beat you up is one thing; putting a dull shine on you in the Imperial Palace is something else again."

"A dull shine. I've never heard that euphemism before. It's very, uh, vivid."

She shrugged. "The fact that it has to be Morganti is protecting you. Isn't that amusing?"

"I'm laughing on the inside; laughing on the outside hurts too much."

She winced in sympathy. "Anything broken?" she asked.

"A rib cracked, I think."

"Let me bind it."

"You know how to do that?"

"You pick up a bit of everything, after a while. Take your shirt off."

I sat up without assistance, but she helped in the shirt removal process. When a dagger dropped out from under my left armpit, she pretended not to notice. She also pretended not to notice various things strapped to my wrist. She pressed on the bruise, and when I hissed, she nodded sagely, just like a real physicker. She allowed as to how she'd be back shortly, and then teleported out. She was back shortly—under a minute—with a roll of bandages.

I declined her help in standing up, for what reason I couldn't say. Raising my arms hurt a lot. The process of wrapping the ribs wasn't any fun, but I did feel better afterward, and even remembered to tell her so. She said, "Good. I'd give you all sorts of instructions about what to do and not do, but I don't actually know them, except for the ones you're going to ignore, and the ones you can't help but follow, so let's just pretend I did."

"We also could have pretended to do the part where you poked my cracked rib."

"Then how could you have trusted me to bind it? Let's get back to untangling this mess."

"I'm not sure I can think about anything except breathing right now, but I'm willing to try."

"If you'd take that amulet off for a minute, I could—"

"No, thanks."

"As you please. So, why were you beaten by people pretending to be Dragonlords?"

"Pretending."

"Yes."

"You just seem awfully convinced of that."

She gave a Kiera shrug—more implied by the twitch of her lips than by any movement of her shoulder—and said, "I won't say I can't be wrong. I just don't think I am."

"Then you think it was the Left Hand?"

"Thugs hired by them, yes. At least, that's the first thing that comes to mind."

"So then, why?"

"To get you to do something you wouldn't otherwise do. What did you do?"

"I saw Norathar, and used the event to pry some information out of her."

"What information? Oh, right. You won't tell me."

"I'd rather not. It wasn't anything she wanted to tell me."

"So?"

"If you need to know—"

"I will never, ever, understand Easterners."

"What, that we have scruples?"

"Not that you have them; where you keep them."

Sethra would have understood completely, but this time I kept my mouth shut about it. "So, anyway, there's your answer: I was able to get information from Norathar that I wouldn't otherwise get."

She nodded. "And does the Left Hand know you well enough to have predicted you'd do that?"

I started to say no, stopped, considered, and said, "It's not impossible, I suppose. But it's a little scary if they do. Think of how much they'd have to know, how many implications, how many possibilities."

"Maybe. But, you know, they wouldn't have had to *know* you'd do it. Just knowing you might do it would be enough."

"Enough for what?"

"Vlad, I understand that you might not pay attention to what I say, but you ought to pay attention to what *you* say, don't you think?"

"Kiera, you know I love you. But I swear by all I despise that I would hit you over the head with a chair if I could lift one right now. Please just explain it? Please?"

"You've just said that, after the beating, you got Norathar to tell you things she wouldn't have otherwise."

"So? How does that benefit them?"

"The Left Hand, Vlad. What do they do?"

"Illegal magic. Devices for gamblers to cheat. Defeating spells to prevent eavesdrop—oh."

"Yes."

"They were listening."

"We'd best assume so."

"Norathar is going to kill me."

"I don't much care about that," said Kiera sweetly. "I'm worried about who else she's liable to kill."

"Oh. Yes. Um. If they're clever enough to know what I'd do, aren't they clever enough to know what Norathar will do?"

"You'd think so."

"Well?"

She spread her hands. "Maybe they're counting on her years in the Jhereg to have given her some sense. Or maybe they think it's worth the gamble. Or maybe that's exactly what they want."

"Coming up with a complex plan that, if it works, will result in your throat being cut seems like a lot of wasted thinking. But maybe that's just me."

"I don't know, Vlad."

"Can you find out?"

"How? I have no sources in the Left Hand. No one does. However stupid you may think their rituals are, they work: No one who isn't one of them knows anything."

"Ugh," I suggested. I wondered what had happened to the side of my left shoulder to make it hurt so bad; I didn't remember getting hit there. "You can't do what they do without leaving a trace. That means there are ways to find out."

She nodded. "Let me know how that works out for you."

"Kiera—"

"What do you expect me to do about it?"

"I don't know. Kill someone. Steal something. Figure something out."

"The first and last are your business. I'll be glad to steal something as soon as you tell me what you want me to steal."

"Maybe I'll hire Mario."

"Heh. As if—" She stopped. "You might, you know."

"And pay him with what?"

"Vlad, he's Aliera's lover."

"Um. Yeah, I've heard that. Is it true?"

She frowned. "I don't know. It might be worth finding out."

Mario, in case you've never heard of him, is to assassins what Soramiir is to sorcerers. If you've never heard of Soramiir, don't feel bad; I hadn't either until a few days ago.

I thought about it. "It's certainly something to keep in mind. At the moment, however, I'm not sure just who I'd ask him to kill."

She nodded.

I said, "This business of them guessing what I would do, and planning on it, would make me uncomfortable if I believed it. Like, I couldn't do anything because they'd know just what I'd do."

"I think you're overstating it a bit."

"I know. But it's strange. Ever had someone try that on you?"

"No. But then, I've been pretty scrupulous about Jhereg rules."

I winced. I guess I had that coming. "My first reaction," I said, "is to just find some Left Hand business somewhere and start messing it up, to see what they do. Pick one at random, so they can't predict it. It'll give me something to take my frustrations out on. I suppose that would be stupid. Unless I can find some useful aspect."

"There are worse ideas."

"Also better ones, I suspect. But if they really have this planned based on predicting my actions—which I still don't believe—then doing something unpredictable might have some benefit."

"Suppose I'm right—using this to kill you is just a grace note in a larger concert."

"All right. What then?"

"Who is playing the instrument? That is, who in the Left Hand have you especially pissed off?"

"Triesco," I said.

"You don't aim small, do you?"

"What's the point of having weak enemies? They just waste your time."

"It would make sense," said Kiera. "From what I know of her, she's powerful, ruthless, skilled, and not all that nice. And, yes, she's quite capable of hatching a plot like a Yendi."

"Matches what I know," I said. "Think it's her?"

"If you annoyed her, probably."

"Well, then."

"So," she said to the air. "How did it go down? What are they planning? Or her, if it's her."

"Kiera?"

"Hmmm?"

"Thanks."

She nodded absently, her eyes focused over my shoulder, a frown of concentration on her brow. "The more I think about it, the more I think your idea of randomly messing up a Left Hand cover business isn't that bad. It'll make them respond to something new. It could cause a slip."

"*Hear that, Loiosh? It's from Kiera. You can't argue.*"

"*Sure I can.*"

"*But you won't.*"

"*Sure I will.*"

Sure he would. "In that case," I said, "I need to find out a few of their businesses, so I can pick one to mess up. I'm going to enjoy this."

"Are you in any shape to do any messing? Or, rather, will you be tomorrow?"

I grunted. "Maybe not. Maybe that's why they did it. Can't ignore the possibility that they beat me in order to beat me."

She laughed. I hadn't thought it was that funny, but you never know what will strike Kiera as amusing. "I'd volunteer to help," she said. "But messing people up isn't my talent."

"It isn't a talent, Kiera. It's a learned skill."

"I never learned that skill, then."

There was a lot I could have said to that, but nothing that would have been well received. "Do you happen to know any of their places of business?"

"A couple of the more obvious ones: There's a sorcery supply shop on Lockwood, just west of the market. I've seen them go in and out of the place after hours. And there's a tinsmith on Dencel that has to have some other source of income, and I know it isn't Jhereg—I mean, our Jhereg. But give me a day or so and I'll see if I can find a few more, so you have a good list to pick from."

I nodded. "I appreciate it."

"We have friends in common," she said.

"Yes."

"For now, if you won't remove the amulet—"

She broke off with an inquiring look. "I won't," I said.

She nodded. "Then I think you should get up and come with me."

I gave her a suspicious look. "Where are we going?"

"Down two flights of stairs."

"Why?"

"Trust me," she said.

Put that way, I had no choice. I reached for my shirt, but she said to leave it off, so I buckled on my rapier and Lady Teldra, and threw my cloak over my shoulders, feeling distinctly odd with a cloak and no shirt. Then I followed her out the door.

We went back down to the main level of the inn, then followed a vine-covered stone walkway outside and around, back into the building, and down another flight of stairs, at which point I began to smell something rotten and sharp—it nearly stung my nose—and vaguely familiar.

"What am I smelling?"

"Brimstone."

"Oh. Uh, that doesn't bode well."

"Trust me."

We emerged at last into what looked like a wide underground cavern, though some of the walls had been smoothed and there were sculptures here and there of impossible beasts, many of them with steaming water coming out of their mouths. There was a large pool in the middle, and screens set about it. Kiera led me to one of the screens. Stuck into it was a small green flag, upside down. She removed it, stuck it in right side up.

"After you," she said. I went past the screen, which she replaced behind me. In front of me was a small pool; the brimstone smell was very intense here, and the water was steaming heavily and bubbling.

"Get in," she said.

"What will this do?"

"Make you hurt less tomorrow."

"Really?"

"Either that or boil the skin off you. One or the other. Maybe both. Get in."

I started to argue, stopped, shrugged, and removed my cloak. "Are you going to turn your back?"

"No," she said.

I removed my boots and pants with as much dignity as I could; the pain helped keep my mind off my embarrassment. "What about the bandage?"

"Keep it on. I'll change it when you get out."

Loiosh and Rocza complained about the smell and flew over to the side, staying well away from the water. I couldn't blame them.

My first reaction was that it was, indeed, going to boil the skin off me. But it was either immerse myself, or stand there naked in front of Kiera, and I'd rather hurt than look absurd.

It was very hot, and it also stank. I hoped like hell it would do enough good to be worth it.

Soaking yourself in hot, bubbling water is odd: the first touch burns, then you find you can stand it, and then after ten minutes or so it gets too hot again. I have no idea why that is; I just knew I wanted to get out. Kiera explained that if I got out she'd push me back in again, and I didn't think I'd be able to stop her. Loiosh thought the whole thing was pretty funny.

I stayed in there for another five minutes or so, then Kiera produced a towel from somewhere and said, "That should do it."

I stood up and wrapped the towel around myself. "How many sorcerers does it take to keep all this water so hot?"

"None," she said. "It's natural."

I looked at her face to see if she was kidding, but I couldn't tell, so I let it drop.

"How do you feel?" she wanted to know.

"Scalded."

"I suppose."

"But not bad, really."

"Good," she said. "I heard somewhere that Easterners couldn't take that much heat, that their hearts would explode. But I didn't believe it."

I stared at her. She smiled sweetly. I shook my head and decided not to think about it too much.

"Go get some rest," she said as I dressed myself. "I'll try to get you some useful information, and then we'll figure out what to do next."

Oddly enough, I felt like I could rest. I still ached, but I felt relaxed and a little drowsy. Maybe more than a little; I don't remember walking back up the stairs, or even lying down, except that I have a half-memory of Loiosh saying something that, at the time, I didn't think was very funny.

When I woke up, some unknown number of hours later, it was dark outside. A check with the Imperial Orb told me it was still a few hours before dawn, and a check with my body told me I hurt a lot. Logic and experience convinced me I hurt less than I should have, but that was of strictly limited comfort. I guess those hot baths had done something, anyway.

I stood up, and carefully—very carefully—went through what I remembered of the warm-up exercises my grandfather had taught me when I was learning swordplay. He'd told me they worked to loosen up tight muscles, and that no magic was involved. I couldn't do everything—my rib objected loudly to a lot of the positions before I could even get into them; but what I did seemed to help. I took it slow, spending over an hour stretching carefully and fielding comments from Loiosh about my new career as a dancer. I discussed his new career as a wall decoration, but he didn't seem especially scared.

As I made my way into the courtyard, Loiosh spotted some-one who looked like he might be a Jhereg. I waited inside the door while he and Rocza scouted the area, and eventually found a circuitous route out of the place and to the Palace, where no one was watching. I mean, I don't *know* it was a Jhereg, and it if was I don't know that he was going to do any more than watch my movements. But I didn't feel inclined to take chances.

I passed through the Palace like I'd been doing it all my life, out the Iorich Wing, and into the House of the Iorich. There were no mysterious notes outside his door, and Loiosh said Perisil was inside, or else someone who breathed exactly the same. Loiosh once gave me a lecture on how to identify people by the sound of their breathing; I listened to be polite.

I clapped. After a moment, I clapped again. The door opened enough for him to look at me, then he grunted and opened it more. We sat.

"You've been busy," he said.

Either his powers of observation didn't extend to things like how slowly I was moving or how gingerly I sat or the pur-plish bruises on my face, or else it just wasn't something he felt like talking about. I said, "What do you mean?"

"About an hour ago, I got word that the prosecution against Aliera was temporarily delayed, while the Empire carried out 'further investigations.'"

"Um," I said. "Is that good?"

"I don't know," he said. His peculiar eyes narrowed a little and he cocked his head. "What did you do?"

"I spoke with the Warlord. She, it seems, had a plan with the Empress to keep from having to execute Aliera, and I explained why it wouldn't work."

He sat back. "Ah!" he said. "Well, that tells us at least that Her Majesty doesn't *want* to execute Aliera."

"We knew that already."

"Yes, I suppose we did."

"Is there a real investigation, or is it just something they're saying so they can slow things down?"

"Both. There's a real investigation, but it isn't about Aliera's use of pre-Empire sorcery. They're actually looking into the events at Tirma."

I sat back, which hurt more than I'd have thought, and tried to figure out exactly what that might mean. I failed. "There are a lot of angles to that," I said.

"Yes. It means everything to our case if we can draw the connection; nothing at all if we can't. And in the meantime, we can't do anything until we know if the Empire is actually going to follow up on the prosecution."

"I wouldn't say that."

His eyebrows went up. "Go on."

"I just mean we may not have things to do legally, but on my end—"

"The things you won't tell me about."

"Right. On my end, I have a few things to follow up on."

He stared at his desk, then looked up. "I don't like being kept in the dark about things that have an effect on my case."

"I don't blame you."

He grunted. "All right. Do what you have to."

I nodded and refrained from saying that I fully intended to, whatever he said. "Anything else?"

"Not for now. Keep me informed of anything you can keep me informed of."

"You too."

He grunted and I made my way to my feet and left. He never did remark about how I was moving.

I tried to walk as if I wasn't hurt; it made me feel less of a target, though I guess there isn't much logic behind that—any assassin worth his stone would assume I was in top form before making a move anyway.

I needed to know what Cawti and her cute little band of would-be rebels were up to; I also couldn't ask her, since my attitude about them was what had led to our breakup.

I stopped just inside the door of the Wing that would lead me back out toward the Palace. I saw no sign of anyone watching me. That doesn't prove there wasn't anyone, but I'm pretty good at noticing such things when I look. The trick is remembering to look.

"*Where to now, Boss?*"

"*I need to see Cawti again. Right away.*"

Then, "*Sorry, Boss.*"

"*Yeah. Any ideas how to get there without drawing a crowd? I hate to repeat a trick. Besides, I don't think the Jhereg would fall for the same one twice.*"

"*You know I'm not much with the ideas, Boss.*"

"I need to see Cawti, and I very much do not want to direct anyone there. Anything you can come up with—"

"Walk around until you're sure you've been spotted, find whoever is following you, and kill him?"

"I'll consider that option."

Other than Loiosh's suggestion, I couldn't come up with any great ideas, so I went the old traditional route of trying to lose someone in a crowd, alternating with empty streets with a lot of turns so you can see if anyone is staying with you. This can be very effective with one person tailing you; with two or more who are staying in touch, it's less reliable. But I had the Palace right at hand, which had the additional benefit of being pretty much off-limits to anyone trying to take me down, especially Morganti.

I spent a good couple of hours at it, stopping only to get some bread and sausage from a vendor I passed. When I was as convinced as possible that I was unobserved, I ducked out through the Jhegaala Wing because it had a nice shrub border near where the coaches were. Loiosh and Rocza remained outside, flying around and keeping watch. I switched coaches once, near Briisan Center, then finally gave the address of Cawti's house.

11

Lord Carver, presently in the Iorich Wing awaiting execution, has refused to speak to the committee. We can, however, reasonably conclude that his primary motive was financial. It is clear both from the buildup of military force beginning in Zerika 239 and what may be called propaganda efforts beginning in Zerika 249 that the attempt to break away had been planned for some years. What is less certain is that he expected support from Countess Sicera and Barons Highhold and Delora. Whether he did expect such support, what reasons he may have had for such expectations, and why this support was not forthcoming is beyond the scope of this investigation, save to note that, had he in fact had such support the possibility of success of his rebellion would have been considerably strengthened.

I had the coach drop me off a few hundred feet away, so Loiosh, Rocza, and I could take a last look around. It seemed clear, so I approached the cottage. Vlad Norathar was out front, using the niball racquet to keep a ball in the air. He was concentrating very hard, but eventually noticed me, stopped, and gave a hesitant bow.

"Well met, sir," I told him, giving him my best sweeping bow. He grinned, making his whole face light up. The door opened and Cawti came out. "And well met to you as well, madam."

"I didn't expect to see you back so soon," she said, looking at me as if uncertain whether to be pleased or worried.

"Some things have come up. Questions. Do you have time to talk?"

It was the middle of the day; a little ways down the street a Teckla watered a garden, probably for the craftsman who owned the house. A couple of children walked toward us, escorted by a bored-looking nurse.

"Come in, then," she said. "Come inside, Vlad." This last was to the boy, though it jarred me a bit when she said it. She held the door open for him, and I brought up the rear, Loiosh and Rocza landing on my shoulder, at the same moment, as we stepped through the doorway. Vlad Norathar turned when he heard the wings flapping, and his eyes got big.

"Bloody damned show-offs."

Something like a chuckle came into my head.

Cawti asked if I wanted some brandy, and I did. She poured it, neat, unchilled, and got something for herself. She gave Vlad Norathar what looked to be a glass of wine mixed with water. He sat in a full-sized chair and waited, ready to be part of the conversation. I'd heard the expression "I didn't know whether to laugh or to cry," but I hadn't given it much credit until that moment.

Yeah, okay, whatever.

"It's good to see you," she said.

"What happened to your face?" said Vlad Norathar.

"I was beaten up."

"By who?"

"Whom," said Cawti.

"I'm not exactly certain," I said.

"Are you going to find out, and then beat them up?"

I hesitated. When in doubt you can always fall back on honesty. "If I have the chance to hurt them, I will."

He nodded, and seemed about to ask more, but I guess Cawti didn't like where the conversation was going. "So," she said. "What is it?"

I tried to figure out how to express it. "Why am I always in a position where I need to know what's going on, and no one will tell me anything?"

"You aren't actually expecting me to answer that." She phrased it as a statement.

"No, I'm not."

"What is it, then?"

She was wearing an olive-green dress, with a white half-bodice, half-vest that laced up in front; there were a few ruffles from her white shirt showing at the collar, and the sleeves were big and puffy. It was the kind of thing that made you ache to un-lace it. Her hair was looking especially black against it. Damn her, anyway. "Can you tell me anything at all about what, uh, what your people, your group, are doing about this massacre?"

Her brows came together and she looked genuinely puz-zled. "Vlad, there isn't any secret about that. We've been agi-tating about it since it happened, and—"

"Publicly?"

"Of course."

"What about privately?"

"I'm not sure what you mean." She said it as if she really wasn't. I hesitated, and she said, "Maybe you could give me an idea of why you need to know."

"Um," I said. "Some of this I can't tell you."

Her eyes sparkled for a moment, just like they used to. "Explain to me again what you were saying about needing to know things and no one being willing to tell you anything."

I felt myself smiling. "Yeah."

Vlad Norathar remained in his chair, his eyes moving from one of us to the other as we spoke. He had some of his wine, holding the mug in both hands, his eyes watching me over the rim. I've been stared at by a lot scarier guys who made me a lot less nervous. I cleared my throat.

"Everything ties into everything else," I said.

She nodded. "Yes, we'll start with the big generalizations. Okay, go on."

I suppressed a growl. "The Jhereg is up to something big and nasty," I said. "They're working with the Orca. I don't know how unrest among Teckla and Easterners will play into it. It might work against what they're doing, in which case your group will be a target. Or it might work for it, in which case you'll be helping them."

"Vlad, I don't know where you get the idea that we can control popular unrest. We can't. On the day we can, we'll be living in a different world."

"Um. All right, suppose I accept that. I don't think the Jhereg will."

She nodded. "I appreciate the warning; I'll pass it on."

"Good," I said. "But that wasn't actually what I was after."

"All right. What are you after?"

"Trying to figure out what will happen, how the Jhereg will

respond, how the Empire will respond to that, and how I have to respond to the Empire."

She nodded. "Good luck with that."

"I drown in the depths of your sympathy."

"Vlad—"

I sighed. "Okay."

"I just don't know what I can tell you that would do you any good."

"Do you expect riots?"

"I wish I knew. People are angry enough. We're doing all we can to stop them, but—"

"Stop them?"

She blinked. "Of course, Vlad. A riot isn't going to do anything except get some heads broken."

"Um. Okay, looks like I need to re-evaluate."

"Does this throw off your plan?"

"No, not that bad. I hadn't gotten as far as having a plan."

She nodded; she knew my way of working as well as anyone. Better than anyone. "We're not the only group working in South Adrilankha and among the Teckla, you know."

"Um. Actually, I didn't know that."

"There are at least six independent organizations."

"Really. Well. What would happen if you all got together?"

"To do what?"

"Eh, I don't know."

"If we all got together, neither would we. Since we have opposite ideas on what to do, 'getting together' doesn't seem like it would accomplish a great deal, does it?"

"Okay, okay. I hadn't meant to start something. What are these other groups up to?"

She rolled her eyes. "Various things. Some of them are

getting up petitions to the Empire. Some are organizing food and money to be sent to the survivors in Tirma. Some are organizing marches demanding the Empire investigate. Some are encouraging people to individual acts of violence against Imperial representatives. Some—"

"Wait a minute. Acts of violence?"

Her lips pressed together and she nodded. "Politically naive is the kindest thing you can say about it; suicidal is more accurate."

"Can you tell me what they're planning?"

She gave me a hard look. "From what I know of them, they aren't planning anything, they're just encouraging people to attack Imperial Representatives. And if they were planning something, I wouldn't be in a position to know what it is. And if I were in such a position, I certainly wouldn't tell you about it."

She's very good with hard looks. I hadn't noticed Vlad Norathar reacting to her voice, but he must have, because Cawti reached out and stroked his head.

"Understood," I said. "I won't press you on that."

"And if you're going to find them, you'll do it without my—"

"I don't plan to do that," I said.

"All right."

I didn't, either. Whatever their chances were of killing someone, their chances of actually affecting things were nil. But something or someone else might. Maybe. I needed to think.

"You look like you need to think," she said.

I nodded.

She was quiet. So was the boy, except that his eyes were very loud. I stood up and paced; he watched me. After a little bit, I said, "It isn't the group that wants to kill Imperial Representatives that bothers me. It's the group pressing for an investigation."

"Actually," said Cawti, "that's something we're pressing for, too. But we want an investigation by us, by the people; they want the Empire to investigate itself."

I digested that. "Do you think you'll get anywhere with your, ah, independent investigation?"

"I don't think asking the Empire to investigate itself is going to get anything. Do you?"

"That," I said, "is just what I'm trying to figure out."

She snorted. "Even if they could convince—"

"They don't have to. It's already happening."

She stopped. "Is it indeed?"

"So I'm told."

"I hadn't heard about it."

"It's pretty new. Also, probably, pretty secret."

"A secret investigation," she said. "Well, I think we can all have a lot of confidence in that."

"I think the Empress wants to know what happened, and why."

"I'd like to know myself," said Cawti.

"But there are others who don't."

She arched an eyebrow.

"The Jhereg," I said.

"The Jhereg? Why would they care?"

"It might interfere with the schemes they're trying to hatch."

"What exactly are these famous schemes?"

"That," I said, "is exactly what I can't talk about."

She nodded.

"It's better to talk about what's bothering you," said Vlad Norathar.

My first inclination was to argue with him, which is funny when you think about it. But I had the feeling Cawti wouldn't have appreciated that, so I just said, "You're right, but sometimes you have to not talk about things because you don't want to get someone else in trouble."

That seemed to make sense to him. He nodded.

"You have friends, you know," said Cawti.

I nodded. "Hard to forget; it's the only reason I'm still around to irritate the Jhereg. Have you heard anything from the Left Hand?"

She shook her head. "They're keeping the agree—why?" she asked, suddenly looking alert.

"This might involve them, too."

She sighed. "You certainly do make a lot of enemies for a lovable guy."

"It's my burden."

A smile came and went on her angular face, framed in straight black hair, her eyes dark and deep. It was hard to believe one face could convey such a range of—

"Boss, if you can't focus on the problem, I'm going to invoke my executive authority to get us out of this town."

"When did you get executive authority?"

"You should give me executive authority."

I studied the ceiling over Cawti's head. "How would I find these people?"

"They meet at the home of the leader, a printer by trade. Her name is Brinea. She lives on Enoch Way, near Woodcutter's Market. A little cottage painted an ugly green, with a pair of evergreens in front."

"Thanks."

"Do you actually need to see them?"

"I'm not sure. There's too much I'm not sure of right now."

She nodded. "This is liable to get bloody, Vlad."

"Yeah, I had that same thought."

"As long as you know."

I shrugged. "I've done bloody before."

"How recently?"

"I've been trying to use my head more and my knives less."

"That's what worries me."

"What, trying to shake my confidence?"

She shook her head. "Trying to reassure myself that you aren't getting into something you can't handle."

"I'm glad you care."

"You know I care."

"Yeah. I just like being reminded from time to time."

She looked at Vlad Norathar. I followed her gaze; he was looking at me curiously.

"Okay," I said. "I see your point." I got up and opened the door. Loiosh and Rocza flew out. A couple of minutes later, Loiosh let me know the area was safe.

"I'll see you soon," I said. "Vlad Norathar, it is always a pleasure, sir." I bowed.

He stood, carefully set his wine cup down, and did a credible imitation of my bow, his leg back and his hand sweeping the floor. Then he straightened up and grinned.

Cawti smiled proudly at him, then walked me to the door.

"Until next time, Vlad," she said, and the door closed softly behind me.

I had nowhere in particular to be, and reason to believe I didn't have a tail, and I felt like walking; so I made my way to

Woodcutter's Market in South Adrilankha. Enoch Way wasn't marked, but one of those Eastern women who looks like everyone's grandmother grunted and pointed, then looked at me as if wondering why I didn't know something so obvious. I offered her a coin, which she refused with a snort.

Loiosh and Rocza flew above me, in circles, watching as I strolled down the street like any good citizen; except of course that not many Easterners openly wore steel at their sides, and the cut of my clothes was better than most.

It was easy to find the cottage; it was just as Cawti had described it. I stood across the street, leaning against a dead tree in the front of a row of cheap housing, and studied the ugly green. I probably should have been able to deduce things about the person who lived there just by looking at it, but I couldn't. I mean, yeah, the yard was neat; so what? Did she keep it that way, or did a husband, or had they hired someone to do it? The paint was pretty new, but, same thing.

I watched the place a little longer, but no one came in or out. I thought about breaking in. Maybe. Couldn't think what I'd be liable to learn, and to have someone find me would be embarrassing. But if there *was* something to find—

"Boss, hide."

I ducked behind the oak tree. *"What?"*

"You've been found. Dragaeran, Jhereg colors, big but moves well. He's got those eyes."

I knew what he meant by that; there's something around the eyes of someone who's done "work." I guess maybe I have that look, too. Or did. I don't know.

"Find me a clean way out?"

"Looking."

I remained still and waited, my fingers tapping on Lady

Teldra's hilt. I'd been in much scarier situations than just one lone Jhereg. If this was more complicated than that, well, I'd have to trust Loiosh to let me know in time; meanwhile I was ready, but not nervous.

"Boss, uh, something odd."

"That isn't useful."

"He's about twenty feet away from you, stopped, leaning against that empty storefront, pretty well concealed from the street. He knows his stuff."

"All right. And?"

"And when he got there, someone else left the same spot."

"We walked right by someone?"

"Seems like. But that isn't the thing. He's watching the house."

"Oh."

"You think he isn't here for you?"

"Let's stay here for a bit and watch the watcher. What's the other guy doing?"

"Leaving, trying to look inconspicuous. Doing all right at it."

"What are the chances they recognized me?"

"How should I know, Boss? I mean, probably not; you're just another Easterner here. But—"

"Right. We can't know. Okay, let's hang out and see what happens."

On reflection, it seemed that breaking into the house would have been a bad idea after all.

"Is there a way I can get into a position to watch him?"

"I'll check." And, "All right. This way." He landed on my shoulder, and guided me behind the row of housing, through some yards with bits of discarded furniture and broken pottery, and then around. I hugged a house, settled in, and waited, watching.

Well now. Here was an interesting situation.

The solution, of course, presented itself at once, seeing as I wasn't in a hurry. If for whatever reason you are unable to speak with someone psychically, there is a vital tool that you must never be without: a scrap of paper and a wax pencil.

"I'm running an errand?"

"Yes, indeed. Unless Rocza can do it."

"Better be me. Are we in a hurry?"

"Only because I'm going to be really bored until you get back."

I scratched out a note and handed it to him. He took it in a claw and flew off. I squatted down and settled in to wait. I didn't move; the guy I was watching didn't move. I occupied my time with trying to decide whether I knew the guy, and, if so, from where. He looked vaguely familiar; I might have hired him for something once. Or I might have just seen him at—

"Hello, Vlad. You wished something?"

I heard the voice at the same time I felt the pop of displaced air; I didn't quite jump and scream. I'd have glared at him, but it was my own fault for not telling Loiosh to warn me, so instead I just glared.

"Hello, Daymar. Long time."

"What do you mean?"

"Never mind. Yes, I'd like a favor of you, if you aren't busy."

He was floating, cross-legged, about three feet off the ground. It's an easy trick, and I cannot for the life of me imagine why he thinks it might be impressive. Maybe he just thinks it's comfortable, but it doesn't look comfortable.

I'd known him for, well, for years. Tall, dark, and a Hawklord, with all that implies. If it doesn't imply anything for you, I'll spell it out: He's vague, irritating, very good at what he does, and completely oblivious of anything that might be going on around him unless it excites his particular interest. It's good to know people like Daymar, even if it means putting up with people like Daymar. But when it comes to messing around with the inside of someone's head, there's no one better. I've used his skills in the past, and I'll use them again if I don't eviscerate him instead.

I said, "See that fellow over there?"

He looked. "No," he said.

"Look again. There. No, where I'm pointing. Just barely around the corner from the door."

"Oh. Yes. What's he doing?"

"Same thing I am. The question is, who is he doing it for?"

"Should I ask him?"

I took a breath, let it out again. "That wasn't exactly what I had in mind."

"Oh. You mean, something more invasive?"

"Yes."

He paused. "He's wearing protection."

"Oh. Does that mean you can't find out?"

He looked at me, as if trying to see if I was joking. Then he said, "No."

"Okay, but I don't want him knowing what happened."

That earned me another look; which was fine, that's why I'd said it.

I know, I know; it isn't nice to irritate someone who is doing you a favor. It probably isn't smart, either. But if you'd ever met Daymar, you'd understand. Besides, this gave him an excuse to show off, which was what he lived for.

No, that isn't fair. It wasn't about showing off for him, it was his fascination with the thing he was doing—it was a chance to use his skill, to do what felt right for him to do. I could understand that; I used to feel the same way when setting up to put a shine on someone. Not the killing, the setting up: that feeling of everything functioning the way it's supposed to, of your mind going above itself, of—

"Got it," he said.

I nodded. "What did you learn?"

"That he's bored, that this is stupid, that nothing has been happening, and that he's glad he doesn't have to make the report."

"Um. Let's start with the last. He doesn't have to make the report?"

"No, he's just helping out some guy named Widner."

"And he doesn't know who Widner reports to?"

"Nope."

I suggested that my patron goddess should take sensual pleasure, though I didn't put it quite in those terms. "Why doesn't he want to make the report?"

"I can't say exactly; I just got the impression that whoever the report is being given to, he wouldn't like her."

"Her."

He nodded.

"Oh."

I withdrew my suggestions about the Demon Goddess.

Well now, that was all sorts of interesting. "Thank you, Daymar. You've been most helpful."

"Always a pleasure, Vlad."

There was a "whoosh" of air and he was gone, all abrupt and stuff, leaving me with my thoughts, such as they were.

Her.

If it was a "her" that Widner was reporting to, it was the Left Hand of the Jhereg.

Why was the Left Hand keeping a watch on what happened in that little cottage?

Because the Left Hand was involved in whatever the Jhereg—the Right Hand, I mean—and the Orca were doing. And because having Brinea and her people pushing for the Empire to investigate the massacre in Tirma might mess up the plans.

Okay, fine. Why?

Because the Empire, just on the off chance that they were honest (whatever Cawti might say about that possibility), would, by investigating, undercut the pressure the Jhereg and the Orca were putting on them, and their scheme would fall through.

So, what would they do? They'd stop the investigation, if they could.

How? How do you go about stopping an Imperial investigation? And what did it have to do with some weird group of Easterners gathered in a little cottage in South Adrilankha?

Loiosh returned from his errand and landed on my shoulder.

"Is he gone already, Boss?"

"Yeah, and so are we. I have stuff to do."

12

Q: *State your name and House.*

A: *Aliera e'Kieron, House of the Dragon.*

Q: *What was your position at the time of the incident in Tirma?*

A: *As near as I can reconstruct the moment, I was sitting down.*

Q: *Please tell us your official position with respect to the Empire.*

A: *Prisoner.*

Q: *Please tell us your official position, with respect to the Empire, at the time of the incident in Tirma.*

A: *Warlord, although in point of fact, my respect for the Empire is, at this moment, under something of a strain.*

Q: *Were the Imperial troops in Tirma acting under your orders?*

A: *I was the Warlord.*

Q: *I take that as an affirmative.*

A: *You can take that and—yes, they were acting under my orders.*

Q: *What orders did you give with respect to the rebellion in the duchy of Carver?*

A: *To suppress it.*

Q: *Were you specific as to the means of suppressing it?*

A: *I thought perhaps a nice bouquet of candlebud surrounding a bottle of Ailor would do the trick.*

Q: *The Court reminds the witness that copies of her orders are in the Court's possession.*

A: *The witness wonders, then, why the Court is bothering to ask questions to which it knows the answers.*

Q: *The witness is reminded that she may be held in contempt.*

A: *The feeling is mutual.*

"Want to tell me about it, Boss?"

Just to be unpredictable, I filled him in on what I'd put together. When I'd finished, he was quiet for a while; maybe from shock. Then he said, "Okay, what now?"

"Can you think of any reason for the Left Hand to have that cottage watched, except for what I'm thinking? They're pushing for an Imperial investigation, and the Left Hand doesn't want that to happen. Am I missing something?"

"Boss, you don't know anything about those people. That's one thing they're doing. What if it's something else entirely?"

"Like what?"

"How should I know?"

"You really think it's something else?"

"No, I think the same as you. But you don't know."

"Then let's run with that for the moment, and see where it gets us. If the Empire investigates, the deal's off, and the Jhereg, the Orca, and the Left Hand all lose. So, they don't want the investigation to happen."

"But it's happening anyway, having nothing to do with anyone in any little cottage. Where does that leave us?"

"That's what I'm trying to work out."

"Work away."

"Okay. How do you stop an Imperial investigation?"

"You know, Boss, that's something you neglected to cover in my training sessions."

"Can't pressure the Empress directly, we have nothing to pressure her with."

"I don't get it, Boss. Why is the Empress doing this, anyway?"

"So she can get out from under the Jhereg; to look good to the nobles, and maybe to the people too, I don't know."

"Okay, I'll buy that."

"So then, the thing to do is to discredit the investigation."

"Good plan, Boss. How do you do it?"

"Spread rumors that these Easterners are behind it? Maybe plant some evidence?"

"Possible." He didn't sound convinced. Neither was I, for that matter.

"Boss, where are we going?"

I stopped. As I had been thinking and walking, my feet had taken me over the Stone Bridge and were leading me back to my old area—the worst place I could be. The chances of the Jhereg spotting me were too high to make me comfortable anywhere in the city; in my old neighborhood it was nearly certain.

"Uh, nowhere. Back to the Palace, I guess."

I changed direction; Loiosh kept his comments to himself.

I made it to the Palace without incident, entering through the Dragon Wing just to be contrary, and because I was in a mood to glare back. I found some food, then crossed to the House of the Iorich.

I clapped, and, once again, he opened the door enough to peer out, then let me in. One of these days, I was going to have to ask him why he does that.

I sat down and said, "The Empress is launching an investigation into the events at Tirma."

"Yes," he said. "I seem to remember telling you that. What about it?"

"Do you think it's a real investigation?"

He frowned. "As opposed to what?"

"I don't know," I said. "A bunch of running around, closed-door testimony, followed by whatever result the Empress wants."

"I doubt it's that, not from this empress. I should find out who is in charge of it. That might tell us something." He stood up. "I may as well do it now."

"Should I wait here?"

"Yes, but relax. This might take a while."

I nodded. He slipped out. I leaned back in the chair and closed my eyes. I guess I fell asleep, or at least dozed. I had some vaguely disturbing dream that I can't remember, and woke up when Perisil came back in.

"Were you sleeping?" He seemed amused.

"Just resting my eyes," I said. "What did you learn?"

"It's being run by Lady Justicer Desaniek."

He sat down behind his desk and looked expectantly at me. "Sorry," I said. "I don't know the name."

"She's one of the High Justicers. I trust you know what that means?"

"More or less," I said.

"I know her. She isn't corruptible. She's a little fast and

loose with her interpretations of the traditions, but completely unimpeachable when it comes to judgment and sentencing."

"So you're saying that the investigation is straight."

"Probably. She'd be an odd choice if the Empress didn't want to actually learn what happened, and why."

"Might there be other pressures on her, less direct than orders to rig it?"

He hesitated. "Maybe."

"So then, how would someone stop it?"

"Stop it?" he said. "Why would you want to do that?"

"Not me. There are others."

"Who?"

"Let's say powerful interests. How would they go about stopping it?"

"I can't answer that unless you give me more information. What interests? Why do they want to stop it? Powerful in what way?"

"All good questions," I said. I paused to consider just what I could tell him. It was frustrating: he could almost certainly tell me useful things if I didn't have to worry about what he might be made to tell.

"Just suppose," I said, "that there existed a large criminal organization."

I hesitated there; he watched me, listening, not moving.

"And suppose," I said, "that they had come up with a great idea for changing the law in such a way that they made a lot of money, and that they were working with certain other very powerful interests."

"How powerful?"

"As powerful as you can be at the bottom of the Cycle."

"Go on."

"And suppose that this idea for changing the law required putting pressure on the Empress, and that this investigation had a good likelihood of relieving that pressure."

"I'm with you."

"How would such a hypothetical organization go about stopping or sabotaging the investigation?"

He was silent for a minute or two; I could almost hear his brain bubbling. Then he said, "I can't think of any way."

"Heh. Suppose they killed Desaniek?"

"Would they do that?"

"They might."

"It wouldn't work anyway. The Empire would find someone else just as good, and make sure it doesn't happen again, and hunt down whoever did it."

"I suppose so. In any case, I apologize; I understand this is outside of your usual line of work."

He shrugged and a wisp of a smile came and went. "It's a welcome break from thinking about rules of evidence and forms of argument."

"Oh? You don't enjoy your work?"

"I do, really. But it gets tedious at times. This whole case has been a bit out of the ordinary for me, and I appreciate that."

"A pleasure to be of service," I said. "I can't imagine doing what you do."

"I can't—that is—never mind."

"Do you care whether the person you're defending is actually innocent or guilty?"

"Innocent and guilty are legal terms."

"You're evading the question."

"You should be an Iorich."

"Thank you, I think."

"The House has decreed that, whatever a person may or may not have done, he is entitled to be defended. That is sufficient for me."

"But if he tells you he did, doesn't that—"

"No one would tell me that, because I'd have to testify to that fact."

"Oh, right, I knew that. But if, say, the person implies it, or hints at it—"

"I still give him the best defense I can, because that's what the House dictates, and what Imperial law decrees as well."

"And you feel good about that?"

He looked puzzled for a minute. "Wouldn't you?"

"Huh? Me? I'd feel better about it if the poor bastard was guilty. But I'm not an Iorich."

"No, you aren't."

"It feels good if a guy walks away, then?"

"What are you getting at?"

"Nothing, really. I'm making conversation and letting the back of my head work on this problem."

"Oh." He gave me an odd look, then said, "It feels good to make the best arguments I can, and it feels good when, sometimes, it actually has something to do with justice."

"Justice? What's that?"

"Serious question?"

"No, but answer it as if it were."

"I don't know. I don't get into the deeper, mystical aspects. Some do. But justice? Edicts occasionally have something to do with justice, but statutes almost never do."

"Uh, what do they have to do with?"

"Practicality. For example, right here in Adrilankha, when meatpacking became such a big industry, they passed local statutes saying that any peasant who fell short for the year could be kicked off his land. The nobles raised an outcry, but didn't have the clout to do anything about it."

"I don't understand what that has to do with meatpacking."

"Kick peasants off the land, there's your labor force for the packing plants. Along with a lot of Easterners, of course."

"Oh. Are they that, I don't know, obvious about it?"

"Sometimes. In the area around Lake Shalomar—right where Tirma is—they discovered silver. First thing that happened was an influx of miners, the second thing was an influx of merchants selling to the minors. So the Duke passed a statute taxing both the sale and the purchase of mining equipment, set taxes to some absurd level, and provided for the conscription of anyone unable to pay the tax. That's how he recruited his army. I don't think you'd call that justice."

"Um. No, I imagine not."

"There are worse cases. Around the Korlaph, north of the Pushta, they discovered tin, and had a real labor shortage. The Count went on a statute rampage, and by the time he was done, he not only owned all the mines, but had made up the most absurd laws to have a few thousand locals arrested, and then sentenced them to work the mines."

"He can do that?"

"Once in a while, someone has enough family with enough money to bring a particular case to the attention of the Empire, and a particular law gets overturned."

"And I thought the Jhereg was corrupt."

"Law is a reflection of society, justice is a reflection of an idealization of that society."

"You're quoting someone."

He nodded. "Yurstov, Iorich Emperor of the Fifth Cycle, who tried to create an actual justice system. He failed, but he did some good."

"And you stay with Edicts because they aren't as bad?"

He frowned. "I guess that's part of it, though I don't think of it in those terms. I had a client once who annoyed someone, and the someone set him up to look like he'd committed a crime. I got him off. That felt like justice."

"Was it? I mean, what had he done to annoy the guy?"

Perisil shrugged. "I don't know. As I said, the deeper levels I leave to others. But that's justice to me. Suppose some poor fool of a Teckla steals a chicken from his landlord because he's hungry. And some high-and-mighty Orca manages a scheme to cheat his crew out of half their pay. If the first guy gets off with a couple of cuts, and the second goes to the Star, well, to me that's justice."

"How often does that happen?"

"I don't know; I don't deal with those sorts of cases. Those have to do with traditional law, and I work with Edicts. More often it's the other way around, I should think. Is there a point to all this, Lord Taltos?"

"I'm a curious guy, is all. And you're—odd."

"You've met advocates before."

"Yes, but only the ones interested in money."

"Oh," he said. "Yes, I suppose so."

I stood up. "Sorry, I'll let you work."

"And you?"

"I need to think like a Jhereg."

"I imagine that comes easier to you than thinking like an advocate."

"A little," I said. "Oh, one other thing. Desaniek. Where do I find her?"

His eyes narrowed. "Why do you want to know?"

"I'm not sure. But I have no intention of killing her."

"If you even talk to her—"

"I doubt it will come to that."

He hesitated, then said, "While she's conducting the investigation, she'll be working out of the Office of the Imperial Justicer in the Imperial Wing."

"What does she look like?"

He frowned again. He clearly didn't like the way this conversation was going.

"Really," I said. "I don't intend to kill her. Or beat her. I don't know what I'm going to do, but it could end up that I'll be saving her life, depending on how things shake out."

"All right," he said. "But I'm not very good at describing people."

"What's the first thing you notice about her?"

"Um. Her face?"

"Anything special about how she dresses, or what she wears—"

"She keeps her hair up, and she always wears a stickpin in it with a lot of little diamonds."

"Thanks," I said. "That should do it. And don't worry about it too much."

I took myself out of the office and back up to the main floor of the House. I needed to think, and I needed to find a place to do it. I crossed over to the Iorich Wing, stared for a moment at the sculpted thing and wondered what it symbolized, then ended up letting my feet carry me toward the prisons while I tried to put the pieces together.

I hadn't gotten anywhere when I reached the big gates; the same guard was there. He said, "You want to see Aliera?"

"Yes," I said, though I hadn't actually formulated the idea.

I just had to sign and seal one paper, affirming that everything I'd signed before still applied. Someone I'd never seen before guided me in.

I clapped at the door before the guard could; she opened the door and let me in, saying, "One hour."

Aliera was in the same place, the same position she'd been in before. I had the impression she hadn't moved since I'd left. On the table next to the couch were several wine bottles, all empty.

"Well," she said, glaring at me.

"Verra!" I said. "First Sethra, now you. Great."

"Huh?"

"When I spoke with Sethra, she was drunk, too."

"Is there something I should be doing instead?"

"Answering my questions."

"Ask them."

"First question: Did you know the Empress is starting an investigation into the events in Tirma?"

"First answer: Why should I care?"

"Because it was not wanting to run that investigation that led to you being arrested."

"So you say. And by the way, yes I knew. Some Iorich came in here and wanted to ask me questions about it."

"And you were in just the shape you're in now, right?"

She shrugged.

"Perfect," I said. "Can you remember what she wanted to know?"

"Sure. She wanted to know if I enjoy slaughtering innocent Teckla."

"Did she ask that in so many words?"

Aliera made a vague sort of dismissing gesture.

I said, "You're probably too drunk for this to do any good, but I need to point out that if the Empire is investigating the real thing, then there's no need for them to press fake charges against you."

"And yet," she said, "here I am."

"Yes. I'm trying to fix that."

She yawned. "Let me know how that works out."

"If I come back tomorrow, will you be sober?"

"If I stay drunk, will you stay away?"

I could have pointed out that she wasn't helping, but I was beginning to get the idea that this wouldn't be a powerful argument. There needs to be a better word than "stubborn" to describe a Dragonlord whose pride has been offended, and then a better word than that to describe Aliera.

"So tell me," I said. "*Do* you enjoy slaughtering innocent Teckla?"

She stared at me for a minute, then burst out laughing. Since I'd figured it was either that or she'd kill me, I was just as pleased. She laughed for much longer than it was worth, but I attributed that to her state. Eventually she wiped her eyes and said, "Yes, but not by proxy."

"I doubt the Iorich would accept that answer."

"You never know," she said. "They might. I'll ask my advocate if we should base our defense on it."

"Do that. I'll ask the Empress what she thinks."

"Do that. I'm curious about what's behind all of this."

"Me too. That's what I'm doing here."

"What, you think I can tell you something?"

"Almost certainly. And you might even be willing, if I knew what to ask."

She swirled the wine in her glass and stared at it. "Maybe I would. What exactly is the problem you're trying to solve?"

I gave her a quick rundown about things as I saw it.

"So, you think the Jhereg," she almost spat the word, "are going to sabotage this investigation?"

"Have you ever known them, or the Orca, to give up a chance for profit if there was a way not to?"

"No. But I don't see anything they can do that won't back-fire on them."

"You aren't really drunk, are you?"

"No, not really."

"I should probably tell Norathar, or else the Empress, about what I think is going on."

"Probably."

"Unless you'd rather."

"Why would I?"

"I don't know. A way of saying there are no hard feelings?"

"What makes you think there are no hard feelings?"

"Okay, a way of playing politics? My problems aren't the sort that can be solved by having the Empire owe me anything."

"I don't actually care." She hesitated. "But thanks for the offer."

"D'ski!tna."

"What?"

"You owe me no debt."

"I know what it means. When did you learn Serioli?"

"Only a couple of words," I said, feeling my face turning red. "I met a bard who—never mind."

She shrugged. "Anything else, or can I get back to plotting my jailbreak?"

"You can get back to it. Can I smuggle you in a little blue stone or something?"

"They're actually purple, and, yes, I'll take three of them."

"Heh."

I stood up to go. She said, "Vlad."

"Hm?"

I expected her to thank me for all my work. Or maybe announce something profound, like telling me about a vision she'd had of the Demon Goddess. What she said was, "I don't mind my daughter playing with your son."

"Um. Okay, thanks."

I had the guard let me out of the place.

Being in the Palace anyway, I went back to the same vendor and found some sausages that weren't too bad, and bread that could have been staler, then made my way back to my room. Loiosh told me it was empty, so I went in. I lay down on the bed and tried to think. My stomach grumbled a little. I wondered if I was getting too old to be living on bread and sausage; that would be sad.

As I lay there, I found my hand stroking the tiny golden links on the hilt of Lady Teldra. In the years I'd had her, I'd only used her twice; I somehow thought that would please her. Those thoughts led me to another Issola I knew, but I pushed those away: I needed to concentrate on business.

My hand kept stroking Lady Teldra's hilt.

Hey, you in there? Any ideas? Can you help?

Nothing.

I suddenly missed her—I mean, the real person—very

sharply. It's all well and good to think of her personality being preserved inside a weapon, but for one thing, I'd never felt it that I could be sure of. And for another, I didn't entirely believe it. I wonder if she would say murdering a bunch of Teckla was impolite. I wondered if the fact that I didn't much care made me a bad person. Probably.

"*I wonder if she'd say anything about lying on top of the bed with your boots on.*"

"*Probably.*"

My mind wandered, which is a good thing, because sometimes it wanders to where it needs to go and uncovers just the right rock. In this case, it wandered to High Counsel Perisil. An interesting fellow. What I'd said to him had been true: None of the advocates I'd run into before had any interest other than in making themselves rich. This shouldn't be seen as saying anything about the House overall: it's a particular set of them who end up working for the Jhereg. I don't know, maybe the Jhereg exerts an influence on some people, turning them. Or maybe those with such inclinations, in any House, are more subject to working for them, more subject to taking and giving bribes, to stabbing people in the back, to setting up some poor bastard the way Perisil had said—

Oh.

Well, sure. That would do it.

"*You think, Boss?*"

"*Why not? What would happen?*"

"*I don't know. You figure that out.*"

"*I already have, Loiosh. The investigation would be stopped, at least for a while, and there would be all sorts of noise about rounding up and suppressing Teckla and Easterners, and the nobles would* blame Zerika for letting it get out of hand, and it would be a round throw whether she'd be able to get things back in hand, or whether she'd have to cave to the Jhereg to get the pressure off."

"That's the part I don't see, Boss. How does going along with the Jhereg relieve the pressure on Zerika?"

"Now that is an excellent question, my fine jhereg friend. I think I'll go ask her."

"Now?"

"I'll probably have to wait for hours to see her; can you think of a reason not to start the wait?"

"Put that way, I guess not."

It was early evening; just beginning to get dark. I didn't know what hours Her Majesty kept, but it could do no harm in asking, so long as no one polished me up during the walk from the inn to the Palace.

Loiosh and Rocza kept careful watch, and I took the round-about path I'd taken before, and made it to the Palace without incident. I won't bore you with a repetition of making my way to Asskiss Alley. Harnwood was still there; like Aliera, he seemed not to have moved.

"Count Szurke," he said.

I bowed. "Good Lord Harnwood, would it be possible to find out if Her Majesty would consent to see me?"

His face gave no sign there was anything odd in the request. "Is it urgent?"

"A few hours or a day will make no difference," I said. "But I have new information."

He didn't ask about what. Maybe he knew, but more likely he knew it was none of his business. "I shall inquire. Please have a chair."

I did, and waited maybe half an hour.

"The Empress will see you."

I started to follow him, stopped, and said, "When backing away from Her Majesty at the end of the interview, how many steps do I take before turning around?"

He smiled; I think the question pleased him. "If you are here as a personal friend of Her Majesty, then five. If you are here as Count Szurke, then seven. If as Baronet Taltos, then ten."

"Thank you," I said.

If I had the choice between trying to figure out an Issola and trying to figure out an Iorich, I think I'd take a nap.

Harnwood led me through a different route, shorter, and to a cozier room; I had the strong feeling this was a part of her living quarters, which meant I was being honored, or else that I was irritating her, or both. She was waiting. Harnwood bowed deeply to Her Majesty, less deeply to me. I bowed to Her Majesty, she nodded to me. It's just like a dance.

She didn't offer me a chair. I said, "Majesty, thank you for seeing me. I hadn't realized you knew the Necromancer."

She frowned. "How did you—" then looked down at her golden outfit. "You've seen Sethra recently."

"Your Majesty's powers of deduction are—"

"Leave it. What is this new information?"

"There is going to be an effort made to stop the investigation into the events in Tirma."

She frowned. "What sort of attempt, and how do you know?"

I nodded. "Please accept my compliments, Majesty. Those are good questions. I recognize good questions, because I can come up with them myself."

Her brows came together. "Are you bargaining with me, Taltos?"

"No, Majesty. I'll answer yours in any case. I'm hoping Your Majesty's gratitude will—"

"I get it. I'll think about it."

Being Empress means being able to interrupt anyone, at any time. Lady Teldra wouldn't have approved, but I have to admit it was the first thing about the job I'd ever found attractive.

I said, "An attempt will be made on the life of Justicer Desaniek. I know by deduction, from hints I've gotten, and because I know how the Jhereg operates."

She stared. "The Jhereg? They wouldn't—"

"It will look like an attempt by a group of Easterners and Teckla; one of those outfits of political malcontents. It will be very convincing."

She sat back and her eyes half closed. The Orb slowed down over her head, and turned purple. I'd never seen it slow down before. I wondered what it meant. After about a minute, she looked up at me. "What are your questions, Taltos?"

"Just one: Why would they do it?"

"Eh?"

"I know about their attempt to get you to pass decrees outlawing certain chemicals—"

"How do you know that?"

I answered the question she wanted answered, not what she'd asked. I said, "From the Jhereg side, Majesty, not from anyone to whom you entrusted the knowledge."

"Very well."

"As I said, I know about that. And I understand that Your Majesty—"

"Forget the formal speech, Taltos. I'm too tired and too irritated."

The Orb had, indeed, turned icy blue. I bowed slightly and said, "I understand you're trying to break out of the trap by bringing the truth out about the events in Tirma, and I admire that. But I don't understand the other side of it. That is, how it is that if you cooperate with the Jhereg, make the decrees they want and all that—how does that take the pressure off you?"

She was quiet for a long time; the Orb gradually changing from blue to a non-descript green. "My first duty," she said slowly, "is to keep the Empire running. If I fail in that, nothing else matters. To run the Empire, I need the cooperation of all of those I can't coerce, and to coerce those who won't cooperate. To do that, I need the confidence of the nobles and the princes. If I lose the confidence of the nobles, of the princes, I cannot run the Empire."

"Sounds pretty simple. Can the Jhereg really cause the nobles and princes to lose confidence in you?"

"A week ago I thought they could. Now—" She shrugged. "Now I guess we'll put it to the test."

I bowed to her, backed up seven steps, and left.

13

Caltho—*I understand Henish has refused to testify officially. I don't think that will be a problem, but if we're going to do this, we need to know what he knows. Can you speak with him informally and find out just what happened? Let him know we aren't out to stick a knife in him, we just need to know, from his point of view, what the sequence was. In particular, try to ascertain:*

1. *Did the troops have reason to believe the peasants in that shack were working with the enemy?*
2. *Did the peasants do anything that looked like it may have been an attack, or preparation for an attack?*
3. *Were they questioned, and, if so, how did they respond?*
4. *Did the troops see any weapons or anything that looked like it could be used as a weapon?*
5. *Did they violate orders, and, if so, at what point did they deviate from orders or expected procedures?*

Let him know that if we can get straight answers to these
questions, even unofficially, I'm pretty sure we can put this
thing away, whatever the answers are.

—Desaniek (not authenticated)

How do you stop an assassin?

Sounds like it's about to be a joke, doesn't it? But no, I was really asking myself that.

You'd think, what with me having been one for a big chunk of my life, I'd have some pretty good ideas on how to go about stopping one, but it doesn't work that way. When I thought up a way that would have stopped me, I thought up a way to counter it.

The point is, most assassins I know work pretty much the same way: get the pattern of your target's movements, select a spot, pick a time, make an escape plan, choose a method, then, well, you do it. If you want to stop the assassin, and you don't know who it is, you need to do pretty much the same thing and be there first. Good luck with that.

Or else—hmmm—maybe find the assassin while he's setting it up? Yeah, that had some possibilities.

"*Well, Loiosh? Got any better ideas?*"

"*Your job is to find better ideas, mine is to cut holes in the ones you have, and you've already done that pretty well.*"

"*Yeah. Thanks.*"

I wandered around the Imperial Wing until I found a refreshingly snobbish Teckla who, for a bit of silver, was willing to guide us to the office of the Imperial Justicer. Loiosh and Rocza hid inside my cloak, which I should mention isn't terribly

comfortable for any of us at the best of times, and with the added
weight on my shoulders (literally) now was flat no fun at all.

I was just as glad to have a guide—I'd never have been
able to find it on my own. I made a point of noting the twists,
turns, and stairways, and when we got there ("Down this hall,
the double doors with the iorich below the Imperial Phoenix
there, you see, and the gold knobs? That one.") I didn't think
I'd ever be able to find it again.

I dismissed the Teckla and walked into the office, which was
damn near as big as the throne room, and much more tastefully
appointed, gold knobs notwithstanding. A pleasant-looking
gentleman with eyebrows that looked like he trimmed them sat
behind a large highly polished desk and inquired as to my business, showing no signs of discomfort at being polite to me. I said,
"I beg your pardon, m'lord, I'm in the wrong place." I bowed low
and humbly, as befit an Easterner, and walked out.

There was no one outside the office, so I took a good, slow
look around. I was at the end of a long, wide hallway; with no
other doors to the place, the insides probably wrapped around,
with a bunch of internal offices, and also probably went quite
a ways back beyond what I saw. There had been no windows in
the room I was in.

Being at the end of the hallway like that was bad, because
there was no place to hide, but good because it meant there
was no other way out—unless there was a direct exit. I should
have had Kiera steal the plans for the Palace, if there were
any, and if I could have found a Vallista to interpret them for
me. Wide hallways mean important people in the Palace, and
maybe other places too. I'll make no comment on gold door-
knobs; you decide.

It was marginal whether this would be a good place to find Desaniek; someone important is liable to have another entrance or two, but not likely to use it most of the time; this is because they usually want to be seen coming and going, and to check on those who work for them. Not always, but chances were good she'd be coming out this way.

At the other extreme of the hall—that is, past the stairway—were three rooms and a small, short passage ending in a door. I went and clapped at it—which hurt all through my chest and neck—and no one answered; tried the door and it was locked. I didn't feel like being caught picking a lock in the Imperial Palace, so I didn't.

I hate it when there's no good place to hide; especially when I'm standing around somewhere I obviously don't belong. Here is where an invisibility spell would have been useful, if I'd been able to cast one without removing my protections, and if casting it wouldn't have set off every alarm in the Palace.

Yeah, well.

The ceiling provided no good place for Loiosh to hide, either.

"*I beg to differ.*"

"*The hanging lamp? You think you can use that?*"

"*I'd be concealed from one direction, and in shadows from the other.*"

"*You know what would happen if you were spotted? A jhereg in the Palace? Someone would scream, and they'd run and get everybody and—*"

"*Maybe they'd just shoo me out the nearest window.*"

"*I wouldn't bet on it. And you won't be able to follow her without being spotted. And whenever you leave, it'll be problematical.*"

"*Roçza will do it. All she has to do is let me know when she leaves, and which direction she goes. And she can stay here until we can fetch her.*"

"How do we—?"

"*Oh, come on, Boss. There's no one around. She can just fly up there.*"

"You sure about this?"

"*Yep.*"

"Okay."

I walked over to the place where the hall came together, opened my cloak, and she flapped up to the lamp. I studied her. I could see her, but I had to be looking. I felt a little better about the whole thing.

"*What does she think about all of this?*"

"*She thinks it's hot up there.*"

A couple of young-looking Iorich walked by, evidently on the way to see Desaniek, or maybe some other business in that office involving subtleties of jurisprudence. I bowed respectfully. They both glanced at me and kept walking; one might have nodded slightly.

At the bottom of the stairs things became complicated: There were passages in three directions, and I could make out further branchings on two of them; also the stairs kept going down. I checked the nearest doors: one of them was a privy, which I took the opportunity to use, because if you're going to be following someone for maybe hours, that's a problem you don't need. Another was locked, and one was open and empty—it would probably be someone's office when the need arose for legal advice on comparative flower arrangement. I stepped in, shut the door, and let Loiosh out from my cloak; a great relief to us both.

"Oh, do we get to wait now, Boss? You know that's my favorite part."

We waited.

Loiosh kept up a stream of suggestions about how to decorate the empty room, while I tried to think up creative things to say if someone happened to come walking in. Every once in a while, he'd reassure me that Rocza was still undiscovered, and that Desaniek hadn't been by.

We waited a long time.

Either she had a lot to do in the office and was disgustingly dedicated, or she had another way out. After four hours, with my stomach rumbling, I'd about decided it was the latter. After five hours, I was pretty well sure of it. It had almost been six hours when Loiosh said, *"There she is! Coming toward us, Boss,"* and we were off.

Loiosh ducked into my cloak again, and I stepped out of the hall and walked over to the stairway.

"What's Rocza doing?"

"Waiting."

"Good. Tell her to stay with it."

I turned so that when she walked past me I was going the other way; I made a slight bow. My peripheral vision told me only that she was of average height, with a rather light complexion for an Iorich and a firm stride. Once she was well past me, I turned around and followed. This not only permitted me to watch for anyone else who might be following her, but also showed me how to get out of the Palace.

We pretty quickly reached a place where there were lots of people, which wasn't good for me. It's too easy to follow someone in a crowd, which means it's hard to spot someone else doing so. I didn't lose her, of course; I can manage to stay with someone even without Loiosh, thank you very much. But it did get simpler once we left the Palace itself, and I could take a moment when I was unobserved to let him out.

The easy part was following Desaniek. The hard part was spotting someone else following Desaniek. The scary part was leaving the confines of the Palace area and wondering if I had someone following me with unfriendly intentions. The painful part was walking quickly enough to keep up with her.

She didn't go far, as it happened—just outside the Palace district to a place I'd eaten at once before. The food was okay, but the wine list was amazing. Among the things I hadn't practiced lately was following around someone who was eating better than I was.

To the left, however, I could leave Loiosh there in case she was a fast eater, and go retrieve Rocza.

"*Which means you walking through a lot of bad areas without me spotting for you.*"

"*Twenty minutes.*"

"*Think how much you could you do in twenty minutes.*"

"*Did you see anyone on the way here?*"

"*No, but—*"

"*Hang tight. I'll be back soon.*"

And I was, too, believe it or not. It took longer than it should have, because I got lost trying to find the office and had to ask directions three times, but find it I did, and Rocza was there, and I had no trouble getting back out. It's very strange how it can be hard to find your way to a place, but easy to find your way back.

"*Okay, we're about there. Is it safe?*"

"*You're safe from everyone but Rocza, who's hungry, overheated, and bad-tempered.*"

"I trust you to protect me."

"I charge for those services."

I found a safe place to wait while Desaniek finished eating. Loiosh and Rocza scanned the area for anyone watching either her or me.

"How will you tell which it is, Boss?"

"Just spot him, then we'll worry about it."

"In other words, you have no clue."

"Something like that."

But we didn't spot anyone. If there was anyone following her, he could be at the table next to her, eating, and staring off in the opposite direction; I'd done that before.

So I waited some more. Feh.

It might be interesting to give you the rest of what happened that night in great detail if it had turned out to have been interesting, but in fact I never spotted anyone. I was with her for about three more painful hours, as she visited a private club where, I guess, high-powered Iorich like to relax; then eventually she went home. In the end, it was a big nothing.

I went back to the inn, got a little sleep and an early start, and waited outside her home. Loiosh spotted a Jhereg, but it was before we got there, and he was obviously looking for me, based on how carefully he avoided watching the inn. Crap. We lost him on the way to Desaniek's home.

She went straight to the office; I had the jhereg in my cloak and all three of us waited. She didn't eat any morning meal at all, and must have had lunch sent in. What she did in there for eighteen hours I don't know, but there she was, and no one else seemed interested. That night she ate in the same place, but went straight home afterward. She took the same route both times.

Back in my room at the inn, I got a note from Kiera that she had information for me; I wrote back asking her to hold it for a day or two, since I had no time to do anything except follow Desaniek around.

Is it all right if I stop talking about how much it hurt just to walk? You can't be enjoying hearing about it, and I don't enjoy remembering it. Let's just say that, of all the times I've followed people around, this was the least pleasant.

You can repeat the pattern for the day after, except she went to a different place after she'd finished, and ate with an Iorich who was probably her lover—at least, they seemed to be on good terms, and he went home with her. They took a different route, more scenic. I had the impression they always went this way.

The next day, no lover, no Jhereg interested in her, and back to the first route, past one of my favorite bakers, which made it especially trying.

When the same thing happened the next day, I started to get disgusted, not to mention worried.

"What have I missed, Loiosh? They're going to take this Iorich out and make it look like those Easterners are behind it. To do that, they have to know her movements exactly. Why aren't they there?"

"Maybe they are, and you can't see them."

"Invisible? I suppose. But someone would have noticed an invisible guy walking by. I'd think—"

"That's not what I mean. She isn't a Jhereg, Boss. She probably doesn't have any protection spells on."

"What's your point?"

"Maybe they're using sorcery to trace her?"

I used several of my favorite oaths, running them together. I wish I could remember exactly how I put it, because it was very poetic.

"Boss?"

"That's cheating."

"Uh, Boss—"

"I know, I know. I'm just pissed because I didn't think of it."

"That's what you've got me around for."

"Which you'll never let me forget, which is the other thing I'm pissed about. All right, there has to be a way to figure this out. No, we don't, we need to call for help."

"Morrolan, or Sethra?"

"Yes." Before he could say something snippy, I added, "Who would be easier to get to?"

"You could get Morrolan to come see you, instead of you going there."

"Yeah, good point."

I took another circuitous route back to the Palace area, then went into the Dragon Wing by one of the entrances used by the nobility. Two guards in full uniform stood outside the entrance; I wondered if standing outside the Wing for hours at a time is an honor or a punishment, but in any case I put on my full outfit of arrogance and went breezing past them. This was going to be fun.

There was a sergeant at a desk. I knew he was a sergeant because I recognized the marks on his uniform, and I knew it was a desk because it's always a desk. There's always someone at a desk, except when it's a table that functions as a desk. You sit behind a desk, and everyone knows you're supposed to be there, and that you're doing something that involves your brain. It's an odd, special kind of importance. I think everyone should get a desk; you can sit behind it when you feel like you don't matter.

The Empress didn't have a desk. Morrolan didn't have a

desk. Sethra didn't have a desk. They really did matter. Me, when I was running my area for the Jhereg, I had a desk. Now I don't. You can draw whatever conclusions you want to from that.

I went up to the sergeant behind the desk and said, "I am Count Szurke. This is my signet. I wish to see the ensign on duty."

He didn't like it much. The only people who are supposed to talk to you like that are the ones with bigger desks. But the signet of an Imperial title carries some weight with the military, so he nodded and, however painful it may have been for him, said, "Yes, my lord. At once." Then he said, "Flips, bring my lord to the ensign."

A guy who spent too much time on his hair said, "Yes, m'lord," and bowed to me, then led the way down the hall, clapped outside the first door he came to, and, upon receiving the word, opened the door for me. I went into a room where there was a woman behind a desk. It was a bigger desk than the sergeant had.

I repeated my introduction and said, "I require a message delivered at once to Lord Morrolan. I wish him to meet me here. Find me a private room in which to wait, then let him know I'm there."

She didn't like my tone much, but orders, as they say, are orders. "Yes, my lord." She pulled out a piece of paper, scribbled on it with a pen that went into a pen-holder with a dragon's head etched on it, then affixed her seal and stood up. "If my lord will follow me?"

I don't always love throwing my weight around. But sometimes, with some people, it's just fun.

She showed me to a small, comfortable room, surrounded

by pictures of battle, some of them terribly realistic-looking. There was a lot of blood. I didn't find it relaxing. Also, they didn't bring me any food or wine, which I got to resenting after an hour or so. Fortunately, it wasn't much more than an hour before there came a clap at the door. I recognized Morrolan's hands slapping together before Loiosh said anything, which fact might disturb me if I let it.

I got up and let him in, then closed the door behind him. He said, "What is it?" That's Morrolan, all full of flowery greetings and chitchat.

"Those guards who stand outside the Wing. Are they being punished, or honored?"

"What is it?" he repeated. I guess I'll never know.

"There's someone I need to know about." I said, "Her name is Desaniek. She—"

"That's the name of the Justicer leading Her Majesty's investigation into Tirma."

"Oh, you knew about that?"

"I just heard."

"I thought I'd get to surprise you."

"What about her?"

"The Jhereg is going to kill her."

"If the Jhereg does, there won't be a Jhereg."

I rolled my eyes. "It won't look like they did it, Morrolan."

"Oh? How are they going to manage that? A tragic, coincidental accident? She's going to slip under a cart? Fall out of a building? Drown in her bathtub? Accidentally stab herself in the back while cleaning her knife?"

I filled him in on some of the background, then said, "It's going to be blamed on some idiot group of Easterners and Teckla."

He frowned. "Not the one—"

"No, a different group."

"How many are there?"

"Lots, I guess. Stir them up long enough and hard enough, and pretty soon they start listening to the guy telling them how to solve all their problems." I wasn't sure if I believed that myself, but telling it to Morrolan was a nod to Cawti; I'd like to think she'd have appreciated it.

"Do you know where and when?"

"No. That's what I want your help with."

He put on a "this is going to be good" expression, and waited.

I said, "I've been following her, hoping to pick up whichever assassin is following her, hoping to take him out before he moves."

"Well?"

"Well, no one is following her."

He shrugged. "Maybe she has no protection spells on, and they're tracing her movements with magic."

I kept my face expressionless and said, "I had the same thought. Can you find out?"

"Hmmm? Oh, sure."

"Good."

"Now?"

"Up to you," I said. "Now, or else after she's dead. Either way is fine."

"And then," he said, "there are times I don't miss you so much."

"Yeah, well."

"Okay, a moment." He closed his eyes, opened them, looked

disgusted, and said, "Oh, right. I'm in the Dragon Wing. Wait here."

He got up and walked out, so I missed seeing the powerful sorcerer doing his powerful sorcery, which would have involved him closing his eyes and then, I don't know, maybe taking a deep breath or something.

He was back a few minutes later. He sat down opposite me and said, "No one's tracing her."

"Really. Well. Isn't that interesting. Any chance they have a trace on her you don't know about?"

"I checked for sorcery, and witchcraft. I suppose it's possible, but it isn't very likely. Does this mean you're wrong?"

"I don't know. It fit together too well for me to think I got it wrong. But I don't, as Perisil would say, have any evidence that would work in court."

He considered. "If you're right, ignoring the lack of evidence, what happens to Aliera?"

"Good question. In fact, that's *the* question, isn't it? I wish I had an answer. If they get away with it, the Empress has to choose between giving in to the Jhereg, and sacrificing Aliera. I don't know which way she'll jump."

"And if they don't?"

"Hmm?"

"What if you stop them?"

"Oh. Then the Empire runs an investigation into the massacre, and probably drops all those bogus charges against Aliera. She was Warlord when it happened; I have no idea how an investigation like that will work out."

He considered for a moment. "I'd be inclined to think there'd be no blame attached to her."

"Should there be?"

"Pardon?"

"Well, she's the Warlord. It happened. How far up should the responsibility go?"

"Do you care?"

"Not really. Just curious."

"I'm not an Iorich."

"Right."

He said, "What are you going to do?"

"I don't know. Maybe get out of town. I don't want to be here when whatever happens happens."

He stared at me. "What, just give up?"

"I was thinking about it."

"That isn't like you."

"Morrolan, I'm lost. Sometime, somehow, they're going to take out Desaniek. And it will look like these Easterners did it to protest the massacre. It could be anywhere. I've spent most of the last week following her. I counted more than thirty times and places that would have been great to nail her. How am I supposed to know which they'll do? You cannot stop an assassin unless you know the assassin and get to him first. If you have any suggestions on how to figure that out, feel free to mention them. I'm beat."

"Can't help you," he said, dryly. "You're the only assassin I know."

"I know plenty of them, and I'm no better off. The other possibility is that I'm entirely wrong, and in that case I'm even more helpless because I have no clue at all that points to what they're planning, and I can't convince myself they're going to just take this without making a move of some kind."

He frowned. "We need to do something."

"I'm glad it's 'we' now."

His nostrils flared, but he didn't say anything; he knows when I'm just blowing sparks.

"Thanks for coming by," I said.

"Need a teleport anywhere?"

"Yes, but I can't risk it. Thanks, though."

We both stood up. "If you come up with anything, and I can help—"

"I'll let you know."

He nodded and preceded me out the door, heading deeper into the Wing; presumably to find a place he could teleport from. I miss the small conveniences, you know? I took myself out and started back toward my inn, thinking a bit of rest wouldn't be a bad idea.

"*Was that true, Boss? Are you really giving up?*"

"*I don't know. Probably not. But I have no idea what to do.*"

"*I'm with Morrolan. Doesn't seem like you to leave town with things unfinished.*"

"*Would you be against it?*"

"*No! I'm all for it, Boss! This place scares me. But it seems like you showing good sense, and that's not what I expect.*"

I sighed. "*I probably won't.*"

"*You should.*"

"*I know.*"

"*You have no idea where they're going to hit, Boss. What can you do?*"

"*That's what I've been saying. I only know who they're going to nail, and who they're going to—oh.*"

"*What?*"

I stopped in my tracks, and my mind raced. Then I said, "*I know who they're going to blame it on.*"

"*What does that get you?*"

"*A walk to South Adrilankha.*"

"*Uh, care to tell me why?*"

"*There might be things to learn from the people who are supposed to take the fall.*"

"*Like what?*"

"*If I learn them, I'll let you know.*"

"*Oh, good.*"

I was standing in the middle of the courtyard outside of the Dragon Wing of the Palace. The House of the Dragon, dark and oh-so-imposing, loomed over me as if matching glares with the Wing. There were four or five walkways leading out of the area, some to other parts of the Palace, others to the City. For all I knew, there were assassins hanging around all of them waiting to make my skin glisten.

But I had something to do, which is all anyone can ask.

"*Yeah, Boss? What are we going to do?*"

"*I'm going to go back to the inn and drop a note to Kiera asking her to bring by the names of whatever Left Hand businesses she's been able to find, then I'm going to have a decent meal sent up, drink half a bottle of wine, and go to sleep.*"

"*Sounds like my kind of plan.*"

"*Tomorrow is a busy day. I know a couple of places owned by the Left Hand. If Kiera doesn't show up, we visit one.*"

"*Good. Then at least we don't have to worry about a plan for the day after tomorrow, because neither one of us will be around to see it.*"

14

M'lady: Just got word through your office of the event. I'm perfectly willing to attend and answer any questions the mob has, though I cannot imagine what good H.M. imagines such a thing will do. They're going to believe what they believe, and I can talk until my voice is hoarse without changing them; nor do I see what difference it makes what they think, unless H.M. is afraid of more disorders like there were a few years ago. Officially, I have no opinion about that, of course (though unofficially a troop of guards will deal with however many of them take to the street). My question is, if I'm going to do this, how do you want me to handle it? I'd rather not have it in writing. Let me know when a good time is, and I can be in your offices, or wherever else you'd like to meet.

— Unsigned (not authenticated)

I felt a bit better the next morning. I stood up and stretched again, taking it slow and easy. I was still trying to make my muscles obey when there was a clap outside the door; Loiosh told me it was Kiera, I suggested she enter. She asked how I was feeling, and I lied a little. "Did you find out anything?"

"I learned a few businesses that are covers for Left Hand operations. Here." She handed me a sheet of paper with some names and addresses.

I held it out in front of her and tapped one. "You sure about this?"

She studied it. "Tymbrii," she said. "Pre-spun cloth and yarn. What about them?"

"Nothing," I said. "Except Cawti used to go there all the time. I had no idea."

"I don't know who the real owner is, but it's a good place to go if you want to be listening in on someone who thinks he has spells that will prevent that."

I nodded. "It's just odd, is all. The number of times I went in there, and never knew."

I looked over the rest of the list. There were places spread out all over the City, and I recognized a couple from having walked past them, but there were no others I'd actually been in.

"*Now what, Boss? Put the list on the wall, throw a knife at it, and see where it lands?*"

"*Something like that, yeah.*"

"*This is liable to get you killed, you know. You're in no shape—*"

"*Sit on it.*"

He psychically grumbled, but shut up.

"What do you know of these?"

"What do you want to know?"

I hesitated. "I'm not sure what to ask. I know so little of the Left Hand."

"As do I. As do they."

"Hmm?"

"Part of the secrecy thing; most of them know very little other than their own business."

"Oh. Um, how little do they know?"

"What kind of question is that?"

"I guess I'm asking if I were to show up at one of these places, would the individual running it know who I am?"

She considered. "I don't know. Maybe. My guess is not, except by coincidence. Don't bet your life on that, though."

I nodded. "Uh, how do I do this, Kiera?"

"You're asking me?"

"I don't mean that part. But say, this one—" I tapped the list. "It's an inn. Do I walk in and ask for a certain drink? Or—"

"Oh. Sorry. I'd have thought you knew. If you want to reach someone in the Left Hand, ask to see the mistress of the house, and deliver three silver coins, one at a time, with your left hand."

"Left hand," I said. "How clever."

"Imaginative, even."

I sat on the edge of the bed and considered. I took the knife from my right boot, pulled the coarse stone from my pack, and started working as I thought.

"You aren't lubricating it," said Kiera.

"Superstition," I told her. "You don't need to lubricate the stone, you just need to clean it when you're done."

"I know. I wondered if you did. What sort of edge are you putting on that?"

"Five degrees a side." I stopped and studied the knife. It was a wicked thing that I'd found in Shortrest, near Tabo. There was a cheap and worthless enchantment on it that was supposed to help it find a vital spot, and the point wasn't much, but it had a lovely edge and the wrapped antler fit my hand like it had been made for an Easterner. I worked some more, checked the bevel, switched to the other side.

"Where did you learn to do that?" she asked.

"Where did we first meet?" I asked her.

"Oh, right."

I nodded. "Sharpening knives was what I first learned to do after I learned to wash pots and pans, bring trash to the midden, and clear tables. I had one knife I kept a dual edge on: front three-quarters for slicing, back quarter for cutting. Best knife I've ever had."

"Where is it now?"

"Cawti has it. She still uses it. I showed her how to do the dual edge. She—" I stopped and went back to sharpening, switching to the extrafine stone.

"Sorry," she said.

"No, no. Don't worry about it."

"If you slip and take a finger off, I'll feel bad."

I held up my left hand. "That happened once. I've learned my lesson."

I finished sharpening the knife, nodded to myself, and stood up. My rib hurt like—it hurt.

Kiera hesitated, then said, "Do you want me to back you up?"

"Not your skill," I said. "And it won't be necessary. This should be pretty easy."

"As you say." She didn't sound convinced.

She followed me out of the room, and walked down the stairs with me. I went slowly. She said, "I'll be waiting in the courtyard to hear how it went."

I nodded but didn't say anything; most of my concentration was involved in not moaning with each step. Rocza took off from my shoulder and flew in slow circles overhead; Loiosh remained on my other shoulder and was looking around constantly.

In the wide boulevard in front of the Imperial Wing near the park, there is always a line of coaches; on one side those with markings on the door, on the other those that are for hire, all of which get special exemptions from the ordinance forbidding horses near the Palace. I think there are so many exemptions they might as well not bother with the ordinance, but maybe I'm wrong.

I spent some time studying the coaches for hire, trying to decide which looked like the most comfortable, then picked one and made my painful way to it. The coachman was a young woman, a Teckla of course, with the cheery smile and easy obsequiousness of the happy peasant in a musical satire on Fallow Street. I climbed in and gave her the address. She looked at Loiosh, then Rocza as she joined me in the coach, but merely bowed and climbed up to her station. Then she clucked and the horse started plodding along, a lot like I'd been walking.

"Boss, I don't care what Kiera says, you're in no shape—"

"I'm not going to be engaged in any acts of violence, Loiosh, so you can relax."

"You're not?"

"No, the plan changed."

"When?"

"Yesterday, when I was talking to Morrolan."

I settled back for the ride. It was a good coach—the jouncing didn't make me scream.

I stepped out and paid the coachman, who bowed as if I were Dragaeran and a nobleman. She probably thought it would increase her tip, and I guess it did at that.

I was now in a part of the City called the Bridges, probably because the main roads from three of the bridges all led to this area and crossed each other at a place called Nine Markets, which was in fact only about a hundred yards from where I stood. Tymbrii's shop was nestled in among the simple three- and four-room houses of tradesmen, with a few larger rooming houses and an open-air shrine to Kelchor.

"Okay, you two get back in my cloak."

"Do we have to?"

"I don't need to walk in there with two instant identifications on me."

"You think they won't know you just because we aren't with you?"

"Something like that."

"You're dreaming."

"In, both of you."

I felt him start to argue, but he cut it off. The two of them ducked into my cloak as the coach pulled away.

The door itself held a sign that suggested I feel free to enter, so I did. It smelled a bit dusty, and there were oily smells mixed in. It was a single room, well lit, with bolts of cloth and those bunches of yarn that people who use yarn call skeins. There was an elderly gentleman sitting in a straight-backed chair, looking as if he had been doing absolutely nothing until the door opened. Once I entered, he rose, took me in, and did the facial dance I'd come to expect from merchants who don't know quite how to place me, followed by the polite bow of those who decide coins bring more happiness than snubbing one's inferiors. That's the difference, you know, between a merchant and an aristocrat: The true aristocrat will always prefer to snub his inferior.

"May I help you, my lord?"

"I hope so. I'm looking to see the mistress of the house."

He frowned. "I beg your pardon?"

Clink. Clink. Clink.

"I'll see if she's available."

He vanished through a doorway in back, and I looked around at brightly colored cloth. Exotic. That's what Cawti had called these colors: exotic. I guess they were at that. Bright blues and searing yellows and some as dark orange as the ocean-sea.

I waited.

He came out of the door again, bowed stiffly again, and said, "She will see you now. The doorway at the end of the hall."

He stood aside, and I went past him through the open door. I felt uncomfortable as I did, like he was going to bash my head in when I went through. He didn't, though.

There was a short hallway with a closed door to the side, and another door in front of me. This one was open, so I entered.

She was of middle years for a Dragaeran, say a thousand or so, and dressed in the gray and black of the Jhereg. She was sitting behind a desk looking business-like, and she rose as I entered. Nothing in her expression indicated she might know me, although that was hardly proof.

"May I be of service?" she said, with barely concealed distaste. Now, *she* was an aristocrat.

"I seek knowledge, O wise one."

She frowned. "Are you mocking me?"

"Yes, but only in a friendly way."

She sat down again, looking at me through narrowed eyes. "I'm not your friend. Do you have business for me, or don't you?"

"I do. I'm after information, there may be some spells to prevent eavesdropping."

She nodded. "Go on. What are the specifics?"

That set off all sorts of alarms in my head. Was she expecting me to ask her to commit a crime, just like that? I mean, maybe the Left Hand did that sort of thing, but, if so, how did they stay in business?

I looked her in the eye. "I beg your pardon?"

"Before I can accept, I have to know who you want to listen in on. I'll need to get a dispensation from the Justicers."

"Naturally, I wouldn't want you to do anything illegal."

"Naturally."

"So of course, you have to go through the court proceedings."

"Yes."

"I assume there are special fees for the advocate?"

"That is correct."

"How much."

"One hundred."

"That's a lot," I said.

"Yes."

"All right," I said. "I'll give you a draft on Harbrough."

She nodded. She'd certainly know Harbrough: he didn't use names, which made him very popular among the Jhereg—both sides, presumably—and was the reason I still had money available.

She passed over pen and ink and blotter, and I wrote out a standard dispensation then passed it to her. She studied it carefully, I imagine sending the image to someone who'd make sure the funds were there to cover it.

"All right," she said. She moved the draft to a place between us and put the inkwell on it; there seemed to be something almost ritualistic about the act, although maybe my talk with Kiera had me imagining things. Then she bowed her head. "What's the job?" All business; just like the Jhereg.

"What if I said Sethra Lavode?"

She snorted. "I'd give you your draft back and point you to the Nalarfi Home."

"Just making sure *you* didn't belong there."

"Yes, there are things I won't do. Quit wasting my time. What's the job?"

"There is a house at number eleven Enoch Way in South Adrilankha—"

"Are you jesting?"

"Why would I be?"

"You think a house in South Adrilankha has protections against eavesdropping?"

"I don't know that they do, but they might."

"They have the resources for that?"

"If they've gotten support from tradesmen, functionaries, or any of the minor nobility."

"And what makes you think they have?"

"It's a possibility. I'll pay to hear what's going on in there. If there's no protection from eavesdropping, then so much the easier for you."

She hesitated, then nodded. "All right."

"Uh, how does this work?"

"How does what work?"

"How will I know what's said?"

She looked disgusted. "How would you like to know?"

"I'd like to be able to listen myself, but I don't think that's possible."

"Why not?"

"Try casting a listening spell on me, and see what happens."

Her eyes narrowed, and her right hand twitched, and she said, "Phoenix Stone?"

"Yes."

"Well, if you aren't willing to remove it—"

"I'm not."

"Then we can provide you a summary, or a transcript."

"How long does that take?"

"You can have it within a day."

"*Boss*—"

"Is there any way you can, uh, have my familiar listen instead of me?"

"I beg your pardon?"

I opened my cloak. Loiosh poked his head out, then climbed up to my left shoulder; followed by Rocza, who climbed up to my right. I smiled apologetically.

"*See, Boss, you could have saved us all a lot of trouble if*—"

"*Shut up.*"

"I'm not sure what you are asking me to do." She looked like I had offered to share my meal of fresh worms with her.

"Loiosh is fully self-aware, and trained to, well, if you can manage to connect him to the spell, he can tell me what's said."

She didn't much like the idea, but I pulled out my purse and set a nice stack of imperials in front of her. Money that clinks and glitters always has more of an effect than money that exists only in theory.

"All right," she said. "I'll need to, ah, to touch him."

"*Ewwww,*" said Loiosh.

"*Yeah, well.*"

Aloud I said, "How long will this last?"

"If he is aware enough to accept the spell, it will end when he wants it to, or it will fade on its own over the course of the next year or so."

"All right."

Loiosh flew down onto her desk in front of her; she almost managed not to flinch.

"Oh, one thing," I said.

She had started to reach toward him; now she stopped. "Yes?"

"If anything you do causes him any harm, there is no power in the world that will keep your soul safe."

"I dislike threats. If you don't want—"

"I just had to make sure you were informed."

She shrugged. I really don't make threats very often, so I resent it when I do make one and it doesn't impress the threat-enee. But to the left, that's probably why I don't make many.

Her hand was steady when she put three fingers on his back.

"*I need a bath.*"

"*Feel anything?*"

"*Sorcery, pretty mild.*"

"*All right.*"

"You should begin to get sound by morning."

"All right. Be careful, the place is being watched."

"By whom?"

"The Jhereg. That is, the Right Hand, if you will."

She snorted. "That won't be a problem."

"All right," I said. "Anything else?"

"Yes. One question: Who are you?"

"You think I'm going to tell you?"

"You think I can't find out?"

"If it means that much to you, feel free," I said. Then I turned on my heel and left.

The gentleman who sold cloth ignored me as I left, and I gave him the same courtesy, though it wasn't a deliberate snub on my part—I was busy asking myself why I hadn't thought to have the coach wait. Loiosh, as was his custom, wasted no time. *"So tell me, Boss, if the whole idea was for her to be able to identify you, why couldn't we be there?"*

"It would have made it too obvious that I wanted to be identified."

"So, instead, it just matters that you walk into one of the businesses of people who are trying to kill you? Is this what you call high strategy?"

"That's a Dragon term. I never use it."

"Boss, won't they figure out that you wanted them to identify you?"

"Maybe."

"So, how is it that what you just did wasn't stupid?"

"The business of convincing your enemies to do what you want them to is a tricky matter, Loiosh. I wouldn't expect a jhereg to understand the subtleties."

"I trust an education in the subtleties will begin shortly."

"You're starting to sound like Morrolan."

I had to walk to the market to find a coach—a run-down thing that found every rut and hole in the road. Served me right for lack of forethought, though. Things like not thinking to have the coach waiting might seem small to you, but if I went ahead and executed plans without seeing to all the little details, I was going to make what was already a tricky operation downright impossible. I gave myself a stern talking-to about it; my cracked rib and various bruises emphasized the point.

Kiera was, as promised, waiting in the courtyard. "Well?" she said.

"Well enough," I said. "Maybe. Have to see."

She frowned. "What did you do?"

"Started a delayed-action explosive spell."

"Uh, let's go up to your room."

"I thought you'd never ask."

"What?"

"Forget it."

I made my slow painful way to the room. I stretched out on the bed, Kiera took the chair.

"Interesting noise," she said.

"Hmmm?"

"As you lay down. Somewhere between a groan and a sigh. I don't think I've heard anyone do that before. Are you sure you don't want to be fixed up?"

"I'll be fine."

"Unless you have to move fast."

"When have I ever needed to move fast?"

She didn't even bother to give me a look for that one. "What did you do?"

"I hired her."

"To do what?"

"I need to know what's going on in a certain little cottage in South Adrilankha."

"And that was the only way to find out?"

"The best way, under the circumstances."

"Why?"

"I'm trying to do two things at once."

She nodded. "I once tried to steal two things at once. Want to hear what happened?"

"Only if it worked."

"I won't talk about it, then."

"There are two things going on, Kiera. They're probably related, but I can't know that."

"Aliera's prosecution, and the effort to set you up."

"Right."

"And the cottage in South Adrilankha?"

"It's a long shot, as far Aliera's prosecution, but it's all I can come up with. My thinking is this: If the Jhereg wants to blame the killing on one of these people, they'll—"

"Wait. What?"

"The Jhereg is planning to kill the Imperial investigator, a certain Desaniek, and blame it on a group of Eastern and Teckla rebels."

"How did you put that together?"

"When I asked Cawti if she were still giving reading lessons, she said, 'until lately,' which got me to thinking—never mind. It's a long story. The point is, if they want to kill the investigator, and blame it on this group of rebels, they'll need to know what the group is up to. If I know what they're up to, maybe I'll be able to figure out where they'll move."

She looked doubtful. "That doesn't seem likely."

"I agree, but it's all I've got."

"What about the other reason? How does this help you get out of a setup?"

"It might not, but if she takes the trouble to find out who I am, and I did everything but beg her to, it's going to stir up the Jhereg, and maybe throw them off their game."

"That is really thin."

"Not as thin as you think. Something unexpected happens when you're after someone, you slow down and make sure you know what's going on. All I need is for them to slow down long enough to let me finish this business and get back out of town."

"That is very thin."

"Like the other, it's what I have. Do you have any better ideas?"

"This is bigger than you seem to realize, Vlad."

"What makes you think that?"

"Eh? It's the Left Hand of the Jhereg, the Jhereg, and the Orca manipulating Imperial politics. How much bigger—?"

"No, what makes you think I don't realize how big it is?"

"You aren't acting as if you do."

"Kiera, after you've been in battle with gods, you get to the point where the affairs of mere mortals—"

"Can you be serious for two words?"

"Not without effort," I said.

"Apply yourself."

I shrugged. "What do you want from me? Okay, it's serious. It's big. I get that. But I came back here to help Aliera. If you can show me a better way to do that, I'm listening."

"I'll never understand this passion you have for making yourself a target."

"It isn't a passion, it's more of an avocation." She started to say something, but I cut her off. "I didn't create the situation, and no one was doing a damned thing about it, either because they didn't want to offend the Empress, or because they didn't want to offend Aliera. You couldn't fit the hair of a norska's tail on how much I care about offending either one. There's a problem, I'm fixing it."

"You're stubborn, Vlad."

"Is that a compliment?"

"Sometimes. Usually. Right now, I'm not sure. How can I help?"

"You probably can't, but I'll let you know if something comes up."

She sighed, started to say something else, then just shrugged and left me with her Kiera smile and soft kiss on the cheek. I lay on my back and tried not to move too much, and eventually got some rest.

15

Your Highness: I urgently request an immediate review of the entire Imperial prison system. With the suicide of Bryn our investigation—an investigation, Your Highness, instigated by the express wishes of Her Majesty—has been seriously compromised. Permit me to urge Your Highness in the strongest possible terms to form a committee of our own House and some of the more skilled Vallista to see what can be done to make sure this doesn't happen again; it is hardly an overstatement to say that the honor of the House itself is at stake. Any further event of this type and I will not answer for the committee being able to carry out its duties.

I Remain, Your Highness,
Your Loyal and Respectful
Justicer Desaniek

I woke up feeling still better. If this trend continued, I'd be back in shape to fight in only a month or so.

"Boss!"

That was when I realized what woke me up. *"What is it?"*

"Uh, this is weird. I'm hearing things."

"Yeah, that's what was supposed to happen."

"But, it's weird."

"It's just for a day or two. Anything interesting?"

"Depends how interested you are in snoring."

"Mostly interested in my own, but it's too late for that, now."

"Cry up a storm, Boss."

I got up and slowly and painfully took care of morning things. The plan for the day was, actually, to do nothing except to stay as safe as I could: there was nothing to do until and unless I got some information from Loiosh, or until someone made a move at me.

I had them bring me some food. There was klava—good klava—and some hen's eggs partly boiled with salt, and bread with a luxurious amount of butter. They charged too much, but here and there were compensations.

Loiosh reported conversations that were only remarkable in their triviality—the best markets, who had become pregnant, whose uncle had taken sick. Sometimes he identified the voices as male, sometimes female, sometimes mixed. At one point, two women who spoke with an accent that Loiosh remembered as being from some Eastern kingdom got into a conversation that made me blush when Loiosh repeated it. And I don't blush easy.

By the evening, I was starting to wonder if the whole thing were a put-up job—if someone knew I was listening and was staging the conversations for my benefit. But then, I reminded myself that most of these people worked eighteen hours a day or so, many of them at the slaughterhouses, so I wouldn't expect to hear anything of substance until the evening.

And, indeed, in the evening I started hearing things that

were more interesting: Loiosh reported a male voice saying, "They should be arriving within the half hour, we should set the chairs up."

I sent down for another meal to prepare myself; this one a whole fowl done in a sweet wine sauce. I don't actually care much for sweet sauces, but it wasn't bad.

"*Pounding sounds, Boss. Doors. People coming in. Voices.*"

"*What are the voices saying, Loiosh?*"

"*No idea. They're all talking at once. Greetings, I think.*"

"*Any Eastern accents?*"

"*One or two, maybe. It's hard to say.*"

"*All right.*"

About half an hour later he said, "*They're quieting down. Someone's talking. Dragaeran, or at least no accent I can hear.*"

"*What's he saying?*"

"*She. Blah blah blah the Empire blah blah blah Tirma blah blah blah organize blah blah—*"

"*Loiosh.*"

"*Boss, when she actually says anything, I'll tell you, okay? This having voices in my head is really weird.*"

"*You should be used to it. I am.*"

"*It's not the same.*"

"*Okay.*"

About half an hour later, he said, "*They're going to be having some sort of meeting tomorrow.*"

"*How thrilling.*"

"*With an Imperial Representative.*"

"*Oh. If it turns out to be Desaniek, this will suddenly be too easy.*"

"*No idea who it is.*"

"*Guess I'd better find out.*"

"*They're still talking, Boss. Something about meeting before the meeting with the Representative, to, I don't know, I couldn't hear. Something about unity.*"

"Where's the meeting?"

"*Which?*"

"Both."

"*The one with the Representative will be at Speaker's Hall at the fifth hour of the afternoon. The earlier one will be noon, at the cottage.*"

"A meeting before the meeting. Okay. Got it. I may have a bit of an idea, but I first need to make sure that it is Desaniek going to that meeting."

"*What if it isn't?*"

"Then I'll—"

I didn't have to answer the question, because a clap outside the door interrupted me.

"*Who?*"

"*No one I know, Boss. Just one, though.*"

I stirred myself. I had forgotten about the damned rib and sat up directly, instead of turning on my side first. I resolved not to do that again. I hoped I wasn't going to have to defend myself, because I just wasn't in any shape to. Nevertheless, I let a knife fall into my right hand, held it behind the door, and opened the door carefully.

My, my, my.

I didn't recognize her, but I knew what she was. She had a face like a knife's edge, hair swept back and tied, and wore black and gray and rings on every finger including both thumbs.

I stepped back. "Well," I said. "This is unexpected. Please come in."

"Vladimir Taltos?"

"Something like that," I said. "And you are?"

"A messenger." She made no move to come in; the hallway behind her was empty.

"I can guess from whom."

"You have a deal with us," she said. "We have a project
working you know something about. If you interfere with the
project, the deal is off."

Then she turned and walked down the hall.

I shut the door and put the knife away.

"Well," I said after a moment. "*I guess I've been warned.*"

"*I guess so. What are you going to do?*"

"*Just what I was planning to do.*"

"*Now?*"

"*Might as well.*"

Loiosh and Rocza flew out of the door ahead of me, and
announced that things looked good. I made my way to the
Palace. I still walked as if nothing hurt, and I still knew it
wouldn't make any difference. As we walked, Loiosh said, "*Can
I stop listening now?*"

"*Soon. Not yet.*"

"*It's just more of the same, Boss.*"

"*Sorry. We'll be done with this soon.*"

Who would know? Well, the Empress, of course, and I'd try
again to see her if I had to, but one doesn't simply barge in on
the Empress to get a simple question answered if one has any
choice, so I took myself to the Dragon Wing to see if the temporary acting Warlord and Dragon Heir to the throne happened
to have a spare moment. Start small, that's what I always say.

I climbed the stairs to the tiny room that was almost becoming familiar—yea, Vlad Taltos, ex-assassin, ex–crime boss,
wanted by both sides of the law (that last isn't true, but it

sounded good, didn't it?), walked into the inner sanctum of Imperial law enforcement. I clapped.

"Who by the fecal matter of the Seven Wizards is it now and what do you want that can't wait half an hour?" came the cheerful reply from within.

"It's Vlad," I said.

"Enter, then." I did. "My day is now perfect," she suggested.

"Who from the Empire is going to meet with that group of Easterners and Teckla?" As I've said, I'm big on small talk.

Her eyes narrowed and her lips pressed together. "Cawti?" she said.

"No. My own sources. Who will it be?"

"Why should I tell you?"

There were a number of reasons, but I cut to the simplest one. "If it's Desaniek, she's going to be assassinated there."

That made an impression of some sort, but I couldn't judge what it was. "It isn't," she said at last. I'm not sure if I felt relieved or disappointed. It was too pat, anyway. Norathar continued, "It's Caltho."

"Who is that?"

"Iorich. Desaniek's chief investigator."

"I see." Then. "Oh."

"Oh?"

"What would happen if he were killed at that meeting?"

She blinked. "At that meeting? By an Easterner or a Teckla?"

"Yes."

"I don't . . ." Her voice trailed off as she considered it. "It wouldn't be good," she said finally. "What are your reasons for thinking it will happen?"

"You know about the Jhereg, Left Hand, and Orca pressure on Zerika."

"On Her Majesty," she corrected absently.

"An honest investigation would be ugly, but would take away their leverage. An attempt on the part of rebel Teckla to stop the investigation would sabotage it, or at least delay it, and the pressure would be back on."

She frowned. "I don't know. That isn't how the Jhereg operates."

"The Left Hand does." She started to speak but I cut her off. "I don't know a lot about the Left Hand, but I know how they operate, and it's just like that. Not to mention the Orca."

She nodded slowly. "Yes, I can see that. What do you suggest I do?"

"The obvious thing is to arrest the rebels."

"And you know as well as I do why I can't."

"The Empress wouldn't approve?"

"And for good reason: that sort of thing just stirs them up and makes the rest think they must be right. Your peasant is a peaceful, happy sort, normally, Vlad, and having a few malcontents around gives him someone to feel wiser than. Knock ten of those on the head, and now you have a thousand in their place. We don't need that."

I wasn't entirely sure about the whole peaceful happy peasant thing, but I had to agree with the rest. "Cancel the meeting?"

"The same problem, only not quite as bad."

"Yeah. Well, break up this deal with the Orca and the Left Hand? Leave them no reason to go to the trouble? They're practical sorts, you know."

"How do you propose doing that?"

"I don't know. Ask nicely?"

"Can you be serious for two words?"

"Not without great effort."

"Vlad—"

"Okay, I know how to do it. Maybe. I have to make some assumptions, and after learning just now that the target isn't Desaniek, but—what's his name?"

"Caltho."

"Right. After learning that, I'm not so sure about my ability to make assumptions, but I'm going for it anyway."

"What are you going to do?"

"Identify the assassin, and kill him."

She drummed her fingers on her desk. Then, "All right," she said. "Can I help?"

"Yes," I said. "I've been threatened by the Left Hand. Or, rather, Cawti has."

Her eyes narrowed. "And you're going ahead with it?"

"You know her. Wouldn't you?"

She nodded slowly. "All right. I'll watch her."

"She'll need sorcerous protection above all."

"I'm not an idiot, Vlad."

"Sorry. It's just—"

"I know. Anything else?"

I shook my head, stood, and took my leave.

"Boss, I will never, ever understand flightless people."

All I had to do was find the assassin. Should be no problem. Just look for the shifty eyes. Heh.

If you're going up against someone, it's always best to assume he's not as good as you, and a little better than you. You need to figure you're better, because otherwise you start second-guessing yourself, and hesitating, and doing all sorts of other things that don't help at all. And better, because if you underestimate some skill he has, it could be very embarrassing. It's tricky doing both at once.

Put it this way: Could I disguise myself well enough that I couldn't tell I was an assassin?

Easy.

So, how would I get myself to reveal me, in a crowded room? How crowded? I had no idea. It wasn't that big a cottage; you couldn't get more than twenty or thirty people in there.

I ate, and I thought, and I didn't come up with anything better than suddenly pulling a knife and seeing if anyone reacted like he knew what he was doing. I didn't much like it. Then it crossed my mind that perhaps it would be a sorcerous attack, and I liked it even less.

Well, all right. The assassin would be there, or not; the assassin would be a sorcerer, or not. When you're playing Shereba, and you realize that the only way you can win is if your opposing knave is still in the deck, then you play as if it's still in the deck. Therefore, the assassin would be there, and would not be a sorceress.

"Glad that's settled."

"Shut up."

I did some more thinking, and came up with nothing else, and eventually I fell asleep.

When I woke up, I hurt a little less, but I still had no interest in even moving slowly; the idea of moving fast just wasn't any fun at all.

"Boss, if you spot the assassin, what are you going to do?"

"I'm going to say, 'Pointy point, you're the donkey.'"

"I probably don't want to know, do I?"

"I'm just worried about the possibility he never played that as a kid. You don't think about assassins ever being kids, you know?"

"Yeah, that's just what was on my mind."

I stood up, slowly and painfully. "What if I was beaten just for this? I mean, what if the whole point was to make it impossible for me to take out the assassin if I needed to?"

"Yeah, Boss. What if?"

I didn't have an answer, so I slowly got dressed and ready, and then, Loiosh and Rocza scouting for me, I went down the stairs and out. I picked up some warm, crusty bread and smoky, crumbly goat cheese from a vendor outside the inn. I love warm bread more than a lot of things you'd think would be higher on the list, you know?

After I'd eaten, I made my way to the West Palace Market, which is a good place to go for the best ingredients, if you can make yourself get up that early in the morning. I wasn't there for ingredients today, though. In the far southwestern corner of the market, behind a stall that sells the best truffles in White-crest is a ratty-looking permanent store that sells pre-rolled copper tubing, and nails, hammers, springs, and various tools for using the above. It's run by a Tsalmoth named Liska who looks as old as Sethra is and scurries about at a furious pace, her back permanently bent and her eyes looking up from beneath hair so stringy she seems to have lost her noble's point. She keeps her cash in a box beneath the stool she uses on the rare occasions when she sits to dicker with a customer, while the customer stands on the other side of a wooden plank set on two barrels; the plank is a light wood, well-polished, and carved with depictions of a tsalmoth in various odd poses.

"What do you want?" she said when I walked in.

"A knife," I told her.

She scurried onto her stool. She knew me, but admitting it would, I guess, give me a bargaining advantage over her. Something like that. "What sort of knife?" she barked out.

"Nothing fancy; just something to whittle with."

She gave me a look that indicated enough suspicion to prove she knew who I was. I looked all innocent and shit. She showed me a selection, and I ended up picking out a small clasp knife. I tested the edge because it would have looked funny not to, and made sure it opened and closed easily, gave her an imperial and told her to keep it, and headed back out.

"Okay, Boss. I can't wait to see what you're going to do with that."

"It's pretty small; I'll most likely just lose it."

I still had a couple of hours before the meeting was supposed to start. Not far from the West Palace Market is a hostel called the Inkstand for a reason that was explained to me once but I can't remember; I think it was something historical. There's an actor named Ginaasa who lives there from time to time, and with whom I've done business before. Since it was early in the morning, I expected to wake him up, and I expected him to be sober. I was right on both counts, but he took it in good grace when I clinked some coins. I left there a bit later with a cloth bag containing a blond wig and a neatly trimmed matching beard, a bit of glue, and a jar of stuff to lighten my complexion a bit.

That done, I still had the hard part: if it worked, what then? How was I going to manipulate events to get what I wanted, just in case that was a possibility?

"Boss, where are you going?"

"Huh? I don't—oh, House of the Iorich, I guess."

"You think he'll know what to do?"

"I guess if we're going to go into this, we ought to find out what is liable to happen to Aliera. Remember Aliera? She's the one who got us involved in this?"

"Are you expecting gratitude?"

"No. I just know if it were me—"

"Yeah, yeah."

We reached the house safely, and I made the now-familiar trek to Perisil's office and clapped. He peered out the door, then opened it. I went in.

"Why do you do that?"

"Do what?" he asked me. He looked genuinely curious.

"Never mind."

I took the chair opposite him and said, "I have something going that might do, um, something. I need to check it with you."

He nodded. "Well, I'm afraid you'll have to give me at least one or two more details than that if you want an intelligent comment."

It took me a moment to realize he was jesting; I don't know if that says something about him, or about me. I said, "All right, just this once. Here's the situation as I see it, stop me if I'm wrong about something: The Jher—that is, certain groups are trying to pressure the Empress. The leverage they have is the scandal about Tirma, which is going to annoy a lot of the people who matter, although exactly why they care I couldn't say." He gave me a look, but didn't interrupt.

I went on. "The Empress, after you and I started making trouble and kicking things up, reconsidered, and decided to have an official investigation into the events. There will be an effort to stop the investigation and cast blame at some idiot group of Teckla by assassinating Caltho."

"Desaniek."

"No, I was wrong about that. Her assistant, Caltho."

"Hmmm. That would work too."

"Even better, because it will happen at a public meeting where he is supposed to answer questions about what is happening and why."

"I see."

"All right, so, if I manage to stop the assassination, does that give us any leverage to get Aliera released?"

He was quiet for a moment, then he said, "Stop it how?"

"By killing the assassin before he can kill Caltho."

He was quiet for a bit longer, then. "It depends on a number of things. How are you . . . where . . ." His voice trailed off and he looked uncomfortable. I'd never seen him look uncomfortable before; I think I enjoyed it.

"The way I see it going down, I'll take him before he ever gets to the meeting."

"Then, excuse me, how will anyone know?"

"No one will know."

"Then I don't see how it will have any effect on our case."

"Uh. Yeah, there's that. Okay, what if I made it more dramatic?"

"You mean, a rescue at the last minute and all?"

I nodded. "I have no idea if I can, or how, but I might be able to pull something like that off."

He nodded slowly, rubbing his chin, then said, "No."

"No?"

"Legally, it would have no standing. Let me explain. There are three ways this can go: She can be tried for what she was arrested for, or she—"

"Wait, what she was really arrested for, or what the official charges were?"

He blinked, hesitated, and said, "I'll start over. There are three ways this can go. One: She can be arrested for practicing Elder Sorcery, she—"

"It's crap."

He shrugged. "That's as may be. Two: She can be investigated for her role, if any, in the massacre. Or, three: All charges could be dropped and she could be released."

"Eh? Well, that would be best. How can we get that to happen?"

"I've no idea. I'm just listing the possibilities. Now, I can represent her on the charge of Elder Sorcery. If the investigation into the massacre happens, she should find another advocate, because that falls under Military Code, or Imperial Responsibility, or some combination, and in any case I know nothing about it."

"Well, but getting her released—"

"That isn't something we do; that's just something that could happen if the Empress takes it into her head to do it, or if the Justicer decides there's no case. Now, we're going to be appearing before Justicer Moriv. I've tried cases with her before, and we get along all right."

"That's important, I assume."

He nodded. "She's easygoing, for a Justicer, but doesn't tolerate any deviations from strict code; that's probably why they picked her."

"But she has to obey Imperial orders, right? I mean, if the Empress tells her to drop the case, she has to drop it."

He hesitated. "It isn't that simple."

I stifled a groan.

"An order from the Imperial Advocate would do it, certainly."

"Hmmm?"

"The one representing the Empire in the proceedings. My opponent, if you will."

"Oh. Is that something liable to happen?"

"If he thinks he can't win."

"How do we convince him he can't win?"

"In court."

"That doesn't help."

"It's what I've been working on."

"How's it looking so far?"

"Not all that good, but there are a few points that might get us somewhere."

"And if the Empress ordered the, what was it? Imperial Advocate? to stop the prosecution?"

"Same as ordering the Justicer to. Technically, they aren't permitted to. But, ah, it would have a strong influence. I can't predict what would happen."

"So we're back to convincing Her Majesty to drop it, and hoping for the best."

He gave me a look. "Or I might win the case."

"Right. Sorry." I hesitated. "The Empress is under a lot of pressure from a lot of different directions. What happens if she sees a way out?"

"Leading question. She'll take it, of course, barring any significant factors you haven't mentioned."

"How would it work?"

"The best way is to present a request to dismiss to the Justicer and the Imperial Advocate, with a copy to Her Majesty. The trick is finding grounds for the request. We don't actually have any, which puts all of them in a tricky position."

"I have information that the idea of arresting Aliera came from the Jhereg representative; does that help?"

"Is it information from someone who will say so under the Orb?"

"Uh, no."

"Then it doesn't help." He hesitated. "Unless."

"Hmmm?"

"The idea came from the Jhereg representative—to whom?"

"Uh, to the Empire."

"No, no. To whom did the representative make—"

"Oh. To Her Majesty."

"Ah. That's different. Then the Orb will remember it, which means that it happened legally."

"Um, and so?"

"So we present a claim on conspiracy against the Jhereg."

"Oh, they'll love me for that."

He shrugged. "They have a lot of affection for you now, do they?"

"Good point. How does it work?"

"We present a petition to have the Orb interrogated about the source for the idea of arresting Aliera—it doesn't matter how we know about it, as long as we're specific about the request. Then you have to show reasonable probability that there was a Jhereg assassin working against the investigation."

"I can do that," I said.

"If you get lucky."

"Shut up."

I asked him, "How does it work from there?"

"They grant the petition, look at the evidence of a Jhereg assassin, find reasonable grounds that the prosecution was from a private conspiracy rather than cause of justice—what?"

"Nothing. An involuntary noise. Go on."

"And when they've established that, they dismiss the charges."

"What about the Imperial investigation part? I mean, the real charges?"

"I have no control over that, and if there is one, as I said, I'd be the wrong advocate to handle it."

I nodded. "All right. So my part is simple—stop the assassin in such a way that it's known he was an assassin."

"When will this happen?"

I checked the time with the Orb. "Four to six hours from now."

"Oh! Well, if you'll pardon me then, I need to get these petitions drafted."

I nodded and got out of there.

"*Boss, how are you going to identify the assassin, much less prove what he is?*"

"*That isn't what I'm worried about, Loiosh. I'm worried about how to stop the Imperial investigation.*"

"*Why stop it? Will they really convict Aliera just for killing a few Teckla?*"

"*If we're lucky, we'll find out,*" I said.

16

To assert that final responsibility for actions taken by Imperial Representatives rests with the Empress is to state a truism without substance. In this case in particular the discoveries of this committee show that the problem is, above all, that Imperial policies are carried out by human beings, who are necessarily flawed. While incidents such as this are regrettable, the facts do not support blanket condemnations of Imperial policies with regard to rebellion, much less the Empire itself. Rather, incidents such as this must be accepted as in some measure unavoidable.

However, there are, in the opinion of this committee, certain steps which can be taken to minimize the frequency and severity of such events, which steps are listed in Appendix 27.

The big question was whether I had enough time to set everything up: I only had a couple of hours left until the meeting, and if this was going to work, I had to arrive early to try to convince them to let me attend, and to watch everyone arrive in hopes of spotting the dzur among the norska.

The same sergeant was working in the Dragon Wing. He did not look pleased to see me.

"Same thing," I said. "If you would be so kind as to inform the Lord Morrolan that I wish to see him, and add that it is urgent."

He scowled but agreed.

"And," I said. "If I might trouble you for an additional service, please have someone find the Warlord and tell her the following: Vlad has a way out. I'll be waiting in that same room I was in before, if that is acceptable."

Then I wandered for a bit until I found an errand-runner, parted with a few coins, and arranged for a message to be delivered, fast, to a certain innkeeper in a certain hostelry not far from Malak Circle, near where I used to work.

Then I found the room where I'd waited before, and waited again, drumming my fingers on the arm of the chair and hoping everyone would arrive in time.

Norathar was the first to arrive. She entered without clapping and said, "What is it?" without even sitting down.

"I'll tell you when the others are here," I said.

"What others?"

"Just friends."

She sat down facing me, looking like she wanted to read my plan on my face. If it were that easy to do, I'd have no trouble identifying the assassin.

A few minutes later, there was a clap, and Morrolan entered. He looked at me, looked at Norathar, and said, "Well?"

"We're still waiting," I said.

"For?"

"The others," I said, just to be contrary and because turning Morrolan's bait is always fun.

He rolled his eyes and sat next to Norathar. Daymar was there within about a minute. He looked around the room curiously, as if he hadn't realized the Dragon Wing had places to sit. The others, it seemed, didn't know quite what to make of him. Well, neither did I, for that matter.

A few minutes later, there was a soft but firm clap, and Kiera entered; she was the one I'd been most worried about reaching, so I relaxed a bit. "Just one more," I said.

"Who is that?" asked Kragar.

I stared at him. He smiled sweetly and said, "Ah, glorious vengeance," and smirked. I felt better seeing that the others, including Kiera, were also startled. I did not give Kragar the satisfaction of asking when he'd arrived. I just said, "We're all here now."

"Good," said Norathar. "Get on with it."

I outlined the situation as I understood it, except that I made it sound gloomier than it was so it would be more dramatic when I announced that I had a way out. It would have worked better if they didn't know me so well. Kiera smiled a little, Morrolan stared off into space, and Norathar said, "Get on with it" again.

So I did, making it as clear as possible, and only glossing over the part where I had some doubts I could pull it off. I should have known better. "Vlad," said Kiera. "How are you going to identify the assassin?"

"I have some ideas on that," I said.

Norathar said, "He's going to brandish a knife and see who reacts as if he knows what he's doing." That hurt, because I *had* been considering that.

"There are problems with that," I said.

"Yes. Like, if no one reacts right. Or if more than one do."

"Yeah," I said. "Now, Kiera—"

"Hmmm?"

I glanced at Norathar. "Uh, no rudeness intended, Norathar, but in your official capacity, you don't want to hear this. I'll whisper."

She rolled her eyes, and I stood up, leaned over to Kiera, and whispered.

She listened, then said, "Sounds easy enough."

Yeah, I'm sure it was, for any thief good enough to steal the mustache off an Easterner's face. But I just nodded to her and sat down again.

Kragar said, "You never mentioned what I'm supposed to do."

"Keep the Jhereg off-balance while we do the other stuff. We don't want them interfering until Aliera is out, with papers with a big Imperial seal on them saying the matter is over."

"Oh," he said. "Any idea how?"

"Yes. Find the Imperial Representative, and keep her occupied."

"Just how am I going to do that, when I can be interrupted at any time?"

"Kragar, meet Daymar."

"We've met," said Kragar. Daymar, it seemed, missed the inflection in Kragar's voice, and just nodded.

"What's my part?" asked Daymar.

"Dress up as a Jhereg, go with Kragar, and make sure the Jhereg representative can't get any psychic messages. And doesn't know it."

"Dress up like a Jhereg?"

"Yes."

"Me?"

"Yes."

He paused. Then, "All right."

"Good."

"What about sending?"

"She's welcome to talk to anyone she wants. I just don't want any Jhereg telling her to go see the Empress right now." I stopped and looked at Kragar. "Just to be clear, if they figure out what you've done, and I don't see how to prevent that, you might become a target."

Kragar yawned. I shrugged. Then I winced.

"Still in pain?" said Kiera.

"Some."

"Is it going to—"

"I hope not. Morrolan, it's clear enough?"

He nodded. "I go to the advocate's office. What's his name?"

"Perisil."

"Right. I wait there for, uh, three more hours and a bit, then, if I haven't heard from you, I take him in to see the Empress. Sounds easy."

"I hope so. Warlord?"

"Don't call me that."

"Sorry, Highness."

She stared at me. I really, really should learn not to bait Dragonlords. It's a bad habit, and one of these days it could get me into trouble. But it's so much *fun*. I cleared my throat and said, "You know where to be, and when?"

"Yes. I'm to make sure no one tries to prevent Morrolan and the advocate from reaching Her Majesty."

I nodded.

"That's it, then," I said. I checked the time. I could make it if I hurried.

"Good luck, Vlad," said Morrolan. Kiera just smiled her smile. Daymar was lost in thought. Norathar shrugged. They all got up, one at a time, and filed out. When I was alone, I pulled the dagger from my boot and studied it and tested it. It was a stiletto, my favorite weapon for making someone become dead. My favorite target, when possible, is the left eye, because it is back there that Dragaerans keep the part of their brains that permits psychic activity. Not that I'm necessarily trying to cut off psychic activity, but if you take it out, they go into shock instantly. That takes a weapon with reasonable length, and a good point. This one had that, though the edge wasn't anything to brag about.

But I had no time to sharpen it just now. I replaced it in my boot, tested the draw, didn't like it, and ended up arranging a quick rig against my stomach on the left side, hidden by my cloak. I tested it, and it worked, and it didn't hurt much more than a whole lot. Fair enough.

I set out for the Stone Bridge, cutting around the Palace district, Loiosh and Rocza keeping an eye on the foot traffic to make sure no one was interested in my movements.

I was a bit distracted: For one thing, it hurt to move. For another, the trickiest part of the whole matter was just coming up. I thought about asking Cawti to help, but I had the impression a recommendation from her might not go over well with these people. I thought up several possible stories and rejected them.

I still hadn't made up my mind when I got near the cottage.

"Check."

"On it, Boss." And, *"Different guy, same spot."*

"All right."

I stood behind an oak that would have taken three of me to wrap my arms around, and I rubbed a bit of stuff onto my skin, glued on the beard, and set the wig in place.

"What do we do?"

"Your choice: cloak, or outside."

"Neither?"

"Loiosh."

"Cloak, I guess."

"Get in, then."

They did. I approached the cottage and remembered to pound on the door with my fist, instead of clapping. That hurt, too.

The door opened, and a middle-aged woman, Easterner, opened the door. I couldn't guess from looking which part of the East she drew her ancestry; she had a large mouth, and wide-set eyes that were almost perfectly round, like a cat's. The look in the eyes, at the moment, was suspicious. "Yes?" she said.

"I'm called Savn," I said, pulling the name more or less out of the air. "I'd like a few minutes of conversation with you before the gathering here, if you don't mind."

"How do you know about the gathering here?"

"That's the voice, Boss. The one doing most of the talking."

"All right."

"I'm hearing double, Boss. Can I—?"

"All right."

There came the psychic equivalent of a relieved sigh.

I said, "Many people know about the gathering here, and the one later with Lord Caltho."

"Everyone knows about that one."

"Yes, including some people you would probably rather didn't."

"The Empire?"

"Worse."

She studied me for a moment, then said, "Come in."

It was bigger than it had seemed from outside: one big room, with a stove in one corner, and a loft overhead that I'm sure contained the sleeping quarters. There were a lot of plain wooden chairs set out—at least twenty of them. I suspected the chairs accounted for most of the expense of the place.

She pointed me to one. I sat; she remained standing. Heh. Okay, so that's how it was going to be.

"Boss, should you be talking out loud? Here? If I could listen—"

"Um. Damn. Good point."

"Mind if we take a walk?" I said. She looked even more suspicious. I said, "The Empire may be hearing everything we say here, and, worse, someone else might be, too."

She frowned, hesitated, then nodded abruptly. I stood up, we walked out the door and down the street. When we were a good distance away, I started talking, but she interrupted before I had a word out.

"Who are you?" she said.

"I gave you my name. What's yours?"

"Brinea. Now who are you?"

"I'm what you'd call an independent factor. I'm not with the Empire—" she looked like she didn't believe that "—or with anyone else. I have a friend who's caught in the middle of it, which means I'm temporarily on your side."

"My side is—"

"Spare me," I said. "I have information you'll want to

know, and no interest whatever in politics, whether Imperial or anti-Imperial."

She pressed her lips together and said, "What information is that?"

"Is today's meeting, here, to plan for the meeting with Caltho?"

"That's a question, not information."

"All right. If it is, there is liable to be a disguised Jhereg assassin here, who is planning to kill Caltho and blame it on you."

I suddenly had her attention. "Talk," she said.

We turned a corner; with Loiosh and Rocza still in the cloak, I felt exposed, but I tried to stay alert. I only saw a few Easterners.

"The Jhereg," I told her, "is working on a complicated scheme, along with the Orca and the—and another organization. To pull it off, they need to pressure the Empress. To pressure the Empress, they're using the massacre in Tirma. If a legitimate investigation—"

"It won't be a legitimate investigation," she said. "They'll just throw a black tarp over it and say it's fine."

"No, they'll do a real investigation. Not because they care, but because the Empress is trying to get out of a jam, and that's the only way to do it."

"Maybe," she said.

"The Jhereg needs to stop the investigation. To do that, they're going to make it look like your group killed Assistant Investigator Caltho. Much outrage against you, probably a lot of arrests, and the investigation gets put on hold. That's how they're going to work it."

She was quiet for ten or twelve paces, then she said, "Maybe."

"I agree with the maybe. I think I'm right, but I could be wrong."

"How will you find out?"

"With your permission, I'll attend today's meeting here, and try to identify the assassin."

"What makes you think you can do that?"

"I can sometimes spot them," I said.

"What is it you do?"

"Run from them."

"I don't understand."

"The Jhereg wants me dead for personal reasons. So, most of my life is avoiding them. But that's okay, I've been running for so long it feels like walking to me."

She was quiet again for a bit, then she said, "What will you do if you identify the assassin?"

"Tell you who he is, so you can do whatever seems appropriate."

"What if you're wrong?"

"I won't be. I might not be able to spot him, but if I do spot him, I won't be wrong."

We turned a corner and she started leading us back toward the house. No one had yet tried to kill me. Eventually she said, "All right. I'll trust you on that part. You may as well relax; they'll be here soon."

We made it back to the house and closed the door and I felt relieved. I found a chair from which I could be watching the door without appearing to, and I waited.

It was, indeed, only a few minutes later that they began to arrive. The first to arrive appeared to be a Teckla, and suspiciously like one straight out of someone's imagination of what a peasant ought to look like: brown hair, roundish face, leathery-looking skin, sturdy. He greeted Brinea, who introduced me. He gave his name as Nicha, and sat down next to me and began a conversation about needing to watch for trickery at the meeting with the Empire. I grunted agreeing noises and kept watching the door.

Shortly after, a pair of Easterners came in: Katherine was tall for an Easterner, dark, and wore glasses; Liam had the round face of a Teckla, an odd hair color that wasn't quite blond and wasn't quite brown, and a nose that looked to have been broken at least once. They carried flyers in their hands. I didn't ask to see one because I was afraid it was something I was supposed to know about. They were both reserved with me; maybe they thought they should be the only humans there.

In fact, except for the three of us, everyone else was a Teckla. I won't give you all the names; there were twenty-three of them, not including me or Brinea. Eliminating the two Easterners, that meant twenty-one who might be assassins. Nine of them were women, and I almost dismissed them, but for one thing, there *is* the occasional woman working for the Jhereg (as I happen to know better than most), and for another, a Jhereg willing to disguise himself as a Teckla could just as easily disguise his sex, right?

So, there were twenty-one who might be my target; and none of them instantly jumped out at me. I had been thinking I might take a look at their calluses, if I could see them; but it seems I'd stumbled into the largest collection of non-laboring Teckla ever assembled in one place. Some were messengers, some were house-servants, some did menial jobs for merchants, but none looked like he actually did any work. It was terribly disillusioning; I wondered what it meant.

It seemed there were several there who didn't know each other, so my being a stranger turned out not to be that bad.

Brinea made introductions as people came in, and I watched a lot, spoke little, learned nothing.

"I wish I could see, Boss."

"You think you can spot an assassin when I can't?"

"Yes."

"Ha."

The chairs were arranged in most of a circle, three rows deep, only an arc in front of the doorway and into the kitchen area left free. One chair, on the other end of the arc, was unoccupied, as if by unspoken consent. Brinea sat in it and said, "Let's get started."

It started, and it went on for a long time. They spoke of pressuring the Empire, which struck me as an exercise in futility, but what do I know? They spoke about guarding the interests of "the people," but weren't exactly clear on what that involved. Mostly, it went on for a long time. I took out the clasp knife I'd just bought. No one reacted. Damn. I cleaned my nails with it, and no one seemed to notice. Nothing. Oh, well. I closed it and set down next to my chair.

Meanwhile, they droned on, talking about what Lord Caltho—they were careful to call him Lord Caltho—had to be told about and what standards he had to be held to, and about insisting that all details of the investigation be made public. *Let me know how that works out for you,* I thought but didn't say.

I was caught between boredom and frustration. I kept wanting to flourish a dagger just to see who reacted; and it might even have worked. But the thing is, it might not have, and then I'd have lost my chance.

It took a while—it took a very very long while—but at last Brinea said, "I think that covers everything. I propose we go there in a body. If we leave now, we'll be a few minutes early, and we can talk to anyone walking by and explain what we're doing, then go in together. Does anyone object?"

No one did, so we all stood up. I watched as closely as I could to see if anyone seemed unusually athletic or, well, *slinky* when standing, if that makes any sense. And I half thought I noticed someone, too. I studied him as I stood: a guy with long, loopy arms wearing loose clothing; and his hair was shaggy enough to have maybe concealed a noble's point. Maybe. The trick was to keep an eye on him, but not be so distracted that I missed someone else. It was hard, but not impossible. You have to trust your peripheral vision.

I contrived to be the last one out the door except for Brinea and a fellow I took to be her husband. No one else seemed interested in who was the last one out the door. But I guess if you'd been watching me, I wouldn't have *seemed* interested either.

We all trooped out toward the street to head toward the South Adrilankha Speaker's Hall, which is what someone had once built instead of the Speaker's House villages have. It wasn't far away, but at least one of us wasn't going to make it. They waited for Brinea to take the lead, and, as she shut the door, I said, "I don't have my pocketknife."

"You set it by your chair," said a short, elderly Teckla who was about four paces from me.

We assassins notice things like that.

I nodded and opened my cloak as I covered the distance. Loiosh and Rocza flew out very quickly and several people cried out, but by that time I had the stiletto in my hand. I got him up under the chin. I hit him hard, too—I remember feeling the hilt connect with his chin bone, though I mostly remember how much my ribs hurt when I struck. I left the knife there, and started to step back, about to curl myself up into a ball of pain and try to breathe when—

"*Down!*"

I hit the ground and rolled and felt something go "whoosh" over my head. Someone was reacting awfully fast for a Teckla, and my muscles cried out to stop it and

"*He has backup, Boss! Three of them!*"

Sheesh. Was the whole room full of assassins? What was he doing bringing backup along? I never did that. What sort of crappy assassin wants witnesses and needs protection? I'd have given him a piece of my mind if I hadn't left eight inches of steel in his.

I hoped one of them was the guy I'd picked out; that would make me feel better. There was a lot of screaming going on as I continued my roll; some of the screaming was from my rib. My hand found the hilt of Lady Teldra, and I drew her and came to my feet, knowing somehow I needed to duck to my left, and someone yelled "Morganti," which was useless, because once I drew that blade, everyone within a mile who had any psychic sensitivity at all must have been aware of it.

She had taken the form of a rapier, which was awfully nice, since that's what I'm used to fighting with. She fit into my hand like my palm, hilt smooth, and it was like she was weightless. I knew—somehow—that it was safe to take a step backward, and I did, taking my first good look around.

There were several horrified faces, backing away. Brinea, to her credit, was seeing to her people and trying to pull them away and speaking rapidly. Three of what appeared to be Teckla were facing me: each with a fighting knife, one with two of them. They were crouched, alert, and they were staring at Lady Teldra. I didn't blame them.

We stood there, watching each other for half a heartbeat, when a couple of things happened. First, I realized I didn't hurt anymore. I almost looked at Lady Teldra myself. You'd think someone would have told me she could do things like that.

The second thing that happened was someone called out, "You will put up your weapons in the name of the Empire."

I froze.

"What the—?"

"Two of them, Boss; they've pulled gold cloaks out of somewhere and are tossing off wigs and such."

"Great. Half the gathering were assassins, the other half were Phoenix Guards. Perfect."

For a moment, no one moved, then I heard another voice, this one I recognized. "Vlad, put it away."

I looked over. "Norathar? Where did *you* come from?"

"Behind that tree over there."

I wanted to say that hadn't been the plan, but she probably wouldn't have appreciated it. I sheathed Lady Teldra with a flourish.

"Now," she said, "if you gentlemen will put yours up as well, let us all go to the Palace and talk this over. The wagon will be here shortly."

There was a pause, but I had no doubts about what would happen. These were Jhereg; they knew that, whatever else, you do *not* fight with the Phoenix Guards. You can't win. After a breath or two, there was a collective sigh and cutlery vanished all over the place. Norathar said, "Who is the leader here?"

I glanced at the corpse and said, "Uh, I'm afraid—"

"No, not him."

"I am," said Brinea, in an impressively steady voice. She looked at me but didn't say anything. Yeah, I know: I'd told her I was going to just identify him. I'd been lying. I do that sometimes.

I studied the Jhereg who were still alive, standing there like idiots the same way I was. One of them looked familiar. I looked at him more closely, realized where I knew him from, and shook my head. He avoided looking at me. I'm guessing he was disgusted with himself because my disguise had fooled him. I tried to feel smug about that but it wasn't in me. I hate it when my plan goes blooey, even if the results come out okay.

Oh, and to complete my humiliation, the fellow I'd noticed earlier, and thought might be an assassin, was one of the Phoenix Guards.

Sheesh.

Norathar said, "I'd like everyone's name as witnesses. After that, you are free to go on about your business. I think the excitement is over, and Lord Caltho will be arriving shortly."

Briana agreed, and about then a couple of coaches pulled up. The three Jhereg were put into one, still with their weapons and unbound; I got the other. Loiosh and Rocza remained outside, overhead, providing a winged escort.

Norathar climbed in with me, and we started off. I said, "Is there any law against impersonating a Phoenix Guard?"

"Why?"

"One of those Jhereg—the one with the floppy hat—was one of the ones who beat me up."

"Oh. He can be fined for that, and maybe dunked."

"All right." I sighed. "Got through it, anyway."

"I suppose. But, Vlad, that was pretty sloppy. Now what? You've been seen killing someone. I wouldn't have thought you'd have slipped so far so fast."

That was unfair. For one thing, it wasn't fast by my standards; it had been years. For another—

"I'll point out that I was in disguise, and if you'd done what I said—"

"You'd either be dead, or have three Morganti killings to account for. I don't know how we'll keep you away from the Star as it is, but with that—"

"It shouldn't be a problem. He was a Jhereg assassin."

Norathar nodded. "Yes, so he was. He turned out to be not only armed, but carrying a seal of the House with him."

I nodded.

"The only thing is," said Norathar, "that assassins don't carry the House seal when they're working. I happen to know."

"This one did."

"You say that like you knew."

"I had a pretty good idea he would be."

"How?"

"Because I trust Kiera."

"She planted—?" She cut herself off before asking the question. Dragon Heir, acting Warlord, and ex-assassin; had to be tough to be her.

I leaned my head against the hard wall of the coach.

She said, "He had three toughs with him for backup."

"Yeah," I said. "I hadn't expected that."

"I had."

I opened my eyes. "Why?"

"Because they were going to assassinate a public figure in a crowded room. You're used to—that is, you were used to a different sort of thing."

"I did jobs in public."

"Different sort of thing than taking out a guy in the mid-

dle of a restaurant. With a public figure like that, if you're going to get out of it alive and unidentified, you need people to
create enough confusion to get away."

Great. Now I was getting lessons in assassination from the
Warlord of the Empire. "You could have told me," I said.

She shrugged. "How did you identify him?"

I explained about the knife.

"How do you know the guy you got was the one going to
do the work, not one of the backups?"

"Why do I care?"

She inhaled deeply, then let her breath out slowly and
nodded.

"Give me a moment," she said. "I'll find out what happened with the rest."

A bit later she said, "Morrolan brought the advocate in to
see the Empress, presented the petition. The Empress is now
meeting with the Justicer and Imperial Advocate. Morrolan is
confident the charges will be dismissed."

I nodded. "And the investigation?"

"Aliera did nothing wrong as Warlord; she has nothing to
fear from an investigation."

"All right."

"As opposed to you."

"Me? I killed an assassin."

"You also publicly brandished a Morganti weapon. Which
I ought to take from you, only I know better." She looked disgusted.

"Oh, right; carrying a Morganti weapon is illegal, isn't it?"

"Very much illegal."

"In spite of Aliera, Morrolan, Sethra—"

"Yes, in spite of that."

"Just like use of Elder Sorcery is illegal, but no one cares unless—say, I just thought of something. The law against carrying a Morganti weapon, do you happen to know if it is a Codified Tradition, a Statute, or an Edict?"

She frowned. "I believe it's an Edict. Why?"

"I have a good advocate," I said.

17

1. *There were regrettable and even reprehensible actions taken by Imperial soldiers in the village of Tirma on Lyorn 2, 252.*
2. *Responsibility for these actions must end with the individuals directly involved (see Appendix 23 for names and suggested charges).*
3. *Any attempt to lay responsibility for this incident on higher levels of the Imperial military order will be inconsistent with justice, and in addition may have long-term negative consequences for the Imperial army, and cannot therefore be recommended (see Part One, point 1).*

I signed and sealed the oaths saying that as an Imperial Count I promised not to go anywhere until my case had been dealt with, then was permitted to leave the Iorich Wing. My destination was conveniently close, and by now familiar.

I ran into Daymar on the way to Perisil's office. I was going to ask him where Kragar was, but I bethought myself to take a look around and there he was. I studied Daymar in his black

and gray, and thought about telling him he made a good
Jhereg, but he didn't so I didn't.

I said, "How did it go?"

"Went well," said Kragar. "I gave her a good runaround
about rumors of new laws, and how could I profit from them,
and she gave me a good runaround not answering me. I don't
think she suspected anything."

"She will when someone asks her why she was out of
touch right when they needed her to get to the Empress."

"They might." He didn't seem concerned.

"Thanks," I said.

"I'm like you, Vlad; it just tickles me to have Aliera owe
me one."

That was a motivation I could understand.

We reached the office. The door was open, and Morrolan
and Perisil were there. I introduced Perisil to Daymar and to
Kragar, whom he hadn't noticed come in.

Perisil said, "I've just gotten word from the Justicer. They're
releasing Aliera."

"Good."

"And they'll be investigating the events in Tirma."

"Okay."

"And Her Majesty wants to see you."

"Oh," I said. I cleared my throat. "When does Aliera get
out?"

"They've already dispatched the release order; she should
be out within the hour."

"Good."

"Good work, Vlad," said Morrolan.

"And you. All of us."

"I should have more chairs," said Perisil.

"Will Aliera be joining us here?"

"I've no idea," he said.

I nodded. "Because she'd prefer to sit, I'm sure." That earned me a look from Morrolan.

It was like the old days in Morrolan's library, except it wasn't. For one thing, Aliera wasn't there. I couldn't decide if I wanted to see her. Most likely, she wouldn't want to see me. She knew and I knew that, what with one thing and another, thanks weren't appropriate; but you can't help when obligation makes you uncomfortable.

But more than that was the uncomfortable feeling that, while it was over, it wasn't over. We couldn't all relax and laugh and make fun of each other, because there was too much unfinished. What would happen with the Imperial investigation? Would the Left Hand go after Cawti, as they'd threatened? When would the Jhereg finally get me? And then there was the unresolved matter of—

"Kragar," I said. "Do something for me?"

"Hmmm?"

"Some asshole was just arrested for impersonating a Phoenix Guard. He was one of the ones who beat me. Find him, learn who his friends were, and break a few bones."

He nodded. "How are you feeling, by the way?"

"Me? Fine."

"Oh, you healed?"

"I . . . yeah."

He let it go. He knows me. They all know me. Sometimes that's not entirely comfortable. I know them, too, but I don't mind that part so much.

Morrolan said, "I've just heard from Aliera. She went home. Care to join us?"

I shook my head. "I need to speak with my advocate."

"Oh?"

"Long story."

He hesitated. "Will you be around long?"

"Unless they catch up to me."

"I meant, around town."

"Oh. I'll get back to you on that."

"I'll be going," said Daymar. "Good to see you again, Vlad."

"You too."

"Haven't seen you much these last few years. Where have you been?"

"Um. I'll tell you about it sometime."

"All right." He waved and vanished; my ears popped. People shouldn't teleport out of small rooms.

Morrolan was more polite; he thanked Perisil again, bowed, and walked out the door, leaving me alone with my advocate. Oh, and Kragar. I looked around. Nope, just the two of us.

"What's on your mind?" he asked.

"Need another client?"

I gave him the short version, and he agreed to take it on, and I paid him. I was starting to feel a bit of a squeeze with money, which was something I hadn't had to worry about for several years, and thought I'd never have to worry about again. A shame about that. But living on the run can be pretty cheap if you do it right; that's one good thing about it.

We left it there while I headed over to the Palace to have a little chat with the relatively absolute ruler of the Dragaeran Empire.

I reached the place with no incidents, and there was Harnwood, bowing as deeply as he could without having me think I was being mocked, after which he said, "If m'lord will accompany me, Her Majesty will see you now."

My goodness. How the fallen have become mighty.

He led me to a small (for the Palace, at any rate) room done in gray marble, with a six-sided marble table at which sat the Empress, nibbling on bread and cheese. As have done millions before me, before I even bowed I couldn't help but glance at the Orb to see if I could judge the Imperial Mood. I couldn't, really. It was a kind of rusty brown, which might mean anything.

"Your Majesty," I said.

There was a soft click as Harnwood shut the door behind him.

"Sit," commanded the ruler. I did so. "Eat," was the next command. Now that wasn't something I needed to hear twice, so I helped myself. The cheese was very sharp, and the sort I'd normally think too salty, but it seemed to work. The bread had a thin, hard crust and an odd slightly sour taste, reminding me of something Cawti had once brought home years before.

"Good, isn't it?"

"Yes."

"It comes from Naarsten County, in the Sorannah. It's from a special breed of goat, and only the best of the breed. They make five pounds a year, and it only comes here, to the Palace."

"Impressive," I said. Actually, the cheese wasn't *that* good.

"Yes," she said. "Other than the cheese, there isn't a whole lot about this job I like."

"Makes the compensations more valuable, that there are fewer of them."

She had another bite of bread and cheese, and nodded. "By now, Aliera should be home."

I nodded.

"Just like it never happened," she said.

"Uh huh. What of the investigation?"

"She'll be cleared of any wrongdoing, I'm sure."

"How can you be sure?"

"Vlad, a squad of half-drunk, frustrated, angry soldiers in County Nowhere go berserk, and we're going to blame the Warlord? She wasn't even there."

"The squad?"

"One was career military, used to seeing civilians as either inconvenient undisciplined idiots, or else un-uniformed sneak killers. The others were peasant boys who weren't used to seeing their friends die without having anyone to take their frustrations out on. People fight, people die, because the alternative is to let some local baron set his own tariffs for passage of shipwood, which will outrage the Lyorn who own the forests and the Orca who buy the wood. I can't risk offending the Lyorn because they're too high on the Cycle, or the Orca because they're already looking to form alliances with the Jhereg. So a few peasants have to die. More cheese?"

"Thanks."

"It's not bad."

"So, the investigation is rigged after all?"

"Of course not. It doesn't have to be rigged. It just needs to be run by someone with a good sense of justice. But not too good."

"All right."

"When it's over, I'll ask Aliera to be Warlord again. That way, she can have the pleasure of refusing. I owe her that much, at least."

The cheese really was good.

"I can't do anything for you, you know."

"Your Majesty?"

"The Jhereg. The Left Hand. They're going to be after you, and after your wife. I can't help you."

I swallowed and nodded.

"I've done what I can," she went on. "I've made some threats, but I can't carry them out. They probably know that."

"Thanks, though."

She nodded. "What are you going to do?"

"I don't know. If Cawti's in danger, I can't really leave town."

"I'm sure she finds that very endearing."

"As much as you would," I said.

"Or Aliera."

"Or Aliera."

"It isn't that they're ungrateful."

"I know. It's just that no one wants to be the one being rescued, we all want to do the rescuing."

She nodded. "And this job is all about making everyone else do the rescuing. Which is why you're here right now."

"You want me to rescue someone?"

"No. I just know that Aliera can't thank you, and if she could, you couldn't hear it. So I'm saying it. Thank you."

"I'll have some more cheese."

"Please do. It's where your taxes go."

"I've never actually paid much in the way of taxes."

"Then you should enjoy it even more."

"And the Teckla in Tirma are still dead."

"Yes, they are. Do you care?"

"No. Do you?"

"Yes."

I nodded.

"The Empire has compensated the families, of course."

"Good work. We used to do that sort of thing in the Jhereg."

"How'd it work out?"

"Not bad, but people trust the Jhereg, so we had an advantage."

She poured some white wine out of a tall, elegant bottle into a simple blue ceramic cup. She passed the cup to me, and I drank, then passed it back.

"I'll let the Imperial Advocate know to hurry up the case, so you can get out of town fast," she said.

"I just said—"

"I know what you said. Don't argue with your Empress."

"Yes, Majesty."

"That's better."

I leave town for a few years, and when I come back, everyone I know starts drinking to the point of semi-incoherency. Was it that everything was too boring when I was gone? I somehow doubted that. On reflection, I decided it was a good idea not to ask Her Majesty if she was drunk. I put the plan into action at once.

We passed the cup back and forth a couple of times, and she refilled it. "You can't do anything to protect Cawti?" I said.

"Norathar has promised to watch out for her, I can't do better than that."

"All right."

"You know the difference between a decadent Phoenix and a reborn Phoenix, Vlad?"

"Is this about to be a joke?"

"No. Or maybe yes, but no."

"Go ahead."

"A reborn Phoenix knows to get out before the bad decisions start, that's all." I nodded. She said, "I've spent much of the last few days consulting the Orb, looking at memories. As far as I can tell, that's the only difference. Once you start making bad decisions, one things leads to another, and then there are more dead Teckla that you don't care about."

"Do you think you made bad decisions?"

"No."

I nodded. "Good, then. The idea of the Empress making bad decisions worries me. What about the Jhereg, the Left Hand, and the Orca? Are they going to get away with it?"

"No, I think you stopped them."

"Me?"

"I should give you another Imperial title, but what would you do with it?"

"Yes, and how would you explain it?"

"Good point. There's still some cheese left."

"Zerika, are you planning to abdicate?"

"That isn't the proper word. I'm thinking it may be time for the Cycle to turn."

"I doubt it."

"Why?"

"It would look bad."

"Do you think I care?"

"You should. The Empire is all about appearances."

She was quiet for a long time after that, then she seemed to sigh. If I had just talked the Empress out of stepping down, then I had just added to my tally on doing good for the world, and subtracted from my tally of helping friends. How would the Lords of Judgment weigh these things? I'd probably never know.

I decided that, whatever the Empress decided to do, my words made no difference. It was easier thinking that.

I cleared my throat. "The fact is, I'm safe enough if I stay at the inn—"

"As if you will."

"—but that says nothing about Cawti. Can Norathar protect her and the boy?"

"I hope so. Norathar wants to protect her just as much as she wants to not be protected. And you may recall, she isn't exactly helpless."

"I know." I sighed. "The more I do what I have to, the more barriers I put between me and everyone I care about."

She nodded. "And now you know the other reason I asked you here. Welcome to my world. It's better with company. I'm going to ask Laszló to keep an eye on her, too, but I'd rather you didn't mention that to her."

"All right. And thank you. Who is Laszló?"

"An Easterner. A witch. He's very good at what he does." A ghost of a smile crept over her features and I didn't press the issue.

"I'll look forward to meeting him," I said.

She nodded. "Are you planning to say farewell to Norathar as you leave the Palace?"

Actually, I hadn't thought about it at all, but I nodded.

"Don't," she said.

Right. Add her to the list. "All right."

A little later she said, "The cheese is gone."

I nodded, rose, bowed, took five steps backward, turned, and left her alone.

Epilogue

It was no surprise to anyone that, when the investigation concluded, everyone was cleared of any wrongdoing, except maybe the peasants, who were convicted of being in the wrong place at the wrong time. It was no surprise to anyone that there were riots in South Adrilankha in response. It was no surprise to anyone that there was a lot of blood involved in suppressing them. The only surprise was that Aliera agreed to become Warlord again a week or two later, but I think that was as a favor to Norathar.

Aliera has a strong sense of obligation.

Perisil moved out of his basement office and returned to a private office in the City itself, where he's already doing much better than his first attempt. Reputation matters almost as much to an advocate as to an assassin or an Empress.

Two weeks ago I got word that I was cleared of all charges relating to the incident, which is good, but I was pretty much expecting it. So that's done, and those four bastards who pounded me got what they deserved too, which is another one I owe Kragar.

I could leave now that everything's over.

I could. Maybe I will.

I'm still staying here at Dancer's Rest, and money is starting to get tight. Every few days, I find a new way to sneak out and visit Cawti and the boy, and every few days it becomes harder to do so safely, and every few days Cawti says I should get out of town. It's nice that she worries about me, I guess. I hope she thinks it's nice that I worry about her.

We are what we worry about, maybe that's the lesson of the whole thing.

Nah.

If there were justice, someone would have paid for what happened in Tirma. If there were justice, a bunch of Easterners and Teckla in South Adrilankha wouldn't have had their heads stove in. If there were justice, Cawti and the boy wouldn't have to worry about their lives.

If there were justice, I'd be dead.

DELETED SCENES

Various scenes had to be deleted for length or content. I thought some of you might be interested in them. They may appear when I release the Director's Cut of this book. But don't hold your breath.

—SKZB

Prologue, Outside Whitemill, Page 13

I pulled the arrow from my eye, hearing myself scream. At that moment, a blast of magic from one of them hit me, and I saw my leg fly off at the knee. I fell to the ground, reaching for Lady Teldra, but one of them came in with an ax and took my right hand off at the wrist.

The air seemed to take on an odd golden shimmer, and I heard the Necromancer's voice come out of nowhere. "Through the Gate, Vlad. Hurry!"

"Uh, what?"

"You have to get out of here, Vlad. You've landed in a Tim Powers novel."

I moaned even as I felt the Gate form.

Hard gray walls appeared around me, and I heard voices speaking a language I didn't know. "Am I going to be safe here?"

"Well," she said, "Not, you know, *safe* exactly."

"Whose novel are we in now?"

"Uh . . . John DeChancie's, Vlad. Best I could do on short notice."

I whimpered. "You couldn't manage Louisa May Alcott?"

Chapter Two, Imperial Palace, Page 51

"I'm glad you've offered," said the Empress. "Yes, there is a service you could do."

"I'm listening."

"Far, far to the East—well beyond the kingdoms you know—there is ancient evil that is gathering power to itself. Its power comes from an Amulet of Evil that dates back to before the beginning of time. The power of the Amulet grows with each act of cruelty, or thoughtlessness toward another, or abuse of power, or greed. The sell-out of the writers' strike didn't do it any harm either. Soon it will become unstoppable, and using it, the ancient evil will enslave the entire world forever. You must destroy the evil, and take the Amulet and cast it into the Place Beyond Time."

I nodded. "All right."

It took six weeks to get there and an hour to do the job. Fortunately, I was able to teleport back.

"It is done," I told Her Majesty.

"Thank you, Lord Szurke," she said. "Evil has been banished forever."

"Until the sequel, you mean."

"Of course."

I shrugged. "Just proving I'm willing to serve Your Majesty."

Chapter Five, Dzur Mountain Stairway, Page 103

"Well met, friend."

I looked around, and noticed a splotchy brown cat on the landing just above me. I stared at it.

"Something wrong?" it said.

"What the hell are you?"

It rolled its eyes. "This is a fantasy novel. I'm the obligatory talking cat. Get a clue."

"*Boss, can I—*"

"*Sure.*"

When Loiosh and Rocza had finished their meal, we continued up the stairs.

Chapter Seven, South Adrilankha, Page 143

"*Boss, isn't there supposed to be a scene here making fun of the old 'weapons that drink souls' thing that always comes up in bad fantasy novels?*"

"*Loiosh, in case you haven't noticed, there are weapons that drink souls in these books.*"

"*Oh. Yeah. Good point. Guess we stay away from that one, huh?*"

"*Probably best.*"

Chapter Eleven, South Adrilankha, Page 209

"Maybe I'll go walk up to the cottage and ask for sanctuary," I said. *"*And then maybe monkeys will fly out of my butt. Wait. I wouldn't say that."

YOU JUST DID.

"I don't care. I wouldn't say that. It isn't even a Dragaeran idiom."

IT IS NOW.

"That's stupid. There aren't any monkeys here."

SO NOW YOU'RE AN EXPERT ON DRAGAERAN FAUNA?

"I didn't say that. Don't put words in my mouth."

THAT'S WHAT I DO.

"Yeah, you and Tom Cruise. Just lose the monkey bit, okay?"

I LIKE IT.

"You also like it when I figure out how to get out of those messes you put me in. Now, you want me on your side, or not?"

YOU WANT TO BE ALIVE AT THE END OF THIS BOOK, OR NOT?

I sighed. *"Maybe I'll go walk up to the cottage and ask for sanctuary,"* I said. *"And then maybe monkeys will fly out of my butt."*

Chapter Fourteen, Outside the Imperial Palace, Page 262

I cut through the park, smiling at all the butterflies. I started skipping. It was such a beautiful day. A puppy barked playfully at me and I stopped to pet it. It seemed so happy, I couldn't help but sing a cheerful song to it before I went on my way, still skipping.

Chapter Seventeen, Perisil's Office, Page 307

"I have something to tell you."

"How, you have something to tell me?"

"You have understood me exactly."

"Well, I am listening."

"Listening? Then, you wish me to tell you?"

"Yes, that is it. I am listening, and therefore I wish you to tell me."

"Shall I tell you now?"

"No."